Over the River

Annie Seaton

Daughters of The Darling:2

This is a work of fiction. Characters, institutions and organisations mentioned in this novel are either the product of the author's imagination or, if real, used fictitiously without any intent to describe actual conduct.

Annie Seaton

Annie Seaton lives near the beach on the mid-north coast of New South Wales. Her career and studies spanned the education sector, including working as an academic research librarian, a high school principal, and a university tutor until she took early retirement and fulfilled her lifelong dream of a full-time writing career.

Each winter, Annie and her husband leave the beach to roam the remote areas of Australia for story ideas and research. She is passionate about preserving the beauty of the Australian landscape and respecting the traditional ownership of the land. For those readers who cannot experience this journey personally, Annie seeks to portray the natural beauty of the Australian environment—its spiritual locations, stunning landscapes and unique wildlife.

Readers can contact Annie through her website, annieseaton.net, or find her on Facebook and Instagram. To stay up to date with her new releases, subscribe to her newsletter on the home page of her website.

Also by Annie Seaton

Daughters of the Darling
From Across the Sea
Over the River
By the Billabong

Porter Sisters Series
Kakadu Sunset
Daintree
Diamond Sky
Hidden Valley
Larapinta
Kakadu Dawn

Others
Bowen River
Whitsunday Dawn
Undara
Osprey Reef
East of Alice
One Summer in Tuscany
Four Seasons Short and Sweet
Follow the Sun
Ten Days in Paradise
Deadly Secrets
Adventures in Time
Silver Valley Witch
The Emerald Necklace
A Clever Christmas
Christmas with the Boss
Her Christmas Star
The Emerald Necklace

The Augathella Series

The Augathella Girls
Outback Roads
Outback Sky
Outback Escape
Outback Wind
Outback Dawn
Outback Moonlight
Outback Dust
Outback Hope
Boxed Sets
Augathella Girls 1-4
Augathella Girls 5-8

Augathella Short and Sweet Series
An Augathella Surprise
An Augathella Baby
An Augathella Spring
An Augathella Christmas
An Augathella Wedding
An Augathella Easter
An Augathella Masquerade Ball
Boxed Set
Augathella Short and Sweet 1-3

Sunshine Coast Series
Waiting for Ana
The Trouble with Jack
Healing His Heart
Sunshine Coast Boxed Set

The Richards Brothers Series
The Trouble with Paradise
Marry in Haste
Outback Sunrise
Richards Brothers Boxed Set
Bondi Beach Love Series
Beach House
Beach Music

Beach Walk
Beach Dreams
The House on the Hill Boxed Set

Second Chance Bay Series
Her Outback Playboy
Her Outback Protector
Her Outback Haven
Her Outback Paradise
Boxed Set
The McDougalls of Second Chance Bay Boxed Set

Love Across Time Series
Come Back to Me
Follow Me
Finding Home
The Threads that Bind
Boxed Set
Love Across Time 1-4

Bindarra Creek
Worth the Wait
Full Circle
Secrets of River Cottage
A Clever Christmas
A Place to Belong

To my dear friend, Kristen Woolgar, who proofread this story on a boat on a river.

Over the River

'To the distance of two miles, it retained a breadth of one hundred yards and a depth of twelve feet. Its banks were covered with verdure, and the trees overhanging them were of finer and larger growth than those on the new river by which we had approached it. Its waters had a shade of green and were more turbid than those of its neighbours, but they were perfectly sweet to the taste.'

Charles Sturt when he encountered the Darling River in February 1829.

Prologue

Ceann Mara Station - Christmas Eve.

Caitríona Mary O'Byrne, soon to become Caitríona Mary Wainwright of *Guntana Station*, held out her left hand so her sisters could take turns admiring her amethyst and diamond engagement ring.

'Well, you're a dark horse, Cat,' Róisín said. 'We had no idea that you'd met someone until that awful day when Mum called to tell us all what happened. Mum and Dad haven't stopped singing your praises yet, Logan. But it's lovely to meet you finally.'

Logan and Cat smiled as Caitríona's four sisters gathered around them. Róisín and Erin had arrived within half an hour of each other that morning and had both been anxious to meet Logan and see the engagement ring that Cat was sporting.

Shea and Bridget had been home for two weeks, and both had fallen instantly in love with their brother-in-law-to-be.

'Too late, girls, get your eyes off him,' Cat had teased.

'It's okay, Cat, we'll love Logan like a brother. Like we love Jack,' Shea said.

Erin grinned, and her husband, Jack, nodded at Logan. 'They're a good bunch, mate.' He held out his hand. 'Welcome to the family.'

Logan shook it and grinned, slightly overwhelmed by the arrival of the whole family.

Dad was in his element, hugging each of his daughters, coming back to Cat frequently to make sure she was alright, as he had done for the past three months, and thumping Logan on the back each time he walked past.

'So, my second daughter is about to get married,' he said to Jack. 'You're going to have a brother-in-law. And I'm going to have another son-in-law.'

Mum had been cooking for a week, and Cat, Shea, and Bridget spent a lot of time in the kitchen helping her.

Cat hadn't been this happy for as long as she could remember. The trauma of the past five months had taken its toll, and she had agreed to see a counsellor in Broken Hill. Every time Dad flew her down, Logan insisted on coming.

After a few sessions, she was feeling much better. Her injuries had healed, and the hair, which had been pulled out of her scalp above the back of her neck, was growing back.

The scars from the night in her Sydney apartment had faded to thin silver lines, and she could look at them now without getting upset.

But now it was Christmas Eve, a happier time, and everyone was home. Cat and Mum had been Christmas shopping in Broken Hill last week after her last appointment with the counsellor. The huge Christmas tree that filled a corner of the living room had dozens of presents beneath it.

Dad and Logan had gone to the heritage room in the library together while Mum and Cat shopped. Logan was as enamoured with their family history research as Cat and Dad were, and Mum constantly rolled her eyes.

'And the best thing, Dad,' Cat said, 'I'm going to be living over the river, so I'll be over here often helping you.'

'Just the two of us again, Tom,' Mum said.

Christmas Eve dinner was served in the formal dining room. Four roasts—including the inevitable goat—sat on the sideboard, surrounded by baked vegetables, a steaming pot of green peas and several gravies. Dad stood with the carving knife, ready to carve the roast beef.

Mum shook her head as they all squeezed around the table. 'If it wasn't for your family history, we could all be in that lovely big study of yours, Tom O'Byrne,' she said with a smile, knowing how much the family history meant to Dad. The girls had all giggled when Dad put the knife down on the sideboard, swept Mum over his arm, and kissed her soundly.

The sound of a spoon clinking on a wine glass silenced the noise of her sisters all trying to talk over each other. Cat smiled. It was lovely to have her family home.

Róisín stood at the side of the table and grinned at Cat. 'Well, Cat, as you always have done since you were a baby, you've stolen my thunder, but sweetheart, I can think of better ways you could have done it. First up, I'm speaking for the four of us when I say how much we love our fiery red-headed sister. And my sisters and I would all like to welcome you to our family, Logan.'

Glasses were raised with shouts of 'Welcome, Logan!'

'Thank you, Róisín.' Cat smiled at her big sister. 'What do you mean stealing your thunder?'

Róisín walked over and stood between Mum and Dad at the end of the table. She put one hand on each of their shoulders. 'Well, if it's alright with Mum and Dad, I'm coming home,' she said.

Mum's mouth dropped open. 'Coming home? To stay?'

Róisín nodded.

'But what about your job with that famous law firm?' Dad

asked.

'I don't like it. I'm sick of divorce settlements, celebrity litigation cases and dealing with city people. I've got a new job.' Her smile was wide as she looked down at Dad. 'Cat is passionate about the family history, but Dad, I know you're just as concerned with the health of the Darling.' She lifted her hands and placed them on her chest. 'Meet Róisín O'Byrne, dear family, the new Murray Darling Basin Authority lawyer.'

Chapter 1

One month later.

Ceann Mara Station, Darling River - Tuesday, mid-January.

Caitríona O'Byrne put her hand to her eyes as the sound of the quad runner drifted across from the levee bank between the billabong and the airstrip; she was waiting for Logan to come back from the bin run at one of the billabong campsites.

Mum had been in a panic when Cat walked into the kitchen twenty minutes earlier. 'Bloody hell,' she muttered when the oven timer went off as she opened the fridge.

'What's wrong, Mum?'

'I haven't whipped the cream for the scones yet. I have to get the sheets off the line for the guest room and make the bed. The scones are ready to come out, and I just heard your father and Logan drive into the shed. I haven't done the bin run yet. That young couple in the Kombi drove out half an hour ago.'

'Yeah, I saw them drive out.'

When they'd come across the river this morning to help Dad drench cattle, Cat had been surprised to hear that someone was camped at the far billabong campsite. A couple of backpackers with kayaks on top of an old Kombi van had booked for one night, Mum had said. At this time of the year, the unpowered campsites were rarely booked; it was too hot to camp there. The few campers who came through in the summer usually camped at the powered sites at the campground near the house so they could run their air conditioners in the unrelenting summer heat.

'Mum, calm down; there's no need to do all that. It's only Róisín.' Cat picked up an oven mitt and opened the oven door. 'They smell good,' she said as she lifted the tray of scones out of the oven.

'They will be with cream and the lime and ginger marmalade I made last week. It's pretty good if I do say so myself.' Her mother turned to go into the laundry.

'Leave that, Mum. I'll get the sheets in. And Róisín can make her bed.'

'No, I'll get it all done after smoko.'

'Why?' Cat shook her head.

'I want everything perfect when she gets here.' Mum pursed her lips. 'I want her room to be nice. So she feels welcome at home. It's a big move, coming from her flash apartment in Brisbane back to *Ceann Mara.*'

'Her choice, Mum.' Cat rolled her eyes.

You would have thought someone important was coming to stay, not one of my sisters, Cat thought. Mum had been in a tizzy all week. The vacuum had been rolled across every carpet every day, and she was sure Mum had filled all the cake tins in the kitchen.

Waste of effort because Róisín was usually on a fitness kick. *Not that I'm jealous*, Cat chided herself. She and Róisín had been close growing up, but her older sister had changed when she moved to Brisbane for uni. These days, now a lawyer, Róisín mixed with other professionals, wore designer labels and owned more shoes than her four sisters combined. Cat knew Roisin would never tell their parents because Mum and Dad had supported her financially during her years at university, but Cat knew the work in the celebrity law firm had jaded her sister.

Cat hadn't been keen on her choice of partner either; the guy who had moved into Róisín's riverside apartment last year had not impressed her. Greg Henderson owned the celebrity law firm where Róisín worked. Cat didn't like him, nor the way Róisín had changed since she'd been with him. She knew she had to let go—love was different for each of them, and it was Róisín's life and her choice. She was simply grateful for Logan;

their love was steadfast, and she knew his commitment to her was unwavering.

'Bit of a risk moving in with the boss,' she said to Róisín on the phone last year when Greg had moved in with her.

'He moved in with me, so I still have my own apartment,' Róisín retorted. Each of the girls had received a share of their grandmother's inheritance, and Róisín had used hers as a deposit on an apartment overlooking the Brisbane River.

'I thought he'd have his own luxury apartment.'

'He's looking to buy again,' her sister had justified. 'He used to live on a large property near Mt Coot-tha, but it was too far to travel into the city every day. He sold it, and he's got his eye on a penthouse in Kangaroo Point, and then he'll only have to come across the river to work.'

'And I guess you'll move in with him?'

'Maybe.'

Bit different to our rowing over the river in the punt to work with Dad. Cat came across to *Ceann Mara* each day with Logan; she took every opportunity to get into Dad's study and continue the family's historical research. Since she'd moved to Logan's place, *Guntana Station* on the other side of the Darling River last year, they spent most of each week over the river at her family's cattle station. After five daughters, Dad enjoyed having an 'almost' son-in-law who was keen to learn as much as he could about looking after the cattle, sheep, and goats. Erin's husband, Jack, was more interested in travelling than settling on the land. They'd been away for a couple of years.

Greg, Róisín's partner, was totally up himself, but they had been together for almost a year. Cat hadn't liked the way Greg treated Róisín the one time she'd visited them in Brisbane, and she couldn't imagine what he'd think of their remote cattle station on the Darling River.

The family hadn't been told any details of the breakup, but Mum and Cat both breathed a sigh of relief when Róisín let slip casually in a phone call that they were no longer together. When she'd come home at Christmas and dropped the bombshell that she was coming home, there'd been a glimpse of the Róisín of old. It would be good to have her home and working locally. Cat wondered whether she'd work from *Ceann Mara* or be based in one of the offices around the basin.

She walked over and put her arm around Mum's shoulder. 'You whip the cream while I do the sheets. Here comes Logan now; he can do the bin run while you get smoko organised.'

'Thanks, love. You're a sweetheart. Put them in the dryer before you come over to the shed. That wind came up quickly; the sheets are going to be full of red dust. I was tempted to put them in the dryer instead of hanging them out, but they'll smell fresher from being in the sun.'

'What time are we expecting Róisín?'

'She stayed in Cobar last night, so I'd say she'll be here for lunch. She loves your grandma's potato salad. I've done the potatoes, but I still have to make the dressing.'

'I can do that after we have smoko. Come on, Dad will be hanging for a cuppa.'

'We both are. I came over to get it.' Logan poked his head around the laundry door. 'Smells good, Laura.'

'I'm coming with the scones as soon as I whip the cream,' Mum said.

'I thought Tom was on a diet,' Logan said with a grin. 'He's expecting Salada crackers and tomato.'

'Tom's been good all week, and it's a special day with Róisín coming home. But he only gets one scone; he's put on too much weight lately.'

'Jug's on in the shed, and he's gone on the ag bike to check the mailbox. He said he'd only be a few minutes.'

'He's waiting for some photocopies from the National Library. We've got a new lead on Samuel.' Cat grinned when Mum shook her head. 'It's the best we've had so far. Dad found—'

'Later, Cat. Logan, can you do the bin run for me? The last site on the billabong where we usually keep the kayaks. And Cat, when you come over, pick some mint from the herb garden for me, will you? I'll whip the cream and take the scones and milk over.'

'Yes, Mum. Now scoot.'

Cat went to the clothesline, and Logan jumped in the quad runner and headed to the billabong. It was only a couple of minutes before she heard the back screen door open as Mum headed for the shed.

'I'll see you over there, Cat. And thanks, love. I appreciate it.'

'No prob. I can hear Logan coming back now. I'll put the sheets in the dryer. We'll only be a couple of minutes behind you.'

Mum opened the side gate and disappeared behind the house, heading for the big shed close to the river.

It wasn't long before Cat heard the putt-putt of the quad runner heading up the road, and Logan parked outside the house fence and came in through the gate. The washing was dust-free, and Cat folded the sheets and pillowcases and put them against her face, inhaling the fresh smell.

'Did I tell you how lovely you look today?' Logan put his arm around her waist and kissed her cheek.

'I had to get out of my work clothes to welcome Róisín

home,' she said.

'Mum's gone over—'

A bloodcurdling scream came from the direction of the shed. For a second, Cat and Logan just stood there, staring at each other, and then they turned and ran.

Chapter 2

Louth, Darling River - Tuesday, mid-January.

Róisín was delayed at Louth. A red ute that had tailed her all the way from Bourke had overtaken her just before the sixty-kilometre zone and pulled up at the fuel pump ahead of her. The driver left his vehicle at the bowser while he went in to pay, and Róisín climbed out of her car for a breath of fresh air while she waited.

'Don't you just hate it when they do their shopping while they're paying for fuel?'

Róisín swung around to face the man who was standing beside a white ute in the other fuel bay. 'Well, will you look what the cat dragged in?' she said with a smile; she knew that voice well. 'It's been a long time, Teddy Brewster, but I'd know that voice anywhere,' she said.

The tall, broad-shouldered man came over, holding out his hand. Róisín shook her head, stepped forwards, and hugged him.

'My God, it's good to see you, Teddy. How long has it been?'

'Well, how long has it been since you left the best place in the world to go and be some highfalutin' lawyer in the city?'

'It is the best place in the world, isn't it?' Róisín stood back and looked at him. 'You're looking good, Teddy. What are you up to these days?'

As they looked at each other, the guy in the red ute walked out, climbed in and took off in a cloud of red dust.

'Takes all kinds,' Róisín said. 'Wait there while I move up to the pump.'

Róisín O'Byrne and Teddy Brewster had sat next to each other at the small, one-teacher school in Louth for most of their primary schooling and stayed good mates when they moved on to their respective boarding schools.

Teddy's parents owned the Louth pub in those days, and as the town was only a half-hour drive from *Ceann Mara Station*, Róisín and her sisters spent much of their childhood there, attending primary school, playing sport, and staying with friends.

Not that it could be called a town. The town had a pub, a fuel station, a small general store, and a tiny population until the Louth races in August each year, when the population swelled to thousands.

'I'm still here.' His eyebrows raised. 'See your dad

sometimes. Haven't seen you back here, though.'

'I was home for Christmas. I thought your parents sold and you moved away. I don't think I've seen you since before I left for uni.'

'And how long ago would that be?'

Róisín tilted her head to the side. 'I did four years at uni, and I've been working in Brisbane for the last three years, so I guess it's almost eight years now since I saw you at the races the last year I was home.'

'So how come you're home now? Everyone okay?'

'Yes, all good. Did you know Cat's moved home?'

'Yeah, I've met her bloke. Logan's a nice fella.'

Róisín was pretty sure no one knew why she was home. She'd asked her family not to talk about her moving back to the district. The position she had accepted was part of an investigative team that was operating under a reasonably innocuous name. She wasn't going to say much about her position until she had her first meeting with Seth Brodie, the team leader. She would find out where she was going to be based and would know more about the position this week.

Plus, she didn't want Greg to know where she was.

'I'll tell you more when I know a bit more about how long I'm staying. And yes, Logan's a great guy, and they're really happy. Did you know they're getting married in June?'

'I did, and I hear your mum's getting ready to have a big wedding at the station.'

Róisín pulled a face. 'I'm not surprised she's talked Cat into it. Mum was so disappointed when Erin and Jack eloped, and she missed out on organising a wedding. Now Teddy, tell me, what have you been up to?'

'When Mum and Dad sold the pub, they retired to the coast. Hervey Bay. God knows why you'd want to live there—crowds, sand and sandflies. I stayed.'

Róisín glanced at his left hand and smiled when she spotted the gold wedding ring. 'You're obviously settled,' she said.

'Married, yup,' he said, noticing her glance.

'Kids?'

'Yup,' he said.

'Land?' she asked.

'Twenty questions today, hey, Ro? Yeah, I married Mandy Sullivan. We have two kids: Brittany, three, and Liam, two—one of each. And yes, I bought myself a bit of land.'

'Well, we'll have to catch up.'

His smile was wide. 'And Mandy and I bought the General Store from Eleanore Higgins last year.'

'Wow, that's great news.'

'We'll make a time if you really do want to catch up.'

'I do. I'd love to see Mandy again, too.'

'How long are you home for?'

Róisín smiled. 'I'm in the district for a while. I'll be down at *Ceann Mara* for a week or two, at least,' she said.

'Do you still fly? I remember how all us guys were green with envy when you got your pilot's license.'

'My license is still current, but I don't fly anywhere near as much as I'd like to.' *Maybe I will now that I'm home,* she thought. That was another thing she'd let go of when she started seeing Greg. 'Anyway, I'd better fill up and hit the road; Mum's expecting me for smoko.'

'I'd better shake a leg, too. I'm on the way to Tilpa—a load of sheep to pick up. I left my truck there with my mate the other day. Mandy's looking after the store for me today. Great to see you, Ro, and we'll catch up for sure.'

'Right, see you soon, mate.' After paying for the fuel, Róisín stood beside her car and looked around. This land had always tugged at her heart. The red dirt, the river gums, and the coolabah trees, with their smooth, powdery cream bark, told her she was home.

It would be a very different life being back here, moving from a thriving city centre office in Brisbane to a nearly two-hundred-year-old sandstone building on the banks of the Darling

River.

Much to Mum and Dad's disappointment, Róisín had left home on Boxing Day after only a few days at home, claiming that she had much work to do before she left the firm to come home to her new job. Her family didn't know she'd already left Henderson and Associates; she'd put on a great front in the few days she was home over Christmas. Maybe she could take up acting as a career if the new job didn't work out. She had to go back to Brisbane, sort out the rest of her apartment and decide what to do with it. The way she felt now, she didn't want to go back to city life ever, but maybe that was a knee-jerk reaction.

Her work over the past three years had been disappointing and unfulfilling. Her days were more like that of a clerical officer keying in data. These days, artificial intelligence had changed the landscape of law work, and to be honest, the work at Henderson and Associates was boring and held no challenges for her. Much of her work was automated, with AI tools sorting through financial documents, text messages, and emails to identify key evidence, especially in contentious divorce cases where assets and communications were critical. There was little legal work for her to do. It was all neatly presented to her after a search where all she had to do was put in key terms, and then the program would predict potential outcomes based on similar case data. Settlement options and court strategies were all presented neatly in a strategic package.

Róisín had often wondered what Greg did in his office all day. He was always busy, either on the telephone or in meetings, but she'd soon learned that he wouldn't talk about it when she asked him about his cases. She suspected it made him feel important, mixing with the higher echelons of the society he considered important.

It was not a life she wanted.

A quick search of *booking.com* found an apartment at the Gold Coast for when she came back after Christmas. She didn't want to be in her apartment when Greg tried to come back. She would be long gone; she wouldn't see him again until she saw him in court.

If it got to that.

Chapter 3

Ceann Mara Station, Darling River - Tuesday, mid-January.

Cat had never run so fast; she and Logan were side by side, covering the distance to the shed in seconds. The whole way, she could hear Mum crying and calling them. 'Help me! Cat, Logan. Help. Help. Quickly!'

Cat's blood was running like ice through her veins, and she knew that something dreadful had happened. It had to be Dad.

'Mum, we're coming. What's wrong?' she yelled as the fine red dirt rose around their legs as they ran across to the shed.

She and Logan rounded the side of the shed together, and for a moment, she couldn't see either of her parents.

'Laura? Tom? Where are you?' Logan called as he ran past the Cessna to the far bay of the shed.

'Help me!' Laura's distressed call came from the other side of the big tractor at the far end. 'Over near the bikes.'

Logan took off, but Cat was close behind him.

'Oh, shit,' he said. 'Oh shit, shit.'

Cat's heart almost stopped as she went around the back of the tractor. Dad was lying on his back, the bottom edge of his shirt soaked with blood. The ag bike lay awkwardly across his legs, its weight pinning him to the ground. His face was pale, lips faintly blue, his breathing shallow. Mum was at his side and had started chest compressions.

'Heart attack, not breathing. We need to get the bike off him!' Mum grunted, her eyes darting towards the bike.

Cat's heart was thumping so hard it hurt as Logan quickly moved towards the bike. 'I'll be careful,' he said quietly, his face tight and worried. 'We don't know how bad his leg is.'

With a mighty heave, he lifted the bike and rolled it aside. Dad's leg was twisted at a strange angle, the skin around the crushed area already darkening.

'Laura, move back. I'll take over!' Logan said urgently. 'Cat, go for the defibrillator. Quickly.'

'He's still not breathing.' Mum let out a soft sob as she rocked back on her heels, her hands clutched to her chest. 'Tom . . . please, no . . .' Her voice cracked, filled with fear and grief.

Oh God, Dad. Please no, no, no. Cat couldn't think straight.

Logan jerked his head to the quad runner at the front of the shed. 'Cat. Go now. Fast!'

Her breath hitched as she took a last glance at Dad and then ran for the quad runner. The grey pallor of his skin and his blue lips didn't leave her as she roared up the road as fast as the small vehicle would go.

'Three-minute rule, three-minute rule,' she muttered as she pushed the throttle. From the first aid training they'd done when the defibrillator was installed, she knew she had to hurry. The quicker the defibrillator was used, the more chance Dad had. Her breath hitched with a sob as the voice of the local St John trainer came back to her.

'For every minute that passes, the chance of survival reduces by ten percent.'

Red dust filled the air as Cat swung the handlebars hard and parked on the path beside the camp kitchen door. She jumped out, ran to the wall-mounted cabinet, and wrenched open the door. The battery-operated alarm sounded, and a red light flashed.

Three minutes. Three minutes. The mantra stayed with her the whole way.

In less than two minutes, she was back at the shed and out of the quad runner, the defibrillator clutched in both hands as she ran across to Logan.

Mum knelt beside Dad, her hands trembling as tears

streaked down her cheeks. Logan's focus remained on Dad's chest, rhythmically compressing it with determined force, his shoulders straining with the effort. He was still counting chest compressions, pressing his hands down on Dad's sternum. 'Good girl. Come on, Tom, don't do this to us,' he muttered under his breath between counts as beads of sweat dotted his forehead.

Laura reached out and grabbed Cat's arm. 'The RFDS—Cat—we need them now. You call. I—' Mum's voice wavered as Cat carefully placed the defibrillator on the ground beside Logan. 'I don't know what to do.'

Cat leaned down and put her arms around her mother's shaking shoulders. 'We've got this. Mum. He'll be okay.' Her voice held more hope than she was feeling. 'Logan. Do you need me to take over, or will I call first?'

He grunted. 'Call now. Use the phone in the office. Too far to go to the radio.'

Cat ran across to the small office in the corner behind the tractor. She looked up at the list of numbers on the wall, and her fingers fumbled on the telephone pad. Dad had installed a landline in the office in the days before mobile phones.

Thank God.

RFDS was top of the list.

1800DRSFLY

Or Dial 000 was on the next line.

Dad had been prepared for emergencies since the accident on the station when Róisín and Cat were toddlers. Róisín could quite easily have died that day, but Dad's quick thinking had saved her life. Since then, various incidents with shearers and stockmen had resulted in the list being put up in the shearing shed, the old store, and at each gate between the hundreds of paddocks at the station.

She managed to dial the number of the Royal Flying Doctor Service.

'We have an emergency,' she said as soon as the call connected. 'My dad has had a heart attack, severe leg injury—he's not breathing, we're performing CPR and about to defibrillate. His back has been bleeding, too. I think he's landed on something when he fell.'

'Okay, stay calm. Where are you located?'

'Ceann Mara Station. Thirty ks south of Louth on the western side of the river.'

'Right. You're in luck. We have a fixed-wing aircraft just about to leave Tilpa. We'll redirect them.'

'Thank you.' Relief flooded through Cat. Sometimes, it could take hours for help to arrive.

'Please stay on the line. You're doing well. Let's take this step by step. Can you confirm CPR is ongoing?'

Cat stepped out of the office as far as the cord would stretch. 'Yes. My partner is doing chest compressions, Mum is doing the breaths now, and Logan's about to deliver the first shock.'

'Okay. Tell me what it says when delivered.'

'Will do. I'm going to take over the compressions.' Cat went back to the office, put the phone on speaker, and then stretched the phone cord out as far as it would reach.

Logan nodded, and Cat took over the compressions as he opened the defibrillator. He placed the pads on Dad's chest, following the illustrations on each pad: one on the upper right side of his chest, one below the collarbone, and the third on the lower left, a few inches below his armpit. The machine blinked to life, beeping in preparation.

Although he moved quickly and efficiently, it seemed like hours to Cat.

Charging. Stay clear of the patient, the robotic voice of the defibrillator instructed. Cat reached out and put her arms around Mum as they stood and stepped back.

Shock advised. Press the shock button.

Logan's voice was tight. 'Here we go. Shocking now.'

'Good.' The operator must have heard Logan, and the

speakerphone was working well enough for them to hear her. 'Did the defibrillator analyse and prompt for a shock, or did it say to continue CPR?'

They all watched, frozen, waiting. The defibrillator resumed its mechanical assessment.

'*Continue CPR,*' it instructed.

Laura yelled. Her voice was shrill. 'We have to try again. It says to keep going! Please don't stop, Logan.'

Logan crouched beside Tom and the machine. 'It's recharging.'

Cat watched helplessly as the machine went through its cycle; her head was spinning from the tension, but she fought the light-headedness that was threatening.

Continue chest compressions. Reanalysing.

Logan and Cat began CPR again as the machine reanalysed. Laura stood behind them, her hands over her face.

'Come on, come on,' Logan murmured, his movements growing more frantic. 'Don't give up on us, Tom…'

Shock advised. Charging. Stay clear.

Logan pulled Cat up to her feet and leaned over the defibrillator. His hands hovered, ready. The defibrillator beeped again.

Shock now. Press the shock button.

Logan's voice shook. 'Shocking now.' He pressed the

button. Tom's body jolted, his chest arching up slightly as the second electrical shock surged through him. Cat's hands went to her mouth when Dad's chest began to rise.

'Mum, Look! He's breathing by himself.'

'Okay, stay with it,' the operator said. 'The aircraft is in the air and should be with you in fifteen minutes. Is the runway close to where you are?'

'Yes, I'll go over in Dad's ute when I hear the aircraft approach. Logan and Mum can resume CPR if necessary.' This time, Cat's voice was calm as she watched Dad's chest rise and fall and his eyelids begin to flicker. There was no way Mum would be capable of driving to the runway. Her face was white, and her hands clenched together.

'Keep the defibrillator ready for further analysis. Follow its instructions. It will monitor the patient. Stay on the line.'

Laura kneeled close to Tom's head. 'Please, wake up, darling. Please . . . we need you.'

'Hold on, Dad. It won't be long now.'

Logan put his arm around Cat, and she turned her head into his chest. He was slick with sweat.

'Hold on, Tom. Hold on,' he said quietly.

Tom's eyelids started to open, and he looked at them, confused, before they closed again. Laura put a hand over her mouth and stood, and Cat could see her trying to compose herself as she took in deep, shaking breaths.

'Come over here with me, Mum. I'll get you some water, and I want you to sit down. Okay? Logan's got Dad under control. I want you to calm down.'

Laura shook her head. 'No, I want to stay close.'

'Okay.' Cat went over to the bench and was surprised to see her hands were steady again. She filled the kettle and turned it on. It didn't take long to boil, and she poured a cup of black tea, adding four sugars to it. As she walked over to Mum, she passed the tray of scones and jam and cream lying in the dirt on the shed floor. It felt like hours since she'd taken them out of the oven, but it couldn't even be half an hour.

Logan had his arm around Laura.

'I want you to drink this, Mum. You're white as a ghost.'

Mum's breath drew in on a gasp as Dad spoke.

'Bastard bike fell on me,' he said, his voice thready, his eyes still shut. Laura dropped to her knees beside him.

Chapter 4

Louth, Darling River - Tuesday, mid-January.

Róisín waved to Teddy as he drove out, and when she'd paid for her fuel and was about to start her car, she remembered she'd promised to text Mum when she left Louth. She glanced at her watch; she would arrive in time for smoko. She hoped Mum hadn't gone overboard with preparation for her stay, but knowing Laura O'Byrne, the fatted calf would have been metaphorically killed to celebrate her eldest daughter's long-awaited return home.

Too long. Every time she mentioned coming home for a visit, Greg organised a trip away: to Cairns, Fiji, or New Zealand. The Darling River and meeting her family didn't appeal to him at all.

And she'd gone along with him. Every time.

With a sigh, she pushed those thoughts away. She wasn't

proud of the person she'd become over the last few years.

She quickly sent a text: **Just leaving. Put the kettle on. Can't wait. Love. R**

Róisín started the car, but before she could reach the road, her phone rang on the seat beside her. She'd expected Mum to text back, not ring.

For a moment, she hesitated, keen to get on the road, and then thought twice. Mum might need something from the store.

'Hi, Mum. Do you need something from the store?'

'Róisín!'

Her heart sank when her ex-partner's voice came through the phone. For a few seconds, her finger hovered over the 'end call' button, but she thought twice. It might be something to do with work. She had to remain professional, no matter what she was feeling. She'd told Greg—by email— he could contact her if he had any questions about the cases she'd passed on to her colleague at his firm and hadn't expected him to call.

Róisín made it clear in her resignation email that any future contact was to be by email or text. HR would have notified him immediately when she resigned, but surprisingly, this was the first time he'd called.

Maybe he thought I've still got COVID, Róisín thought with a grim smile.

'Greg. What can I help you with?' Her voice was brisk.

'What can you help me with? For a start, you can bloody talk to me and tell me what you're doing, quitting the firm and heading off to wherever it is in the boondocks you are.'

Róisín hadn't shared the news about her new job with anyone apart from her family. She had her family's promise that they wouldn't tell anyone until she told them they could, not wanting word to get out in the local paper, especially with Greg's habit of Googling her to find out what she had been up to.

The first time he'd done that and mentioned that he wasn't happy with her being on the social committee for her local gym, Róisín had been quite taken aback.

As a result, she was very careful; she didn't want Greg to know anything about her new job or that she'd headed home. She'd asked Seth Brodie, the convenor of the interview panel, not to publicise her appointment until she officially started next week, even though she had signed the contract.

'That's not a problem. It's not the way we operate. Given the nature of our work, you'll find that we are a very low-key operation that keeps under the radar,' her new boss said. 'I'll fill you in when you come to the office.'

When he'd interviewed her during the Zoom meeting, Seth's professionalism impressed her. Quietly spoken, he had held her gaze as he'd spoken and asked her some deep questions about her legal philosophies and the environment. His questions had been probing, and Róisín had answered from the heart and not referred to her previous employment.

'How do you view the role of law in protecting environmental resources like water, particularly in areas facing exploitation or overuse?' had been his final question. His eyes held hers through the digital connection.

'For me, the law plays a critical role in protecting water because it is the only force strong enough to hold those who exploit it accountable. Laws can ensure that everyone, from farmers to corporations, uses water sustainably and fairly, and it can safeguard the river for future generations. And it's not just about rules. We have to consider justice not just for the property owners but for the land itself. That's why I am interested in this position: without strong legal protections—and *federal* legislation—the river's future, and the future of all who depend on it, is in jeopardy.'

'Wherever you are in the boondocks.' Greg's words now said it all. She should have accepted how shallow he was a long time ago.

Now, his voice nagged at her over the phone.

Róisín kept her tone flat; she wasn't going to let Greg Henderson unsettle her. He was a master of manipulation, but now that she knew what he was capable of, she would never fall for it again. 'I told HR that contact was to be by email only.'

'Come on, Roy! Don't leave me hanging like this! Tell me what I did! Tell me why you packed up and left me, why you changed the locks on our apartment?'

How many times had she told him not to call her Roy? She loathed it.

'*My* apartment, Greg. If you recall, it was always mine. I put all your stuff in suitcases in the basement where you park. I'm sure you found your belongings in the basement.'

'I did, but I want to know why. Why are you leaving me? Why did you chuck me out? Why did you quit the firm? Where are you going? I'm worried about you—I love you.'

'Do you, Greg?' she asked. The coldness in her voice spread to her blood.

'You know, sweetheart, we were building a good life together. I was going to ask you to marry me, and now, what have you done? Thrown away everything! I've even bought your engagement ring.'

When he said that, she knew Greg was being his usual manipulating self, lying to get his way. He'd told her that he'd never marry and that had suited her. Deep down, she'd always known that he wasn't the right partner for her. But their life together had been fun for a while.

'Where are you? Or are your parents with you in Brisbane?'

Ah, he doesn't know I'm out here. Good.

'Greg, I will not speak to you on a personal basis. If you have any questions about the cases I've passed on to Jodie, email me.'

'Just tell me why you left. Were you screwing someone else? Tell me because I'll be after him.'

'Goodbye, Greg.'

'Bitch. You'll pay for this.'

Before she could disconnect, he ended the call. To Róisín's dismay, her hands were shaking. She was angry with herself for letting him provoke such an emotional reaction.

She gripped the steering wheel to stop the shaking and glanced at the screen to see if a reply had come in from Mum, but there was nothing. Taking a deep breath, she started the car, turned left, crossed the bridge to the west side of the Darling River, and headed west along Weelong Road. When she reached the junction with Toorale Road, she calmed a little. This was the road that took her home.

Twenty kilometres along and almost home, Róisín was still unsettled; she knew she had to calm down before she reached the station. Mum would know there was something wrong as soon as she walked in, and she wasn't going to tell her family what a mess she'd made of her personal life.

She turned off towards the free camp at the end of Gentle Nellie's Road and drove over to a spreading river gum where she could see the gently flowing river. Reaching for her water bottle, she took a big swig and forced herself to calm down before she drove the last six kilometres home.

I won't let him have a hold over me anymore.

Maybe she should've told Greg she knew the truth. And if she was honest with herself, she knew with the sway she had let him have over her, he might have even talked her into staying. If he knew what she was planning to do, it wouldn't help Linda's case. Greg Henderson's reach was far and wide.

This was a new start, and she would succeed and overcome her disappointment for letting him fool her for so long. It was a wonder she had been capable of performing successfully at the interview.

But I did, and I'm here now. And he doesn't know where I am.

***

Greg Henderson threw the phone onto his desk. It bounced off the water carafe and slid onto the floor.

Bloody bitch. If he could have got his hands on Róisín

O'Byrne at that moment, he would have choked her until she begged for mercy.

She'd lied to him. Taken everything he'd given her, a senior job at the top law firm in Brisbane, the firm that he had built himself, and the entry he'd given the little country bumpkin into the top echelons of Brisbane society.

Now, he was running short of cash until the next delivery came in, and in the meantime, since she'd changed the locks on the apartment, he had nowhere to live.

How dare she, the stupid bitch?

He'd already tried to call in a favour with a real estate mate, but he wouldn't give him access to an apartment without a hefty bond. After the bitch had drawn the three grand from his credit card when she'd taken off, the bank had put a block on it, and now he had no access to ready cash.

But his biggest worry was that she could bring him down. When Mitchell Bryant called him and told him where Róisín had accepted a position, his blood pressure went through the roof.

How the hell had she found out about his business? She hadn't even known about his pub and restaurant, let alone his business out west.

What was she going to do? Was she going to bring him down? He would stop her, no matter what it took. In the meantime, he would cover his tracks as best as he could.

Reaching down to the floor, he picked up his phone and hit speed dial.

'Wilson,' the gruff voice barked out.

'Update me.'

'She left the Gold Coast three days ago, and now she's headed out past Bourke.'

'Have you been careful?'

'No need to ask that, boss. The only time I've been within view of her car was when I overtook her to get fuel a while back. I don't know how far into the bush she's going, so I needed to fill up. I've got a tracking device on her car, so no wuckers, I won't lose her.'

'Tell me where she stops. If she heads towards Wilcannia, make sure she doesn't get there. I hear the roads are bad out that way.'

'My pleasure. It'll be good to leave this fucking red dirt behind.'

'Don't lose her.'

Chapter 5

Darling River, Tuesday, mid-January.

As Róisín sat in the car beneath the huge red river gum, she thought back to that fateful day on the nineteenth of December. She remembered every moment so clearly. She'd left work early to get ready for the law firm's Christmas party. Greg had selected the dress and shoes he wanted her to wear. When she'd collected them from the boutique, she'd been astounded at the ridiculous amount of money he'd spent. He sent her home from work at two o'clock so she could get her hair and makeup done at the salon on the ground floor of the apartment building—the appointment *he'd* made for her. Before Greg, Róisín had always done her own hair and makeup.

'We're the face of Henderson and Associates, sweetheart, and we have to look perfect,' he said.

After checking that the evening gown was hanging on the bedroom door and that the few crush marks had fallen out, Róisín took a quick shower and washed her hair. Leaving it wet, she picked up her handbag and opened the door to head to the salon on the ground floor. Her morning had been busy, trying to wind up as much as she could before the Christmas break. She was going home for a quick visit for Christmas—much to Greg's disgust—and then they were flying to Los Angeles on New Year's Eve, where he apparently had some business meetings that had to be held in person.

'Do you really have to go home?' he said as she was working on her laptop in the apartment the night before the Christmas function. Honestly, sometimes he was like a child, and Róisín was over pandering to him.

'Yes, I do,' she said, focusing on the screen.

'If we go a bit earlier, you can hit Rodeo Drive and get your winter wardrobe sorted while I meet my colleague.'

'I have enough clothes and shoes to last me a lifetime. Besides, I'm going home on Saturday. I'll be back a couple of days before we fly out. It would be nice if you came with me.'

'Oh, God, I don't do families. You know that.'

Sadly, she did, and that was another reason she knew this relationship wasn't going to be for the long term. Róisín knew that if she asked Greg to move out, she would no longer have a job. In the New Year, she'd start looking for another position.

With a sigh, she pulled the apartment door shut behind her as she headed down to the hair salon. She'd much rather stay in and watch a movie tonight. Next year, things would be different; she'd start looking for another job tomorrow. Greg could move out in the New Year.

Róisín stepped into the corridor and noticed an unfamiliar woman, holding the hand of a little girl, walking towards her. Her apartment building was usually empty at this time of the afternoon, so she paused and smiled politely, waiting for them to pass, only to be taken aback when the woman stopped in front of her.

'Can I help you? Are you looking for one of the apartments?' she asked politely.

The woman shook her head and stepped closer. Her eyes were shadowed, her clothes crumpled, and the child's face was dirty.

'Are you Rose-Anne O'Byrne?' the woman asked.

'I'm Róisín O'Byrne, yes,' she said, sounding out her name as it was often pronounced incorrectly. *Ro-Sheen.* 'How can I help you?' She was hoping it wasn't someone from one of the divorce cases she'd handled for the firm, but her face wasn't familiar.

'How can you help me?' the woman said quietly. 'You can listen while I tell you about my marriage. You need to know.'

'I'm sorry. I don't recall your case. I think you might have the wrong lawyer.'

'No, I don't have the wrong person. You don't know who I am?'

Róisín shook her head. 'I'm sorry, should I?'

'Probably not. But I believe you know my husband very well.'

'I'm sorry, I'm not sure who you mean.'

'Gregory Henderson? Of Henderson and Associates.' The woman took a step closer, and the little girl followed her.

The blood drained from Róisín's face, and she felt slightly faint. 'I beg your pardon? I'm sorry, you must have the wrong person.'

'No, I haven't. I've seen your photo with him in the *Courier Mail* on the social pages quite a few times this year. It just took me this long to find out where you lived. They didn't ever put your name in the paper. You were always referred to as his "beautiful mystery woman." I didn't realise you worked at the firm until I read an article about you last week and recognised you. If I'd known that before, I would have been much quicker finding you. I might have saved you some grief.'

'Some grief?' Róisín parroted. Her head was spinning. 'I'm sorry, but I really don't understand. What are you talking about?'

'I'm talking about my husband, Greg,' the woman said.

'You do have the wrong person. *My* Greg is not married.'

'Oh, yes, he is. I'm sorry to be the one to tell you,' the woman said with a sad smile. 'Not that I want him back. God, that would never happen.'

Róisín stood there, unsure of what to do. Should she continue this conversation in the hallway or invite the woman inside?

No, she couldn't do that. She didn't know if she was even telling the truth or if she could be dangerous. But with the little girl hanging tightly to her hand, Róisín soon discounted that.

'Look, I have an appointment I need to go to, but I'll call and tell them I'll be a little late,' she said. 'Perhaps we could go downstairs to the coffee shop and have this conversation.'

The woman's eyes filled with tears. 'Okay, I understand why you don't want me inside. I suppose he's been living here too.'

Perhaps she was delusional.

But when she looked closely at the little girl clinging to her mother's hand, Róisín saw something very familiar. She nearly gagged, feeling nauseous. The child's wide, brown eyes and arched eyebrows bore a striking resemblance to Greg's—the same eyebrows Róisín had often traced with her fingers, telling him that some women would kill for those arched brows.

Maybe there was some truth in the woman's story.

Her stomach churned.

They walked to the lift in silence. Róisín pushed the button for the ground floor, but neither spoke as the lift descended. When they reached the ground floor, she stepped back to let the woman and child walk out ahead of her.

'What would you like to drink?' she asked when they reached the coffee shop.

'I'll have a black coffee, thank you.' The woman's demeanour was strange. She wasn't angry; it was almost as though she felt sorry for Róisín.

'What would you like, sweetie?' she asked the little girl.

'Can I have a banana milkshake, please, Mummy?' the child asked softly, not looking at Róisín.

'Yes, you can.'

The little girl's face lit up, and she clapped her hands.

'A black coffee and a banana milkshake,' the woman said. 'Thank you, Róisín.' This time, she pronounced her name correctly.

Róisín placed the order at the counter—plus a double shot espresso for herself—and walked across to the secluded booth in the back corner of the coffee shop. It was quiet there; the lunch rush had passed, and the afternoon coffees were usually takeaways.

'Excuse me for a moment.' Róisín pulled out her phone and quickly called the hairdresser next door. 'Hi, Mary, I'm running a little late. Can you give me half an hour, please?'

'No problem. I'm running behind anyway,' Mary replied.

The next hour was the worst of Róisín's life.

Sixty *life-changing* minutes.

When she sat down, the woman had picked up a napkin, and the little girl's face was clean. 'Aurora had a chocolate biscuit on the bus, and I didn't have a tissue to wipe her face,' she explained.

'You've got a pretty name,' Róisín said gently to the little girl.

Aurora smiled back at her, and the resemblance to Greg was even more pronounced.

'What's your name?' she asked the mother.

'Linda. Linda Henderson.'

Henderson.

Róisín took a deep breath. 'And tell me why you came looking for me?'

Linda's eyes filled with tears, but she quickly wiped them away with the napkin she was still holding as their order was delivered to the booth. 'Because I don't want to see more women get hurt. Greg is a smooth operator and such a liar that it is almost impossible not to fall for him. I'm gradually rebuilding our lives'—she looked at Aurora, who was quietly drinking her milkshake— 'but I hate to think of others being conned and ending up under his control. And Róisín, trust me, you're not the first woman he's lived with since he left me.'

'Look, Linda. I have to be honest. I have no idea what you mean.' Even as she spoke, Róisín was recalling the control that Greg had taken over her life in the past year.

The flattery. How beautiful she was. What an excellent lawyer she was and what an asset to his firm. How he'd fallen in love with her the instant she'd walked into her interview, and how he couldn't stop thinking about her. The life they would make together, the new penthouse, and the overseas travel. How lonely he'd been, but now he'd met her, he'd found his soulmate.

As the months had passed, she'd been busy, and the gradual coercive control had been an insidious addition to their relationship.

The gradual separation from her family, Greg's decisions about where they would eat and what they would order, what Róisín would wear, what they would buy, and how they should decorate *her* apartment, selling her car and buying the one that he wanted—occasionally with his money, but mostly with hers—intensified the sick feeling in her stomach as she listened to Linda.

'Greg and I married when we were twenty, and we were together for eight years. I supported him through university with my wages, and we lived in my parents' house after they passed away. I discovered I was pregnant, but I didn't tell him straight away. Something held me back. By that stage of our marriage, I knew what he was like, and I knew he didn't want children. I was working two jobs when his father died and left him a sizeable inheritance. Enough money to become quite the man about town. He started the celebrity business in that posh office in the city, and then he wanted to sell my parents' place.'

'Were you happy about that?'

'No. He lied to me, Róisín. He sold *my* property at Mt Coottha—the land and house my parents had left to me. Then, when I told him I was pregnant, he walked away and took everything we had.'

'How could he do that?'

'Walk away?'

'No, sell your house.'

Linda held her gaze steadily. 'He finally talked me into selling. I'm sure you're familiar with his persuasive arguments, and the way he can exert control? The day the house was settled, the removalists had packed up everything, and I wondered why some of the boxes were left out of the truck. When Greg came home from work, I was expecting to go to the place he'd rented for us, but I soon discovered that I wasn't going with him. He handed me a thousand dollars and left me with the boxes holding my possessions. I'd trusted him so much I didn't even know the address we were supposed to be moving to.'

'What about the proceeds of the sale of the property? Your parents' place?'

'He took it all. He said he'd put the proceeds of the house sale in a trust fund. I wasn't well when I was pregnant—I had a slight breakdown from the shock of what he did. I'm ashamed to say I didn't follow it up until after Aurora was born. That's when he told me it was all gone.'

'The money?'

'Yes, he'd invested it unwisely—or so he told me—and there was nothing left. It had never gone into a trust fund. That was simply another of his lies.'

Róisín shook her head. 'But you have rights. It's a shame you didn't get legal representation.'

'I wasn't in a good place.'

'How much was the property worth?'

'Five million dollars.'

Róisín stared at Linda, shocked by her answer. 'Five million dollars?'

'Yes, it was bought by some developer Greg knew.'

'And you got nothing? And he says he lost the money you were entitled to?' All Róisín could think of were the designer labels, the overseas trips, and the many nights at expensive restaurants.

And Linda and Aurora—she now accepted that they were his wife and daughter—had been living in poverty. Guilt gripped her chest, and she felt physically ill. Her hand shook as she put her coffee cup in the saucer. The bitterness was making her feel even sicker. She picked up the napkin and dabbed at her mouth.

Linda shook her head. 'I'm sure you know what a clever man he is. He's the top divorce lawyer in the state, remember? I used to be proud to say that. Now, it disgusts me. How do you think he got there? Can you imagine any lawyer wanting to take Greg on in our divorce? They'd be blacklisted. He always bragged about the power he had. He threatened me the day he left me. He told me I'd be very sorry if I told anyone. He said he told everyone at the office that I was having an affair and that we were getting divorced.'

Róisín stared at her; that must have been before she started at the firm. Greg rolled through contract lawyers and receptionists at a rate of knots; most were never renewed at the end of contract, so there was no one working there from before she started at the firm. That was one thing she had always wondered about; his perception of how highly regarded he was by the legal community wasn't illustrated by his employment practices. He employed the first-year out lawyers on contract and then replaced them when their contract was completed. She was the one who stayed, and for a while, she'd kidded herself if it was because she was good at her job. Yeah, using AI programs to get a result.

'I'm so sorry, Linda. I had no idea. He told me he wasn't married. He told me he'd built the firm up with hard work and wise investments.'

'Did he tell you what else he owns now?'

Róisín shook her head. 'No, unless you mean his sports car?'

Linda looked at her. Sympathy shone from her eyes. 'The pub at Bulimba and the restaurant in the Valley?'

'No.' Her shoulders slumped.

'In case you doubt me and think I'm just some nutter, I've got this to show you.' Linda pulled a small wedding photo from her purse. Róisín stared at an image of a much younger Greg, and she knew everything Linda had said was true.

For a few moments, she couldn't speak as memory after memory of the last year flooded through her mind.

Her voice broke as she put her hand across the table to clasp

Linda's. She cleared her throat and started again. 'Rest assured, Greg won't be staying in my apartment any longer. And I won't be working with him anymore,' Róisín said, her voice firming.

'He is such a narcissist; he thinks he'll get away with it,' Linda said. 'The photographs on the social pages have been the clues that helped me find his victims. His downfall, eventually, I hope.'

'Victims. Yes. That's the right word.' Róisín dropped her head into her hands. 'I feel so stupid.'

'Don't blame yourself, Róisín. He is very clever, and being such a good-looking man, he attracts women.'

'All that aside, I want you to know how sorry I am. I had no idea. He told me he would never marry; until we met, he said he'd lived a bachelor's life.' Róisín's eyes welled with tears. Sympathy, guilt, and worry for the little girl whose father didn't care about her or provide for her. 'Where are you living now? You are entitled to a settlement and child support.' The professional Róisín kicked in. 'How long have you been divorced?'

'I was living with a friend when Aurora was born, but she moved overseas. We moved around a few house sites, and now we're in a refuge, but we're doing okay,' Linda replied. 'I feel safe there, and Aurora has other children to play with. And we're not divorced. He told me I couldn't get anything if we weren't divorced.'

'That's not true, Linda. Under the Family Law Act of 1975, you can ask the court to make orders for property settlement or maintenance arising out of a marriage, even if you are not yet divorced.'

Linda's eyes widened. 'I should have known he was lying.'

'Do you need some money?' Róisín asked gently.

'We manage.' Linda held her gaze steadily. 'But the main reason I came to see you was that I found out you were a divorce lawyer. I was hoping that maybe when you heard my story, you would represent me if I did decide to go to court. I knew if you'd lived with him for a while, you would understand what I was talking about.'

'He moved into *my* apartment,' Róisín said.

'I can understand that. I do want a divorce. I want to cut all ties, and I want to make sure he has nothing to do with Aurora ever. I have some documents that might help.'

'Linda, I will represent you. But it will have to be as a freelance lawyer because I'll be leaving his firm.'

'I hope I've saved you from what I went through,' Linda said quietly.

Róisín's self-disgust was overwhelming her. 'That's the least of my worries, Linda. We will get back what you are owed.'

'Whatever you can do. I can see you're a good person, Róisín. I'm sorry he took a year of your life.'

Róisín touched Linda's wrist gently. 'I'm sorry he took so much of yours.'

'Can I ask you one more thing?' Linda's hand shook as she put her cup back into the saucer. 'Two, actually. Don't mention to Greg that I've contacted you. And more importantly, please be careful. He has a violent side that he keeps well hidden.'

Róisín nodded, even though she thought Linda was exaggerating; at least, she hoped she was. She'd never seen a violent side to Greg. 'I promise I won't mention your name. But I will fight to get you everything you are entitled to. It might take a long time, but I will work very hard for you.' Róisín's hand was shaking as she pulled out her phone. 'Can I have your contact details?'

'I don't have a phone.' Tears welled in Linda's eyes again as she gave Róisín the name and address of the refuge where they were living.

'I'll only be there for another few weeks. As soon as Aurora starts school after Christmas, I'll be able to get a part-time job and hopefully find somewhere decent for us to live.'

A possible solution came to Róisín, but she didn't want to offer it until she was absolutely certain that Linda's story was true. It wouldn't take much investigating to confirm that, and then she would offer her apartment for them to live in.

'It will take me a while, Linda,' Róisín said, 'but I promise you I'll be in touch within the next couple of weeks. In the meantime, I'd like to make sure that you and Aurora are okay. Would you wait here for a moment?'

Linda nodded and put her head down as the tears splashed onto her cheeks. 'I'll wait. And I'm sorry about the tears; it's just a tremendous relief that you believe me.'

Róisín squeezed Linda's shoulder gently as she left the coffee shop and walked to the ATM on the next block. She pulled out the credit card that Greg used to buy her clothes. It was sheer coincidence that she had it. When she went to pick up the dress that he'd ordered for the function, the woman in the boutique had handed it to her. 'Your husband left this behind. I didn't have a number to call, but I knew you'd be in to pick up the dress,' she said.

Róisín closed her eyes before entering the PIN onto the ATM touchpad. Thank God she knew it.

How had she let Greg turn her into a woman who would happily wear a three-thousand-dollar dress to a party? How had he managed to pull her so deeply into his world? Sickness roiled in her stomach as his daughter's pinched little face stuck in her mind.

She straightened her shoulders as she hurried back to the coffee shop; she half expected Linda to be gone, but she was still sitting there, one arm around her little girl.

Linda cried when she gave her the money.

'I can't take it,' she said, shaking her head.

Róisín's smile was bitter. 'It's not mine. It's from Greg's account, so it's yours.'

Chapter 6

Brisbane - 19th December.

Róisín cancelled her hair and makeup appointments and went straight back to her apartment. She collected the dress, put it into the gold bag of the exclusive boutique and jumped in a taxi to Queen Street.

'I'm sorry,' she said to the woman. 'My husband'—the word almost stuck in her throat— 'didn't like this one when I tried it on at home. He's going to come here with me in the morning while I try some different labels. The function is on tomorrow night.' Róisín smiled brightly. 'Would you please refund this one, and we'll see you tomorrow.'

Greg was obviously such a good customer that the boutique owner didn't hesitate to process the refund to the card.

'I have just the perfect dress in mind. What time will I make an appointment for you tomorrow?'

'I'll call you first thing in the morning.'

As Róisín took a taxi back to her apartment, all she could think of was the look on Linda's face as she'd handed over three thousand dollars to her. Greg could unknowingly fund the bond and rent for his wife and daughter so they could live in a decent place.

Róisín hadn't realised how much he had taken over her life until she started working her way through her apartment.

She cleared out the two-thirds of her walk-in wardrobe where his suits, matching shirts and ties were all lined up and stuffed them into green garbage bags. She pulled out his two suitcases and filled them with his shoes. She quickly ran through the apartment, gathering everything that belonged to him. Greg had been reading yesterday's newspaper this morning as he smoked at the breakfast table—she had asked him not to smoke inside her apartment many times, but somehow, he always managed to get around her. The newspaper *and* the cigarette butt went into the suitcase too.

Within half an hour, she had taken the garbage bags and suitcases down to the garage and put them in his parking space. Then she called a locksmith, offering to pay in cash if he would change the locks on the apartment today.

'Are you sure? That'll cost five hundred bucks this late in the day,' the locksmith said.

'I don't care if it costs a thousand. I need you here now,' she insisted.

'Don't say that—I might charge you that.'

'I don't care, just please do it.'

'Is this a domestic violence situation?' he asked quietly.

Róisín's eyes filled with tears, but she dug for strength. 'You could say that.'

'I'm on my way, and I won't charge you extra.'

'Please hurry,' she said, her voice strained.

Then Róisín did the hardest thing she had ever done: she called Greg at the office and acted as if absolutely nothing had happened. His receptionist didn't want to take the call at first, but she insisted.

'Please, Remy,' she said. 'I need to speak to Greg urgently. It's concerning a case,' she lied. 'He needs to hear this now.'

His phone was picked up instantly.

'What case?' Greg snapped.

'I had to say that because Remy wasn't going to put me through,' Róisín explained.

'That's right, I told her not to,' he replied. 'I'm in a meeting right now. What's wrong?'

'I just wanted to let you know I'm not going to the Christmas party tonight, and you're probably better off not coming home. Can you get changed at the office?'

'What? Why the hell not?'

'I've got COVID,' she lied.

One thing that would definitely keep Greg away from her was his fear of COVID. He'd never been vaccinated and was terrified of catching it.

'In that case, that's a wise move. Okay, I've got some clothes here.'

She knew he had spare clothes and shoes at the office for various meetings.

'I'll give you a call in a few days and see when you're not infectious,' he added. 'I'll stay at the Hilton until then. Text me a copy of your Hilton membership card.'

'On the way,' she said sweetly.

And pigs might fly.

And that was it.

Not a single 'How are you?' or 'Do you need anything?' or 'Are you okay for Panadol?' Just 'I'll see you in a few days.'

Selfish bastard.

After the locks were changed, Róisín stayed in her apartment for three days; she was due home on Christmas Eve. She spent the first day looking at positions vacant online.

Her eyes widened, and her heart beat faster when she saw the job advertised at the Water Integrity Review Panel in

Western New South Wales. With one day to spare before applications closed, Róisín quickly put together her CV. Referees had been a problem, but she'd managed to find a few personal referees not associated with her firm, including Mitchell Bryant, a judge she'd often worked with. Mitchell, with whom she had an excellent professional relationship, was receptive to her request to keep it confidential, understanding she didn't want her current employer to know that she was applying for other positions.

'Good luck, Róisín,' he said when she'd Face-timed him at his chambers before she pressed submit on the online application. 'If you're sure that's what you want, go for it. You are an excellent lawyer, and I know you could apply your legal skills to any environment. A bit over the celebrity divorces?' Mitchell's warm eyes held curiosity.

'At times,' she replied. No one needed to know why she was getting out. She didn't think Mitchell knew about her personal relationship with her employer; they didn't move in the same social circles. Judge Bryant was old school; Greg preferred mixing with the influencer set and the celebrity elite. Actors, footballers, and sports elite made up his client base.

The job in Western New South Wales sounded too good to pass up, and as she pressed submit, she hoped her CV was adequate. It was the sort of job she knew she should have looked for when she'd graduated, but Greg had enticed her with an enhanced description of the work she would do at his firm.

She spent the next morning packing up the kitchen in the apartment and cleaning out the pantry and the fridge; she'd do the rest after Christmas. When it was done, and her bag was packed, she made a strong coffee and sat on her balcony overlooking the river.

Her mobile rang, and she jumped, worried it was Greg. She picked it up; the number was unfamiliar.

It was the recruitment agency.

She was shocked when they asked if she was available for an interview that afternoon via Zoom. The interview went well, and Róisín was gobsmacked when she was offered the job the next morning before she headed off on the two-day drive to *Ceann Mara*. It must have been the fastest interviewing and appointment process ever. She had no hesitation in accepting the position.

She didn't know if she had been successful because of her excellent qualifications or because of the one excellent reference from Mitchell, but in the end, it didn't matter. She got the job, signed the contract online, and sealed her future, but she was still unsure if going west was right for her—maybe she should have taken more time to consider her options. But she knew that the job was what she wanted to do; it was her personal situation that was causing her doubt. Never again would she get her personal life and work life mixed up.

Chapter 7

Darling River - Tuesday, mid-January.

Thoughts of the past wouldn't leave Róisín as she pulled out onto the road home. She'd barely noticed the last few kilometres pass as she headed towards *Ceann Mara.* Clearing Greg and the past weeks from her mind, Róisín switched on the car stereo, found some upbeat music, and continued home on the red dirt highway. She had to stay focused on the positives, her quest to help Linda and Aurora get what they were entitled to.

By the time she turned into the front gate of *Ceann Mara,* she had almost regained her composure, and a trickle of excitement at being home began to flow through her veins.

A big hug from Dad, a home-cooked meal, and lots of heart-to-hearts with Mum would help her begin to heal.

As Róisín stopped at the letterbox, the unwritten family rule made her smile; if anyone came past the letterbox, they had to stop, check, and bring in any mail that might be there.

Sometimes, when they'd all been out on the same day, the mailbox might be checked six times. When she opened the flap, there was nothing in there.

She drove slowly down the road to the house, looking at the feed in the paddocks and shaking her head in amazement at the lush, thick grass. She knew the rain had been way above average over the past eight months, with several floods out west breaking the long drought, but never had she ever seen *Ceann Mara* so lush and green—so much feed for the sheep, cattle, and goats. Dad and the other local farmers would be over the moon.

Her excitement built as she drove through the last gate and approached the shed. It was right on smoko time, and she knew Mum would have cooked up a feast for smoko and lunch to follow. She expected that Cat and Logan would be there too, now that they lived across the river at Logan's property.

As she drove in, all was quiet. No dogs came out to greet her, and there was no sign of anyone on horseback or any utes in the paddocks. She parked at the gate, surprised to see the back door was shut.

Leaving her handbag on the front seat, Róisín walked around to the front gate, past the side of the house, and around to the front door—it was shut, too. She checked her phone again, in case there had been a text from Mum, but there was nothing.

She looked down at the red dust staining her white sneakers as she made her way across to the shed. The satisfaction of being home warmed her chest, chasing away her earlier black mood; it was so good to be here finally. It was a long drive from Brisbane and one she hoped not to do very often from now on.

There was no sign of life in the shed either as she walked past Dad's Cessna and the farm vehicles. When she reached the tractor next to Dad's workbench, she stopped; a tray, some scones and two small dishes with jam and cream lay in the dirt. A jug lay on its side, the milk on the dirt curdling in the morning sun.

Her eyes widened, and her breath caught as she spotted a wide stain on the dirt ahead; it looked like blood. She crouched down and put her finger on it, confirming her fear. As she stood, she spotted the white twirled cable from a phone receiver back to the office snaking out past an ag bike tipped on its side.

Róisín turned to hurry back to the house and cried out in distress. Her hand went to her mouth as she saw the defibrillator from the camp kitchen lying on the ground. Nausea worked its way up through her chest and lodged in her throat.

There was no sign of the Land Cruiser wagon; something terrible must have happened. She ran out of the shed, and the cacophony of noise ahead finally registered.

Róisín was enough of a station girl to recognise the

problem the moment she looked across to the shed paddock. Dad must have brought the cattle in for drenching this morning. The low, urgent bawling of beasts in distress hit her like a wall of sound, reverberating through the still morning air. It wasn't their usual lazy chatter; this was restless and demanding. She could see the beasts crowded in the yard, jostling and pushing at the fences. The red dust they kicked up hung in the air, swirling around their hooves in thick clouds that stung her eyes and throat. They were agitated, pacing with their heads low, nudging at empty troughs. There was no water. There was no one there to see to them. Whatever had happened, everyone had left in a hurry. Someone was hurt.

Her stomach tightened. She knew what needed to be done. Without wasting another moment, Róisín strode around the side of the yard, the dust thick under her sneakers, the air filled with dry heat. The gate creaked as she swung it open, the metal burning hot beneath her fingers. As soon as the gate swung open, the cattle surged forwards, hooves thundering, eager to be released. They pushed past her, one after the other, heading into the open space of the front paddock where they could graze on the lush grass and access the water troughs.

Róisín stood back as the dust settled, and a small sense of relief grew as the yard emptied out. The noise lessened as the cattle spread across the paddock, their bellows fading into the distance. For a moment, the quiet was almost unnerving, but it was better than their desperate cries. Still, she was awfully worried—this wasn't how things were supposed to be. Dad leaving cattle in the yard like that was unheard of. Maybe something had happened to Mum, and he'd taken her somewhere?

Because Róisín was sure now; they weren't here.

She ran back to the house and looked around the back garden, her heart pounding in her chest. The quiet was ominous. She glanced back at the shed, hoping someone might emerge from the shadows, but of course, there was no one there.

With a worried sigh, she headed towards the back steps. The washing basket had blown into Mum's hippeastrums, and two sheets were tangled in the shrubs along the fence. The washing had just been left there, forgotten.

She pushed open the back door, her hand trembling, and called out, 'Mum? Dad?' But she knew there was no one there as her voice faded. If Mum had been there, she would've heard her pull up in the car. She would have run outside, her arms wide.

The kitchen was empty. A bowl holding a small amount of whipped cream was abandoned on the bench, and beaters coated in cream on the side of the sink. Half a dozen scones sat untouched on the tray in the middle of the table. Mum, house-proud as she was, would never have left the kitchen like this. Not without a word. Not without reason.

Róisín swallowed hard, her breath shaky. Something was wrong—very wrong. She walked quickly through the house, searching for a clue, a note, anything. But there was nothing. She patted her pocket. Where was her phone?

Shit, she'd left it in the car. What if they'd been trying to call her all this time?

She dashed to the car, yanking the door open and grabbing her phone. The screen was blank—no missed calls, no messages. The service was fine, so why hadn't anyone called? Her fingers fumbled as she pulled up her shortcuts, pressing the speed dial for Mum's number. Straight to voicemail. Out of range? She tried Cat. Same result. Her heart pounded harder as she dialled Dad's number.

From the back steps, she heard it—his phone ringing inside the study. Typical. Dad never had his phone on him.

Róisín sat down heavily on the back steps, staring out across the paddocks, her mind racing. Should she call Shea? Bridget? Erin? Did they know anything?

Whatever had happened, it had been sudden. The Land Cruiser was gone. Maybe Dad had had an accident, cut himself, and they'd rushed him to the Royal Flying Doctor Service clinic in Louth? That would explain the blood. Or had Mum fallen when she was taking smoko over? But why hadn't anyone called her? Maybe they'd been there when she stopped in Louth for fuel and was talking to Teddy? She hadn't passed anyone on the road.

The defibrillator on the floor of the shed meant there was more than an injury for one of them.

Róisín stood and retrieved the washing basket and the sheets and took them inside. The best thing to do was stay here and wait until someone called because she had no doubt that they would as soon as they could. They knew she was on her way. She went back out to the car and brought her two suitcases and laptop inside.

The house was so quiet. Róisín couldn't remember the last time she'd come home to an empty house. It had been seven years since she moved out, and even during her high school years, when she came home from boarding school, there was always someone there to greet her. Now, the only sound was the floorboards creaking under her feet in the back hallway, echoing in the stillness.

She placed her hand on the highly polished banister at the base of the staircase that led up to the bedrooms where she and her four sisters had their rooms, along with a guest room and bathrooms. The banister that was Mum's pride and joy. It was the original timber staircase, built by Thomas and Samuel

O'Byrne back in the late 1800s, and Mum polished the banister religiously every week.

She climbed the steps and walked slowly past Bridget's room, Erin's, Shea's and Cat's until she reached hers, calling out as she walked along. 'Mum, are you up here?'

Still no sign of life.

One of the loveliest things about coming home was her room. It had remained unchanged since she left for university. Unlike her sisters, she'd never been one for posters or sports memorabilia. Her room was simple, with a lovely green and white checked bedspread and lots of cushions. It was second from the end of the back hallway and the only one with a window seat. She had spent countless afternoons and nights sitting there, watching the sunset or stargazing, dreaming of the life ahead of her.

Opening the door, she took a deep breath. Nothing had changed; the room was spotless, of course—Mum had obviously had a spring clean. She could smell the lemon furniture polish. The bedspread was folded back, and she assumed the sheets draping the shrubs in the back garden had been meant for her bed. No matter; she could easily fix that. She knew the linen cupboard was well-stocked. A huge bouquet of flowers sat on her dressing table, and the old cedar triple-fronted mirror, once her grandmother's, gleamed in the soft afternoon light. She had come full circle. She was home.

But now, her stomach twisted in fear. Where was everyone, and what had happened?

Chapter 8

Louth - Tuesday, mid-January.

When they reached Louth and hadn't passed Róisín on the road, Logan reached over and lightly touched Cat's knee.

'We're back in service now,' he said quietly.

Cat turned from the passenger seat to face her mother, who was sitting in the back seat of the Land Cruiser while Logan drove them to Dubbo.

'Mum?'

'Yes?' Laura's voice was dull, her eyes shadowed.

'Can you read me exactly what Róisín said? We haven't passed her. Maybe she didn't text from here? Maybe it was Bourke?'

'No, it was Louth.' Laura reached into her handbag and pulled her phone out. 'Her message says: Just leaving. Put the kettle on. Can't wait. Love. R.'

'Just leaving where? It must have been Bourke. What time was her message?'

'An hour ago.'

'So, if it was Louth, she would have been there before we left.'

'It was Louth, Cat.' Laura's voice held frustration. 'I asked her to text from there, and she said to put the kettle on. She wouldn't have said that at Bourke. It's an hour away from Louth.'

'We're turning onto the Cobar Road in a couple of minutes, so let's try and ring the girls now?' Logan suggested. 'We've got service for a little while and then nothing until Cobar. How about we have a quick toilet stop and grab some food while you call?'

Laura shook her head. 'I can't do it. And I don't want to stop. I want to get to Dubbo as soon as we can. I want to know what's happening.'

'Mum, we have to take some breaks. If we have one now, we can call the girls and then do a big leg to Nyngan. We'll be in Dubbo before dark. We can call the hospital from Cobar, and they can tell us what's happening.'

Laura sighed, and her voice was muffled as she put her hands over her face. 'Okay. That makes sense, I guess, but Cat, will you call them, please?'

Logan pulled the car up at the General Store and climbed

out. He then went around to the back, opened Laura's door, and helped her out.

'Water or a sweet drink?' he asked Cat as she held her phone in front of her.

'Both, please. Maybe some sandwiches if Mandy has any readymade.'

'Ask Róisín to let the cattle out of the shed yard if you can get onto her,' Logan asked.

'I will. Be quick,' she said.

He nodded, and Cat stared at her phone. Logan and Mum disappeared into the shop. Swallowing the emotion that had been stuck in her throat for the last hour and a half, she pulled up Róisín's number and pressed connect.

It didn't even ring; Róisín answered immediately.

'Cat. Where are you? What's happened? Is everyone alright?'

Cat's voice caught, and she swallowed again. 'Where are you?'

'I'm at *Ceann Mara*. I saw the defibrillator in the shed, and I've been trying to ring you all. I was just about to try again when your call flashed up.'

'We're at Louth. We've just come back into service. Listen, we're on the way to Dubbo. Dad's had an accident, just before smoko. And a heart attack. The RFDS have flown him there.'

'Oh, sweet Jesus. I knew something was really wrong. Is he . . . is he—'

'We don't know much, but he was conscious and talking when they put him on the plane.' Cat's eyes filled with tears. 'But I'm scared, Ro.'

'How's Mum?'

'A mess. She didn't even want to stop here. I don't know how come we didn't pass you.'

'I took a bit of a break and parked down Gentle Nellie's Road for a while after I filled up.'

'You must have been down there when we went past.'

'I must have. I'm sorry. I—'

Cat waited. 'You what?'

'Nothing, it's not important. What do you want me to do? Will I drive to Dubbo? I want to see Dad.'

'First up, Logan said to ask you to get the cattle out of the shed yard.'

'I already have.'

'Thanks. Look, Mum and Logan are coming back already. Can you ring the girls? They don't know yet. We'll be out of service soon.'

'I can do that. And I'll clean up here a bit before I follow you.'

'Stay there. Wait until you hear from us. You've had a big drive today. When do you start your new job?'

'I have to go to Wilcannia sometime this week. Okay, I'll stay here until you call.'

'Do you want to talk to Mum? She's coming now.'

'No, you get on the road. But let me know as soon as you hear anything. I'll text you when I decide what to do. Tell Mum I love her.'

Tears rolled down Cat's cheeks. 'Thanks, Ro. Love you, too. I'll ring you soon.'

Chapter 9

Dubbo Hospital - Tuesday, mid-January.

'Tom, I know you've been through a lot over the past few hours with the heart attack and the fall off your bike. And the transfer in the RFDS plane.'

Cat looked at Dr Johnson as he stood on the other side of Dad's bed. Dad had still been in Emergency when they arrived at five o'clock; he'd undergone a raft of tests throughout the afternoon. Mum had insisted on coming straight here; they could book into a motel later.

'Now, about your leg injury—what's happened is that one of the major arteries in your leg has been damaged, making it hard for blood to get through. This means your leg isn't getting enough oxygen, and that's why you're having pain and other symptoms.

'When parts of your body, like your leg, don't get enough oxygen, the tissue starts to struggle, and if it lasts too long, the cells can begin to die. If we don't treat it quickly, the damage could get worse, and it might affect the use of your leg in the future.

'What we need to do is restore the blood flow as soon as possible to prevent permanent damage. We'll also be monitoring your heart closely since your heart attack and this injury are connected. We're still not sure if it was the accident—the leg injury when you fell that caused the heart attack, or if there is some underlying condition that precipitated it.'

Tom shook his head. 'The last thing I remember is getting a parcel out of the mailbox and then waking up on the shed floor with these three standing over me.'

'We're going to do everything we can to get your leg healed and make sure your heart is stable at the same time.' The doctor looked at Laura. 'We've done everything we can here to stabilise your husband, but we've got some concerns about the damage to the artery in his leg. The injury is preventing proper blood flow, and while we've started treatment to help with that, he'll need more advanced care to fix it fully.'

He turned back to Tom. 'Here at Dubbo, we don't have the specialised equipment or the vascular surgeons required for the kind of surgery you may need. That's why we're going to transfer you to Sydney, where there are specialists and facilities to deal with this. The team there will be able to assess whether surgery or another procedure is needed to restore proper blood flow to your leg and prevent any lasting damage.'

Tom nodded slowly, and his eyes held Laura's. 'You'll come too, love?'

'Of course I will.'

'We'll make sure you're comfortable during the transfer, and we'll keep monitoring your heart closely, too. I know it's a lot to take in, but getting you to Sydney is the best way to make sure you get the right care.'

'Can Laura come with me?'

Dr Johnson turned to Laura. 'Laura, unfortunately, there won't be space for you to go in the air ambulance. Those flights are really tight on room, and they need all the space for the medical team and equipment to focus on Tom's care during the transfer.

'But don't worry—we can help you make arrangements. You can catch a commercial flight from Dubbo to Sydney, which takes about an hour, or you can go by road if you'd prefer.' He looked at Logan and Cat. 'Would you go too?'

Cat shook her head. 'Once we know Dad's going to be okay, we'll have to go back to the station.' She turned to Laura. 'Unless you want me to come with you, Mum?'

'I'll be right, sweetheart. You'll need to help Logan at the station. I know there's a lot to do.'

'If you're going to be down there a while, I'll come down after a few days. I'm sure Róisín will come with me and maybe the other girls too.'

'We'll see.' Now that Tom was in the right place getting taken care of and seemed to be getting back to his usual self, Laura's composure was returning.

The doctor nodded. 'Rightio, Laura. The flights are regular, so you'll be able to get there pretty quickly. We'll make sure you have all the information you need to meet Tom when he arrives in Sydney.'

##

Cat leaned over and kissed her father's cheek as they prepared him for the flight to Sydney. 'Look after yourself, Dad, and do everything they tell you. We'll call you in Sydney.'

'Thanks, love.' Tom reached out and took her hand. 'And I'm sorry I gave you a scare. At least it happened in the shed, and I got our parcel from the letterbox. When you read it, give me a call and let me know if they are letters from our Samuel.'

'Thomas Harold O'Byrne, you just forget all about Samuel and that bloody family history.' Laura's hands went to her hips. 'You just think about *you* and getting better.'

'Sorry, love.' Tom winked at Cat, and her heart swelled with love for her father. The colour was back in his face, but she knew he was still in pain from the injury to his leg.

She leaned down and whispered in his ear. 'I'll have a read and call you.'

As he beamed up at her, two male nurses came into the cubicle.

'Right to go for a little trip, Mr O'Byrne? The aircraft's on the tarmac now.'

Laura's flight to Sydney was scheduled to leave in an hour. She hugged Tom before they wheeled his bed out.

Logan cleared his throat. 'Right. Laura. Let's get you to the airport too.'

Laura put her hands over her face and started to cry.

Cat and Logan stood on each side of her, supporting her as she sobbed. 'Oh, Mum, it's alright. Dad's going to be okay.'

'I'm fine. I just needed to have a cry before we go to the airport.'

Cat met Logan's eyes, and he smiled at her.

'Tom is going to be okay,' he reassured both of them. 'He's a strong man and a fighter.'

'And he needs to see that letter from Samuel, Mum,' Cat said with a watery smile. 'That will get him home in no time at all.'

Chapter 10

Ceann Mara - Tuesday, mid-January.

By late afternoon, Ro had spoken to Cat for the second time and learned that Dad was about to be flown to Sydney, but his condition was stable. She took a deep breath and made the necessary calls to her sisters. Cat and Logan were going to stay the night in Dubbo after Mum and Dad were on their respective flights and then drive back early tomorrow.

'It's been a long day, Ro. It wouldn't be safe to get in the car and drive home. We'll be home late tomorrow afternoon. Then we have to decide what to do.'

'What do you mean?'

'Well, there's a lot of work to do on *Ceann Mara*. It's probably sensible if Logan and I move back into the house rather than having to trek through the scrub and row across the river every morning and afternoon.'

'What about your place?'

'It's a much smaller concern. Logan has it under control, and Dad comes over about once a fortnight to pay him back for the hours he spends at *Ceann Mara.* Will you be staying at home now that you've got the job back here?'

Róisín hesitated. 'I'm not sure where I'll be based or what I'll be doing. I'll be honest, Cat. Applying for this job was a kneejerk reaction to something that happened in Brisbane, and I honestly don't know what the job entails until I meet with my boss.'

'When will that be?'

'I'm going to call him tomorrow. The first office has been set up in Wilcannia. I'll fly down and back in one day.'

'I'll bet you're glad Dad talked you into getting your pilot licence. I remembered how much you fought against it.'

Róisín chuckled. 'Teenage angst. It was much cooler to wear makeup and talk about music bands than to learn to fly back then.'

Cat chuckled. 'I gave into the teenage angst. My biggest regret is that I didn't take Dad up on the offer when I was in high school. I looked into it a couple of months ago, and it was going to cost thousands. But now that you're home, you can fly me everywhere I need to go.'

'I'll be busy working, and I could be living hundreds of

kilometres away.'

'You can fit me into your schedule.'

Róisín laughed; it was good to feel confident about Dad's prognosis and to be able to share a joke with her sister.

When she hung up on Cat's call, she smiled as she called their other sisters.

Erin, Shea, and Bridget were understandably very upset when they received the news, but Róisín reassured them that Dad was in the best hands and improving. Róisín passed on the details of the motel where Mum was staying near Royal North Shore Hospital in case they couldn't reach her on her mobile.

'As soon as they know Dad's room number and if it's okay to call him, Cat said she'd put it on our family chat group.'

Shea had been her usual calm and unexcitable self. Róisín was surprised to hear she wasn't working at the vet clinic in Wilcannia anymore.

'How long ago did you move to Broken Hill?' she asked, surprised. 'You didn't mention it at Christmas.'

'Only just happened. Okay, Ro, it sounds like Dad's in the best spot. As long as Mum is okay. Just stay in touch.'

'Mum's going okay. She's fine now that she's arrived in Sydney. Cat and Logan are on their way back tomorrow, and I will let you know if there is any news. How are you, Shea? I haven't talked to you for ages.'

'I'm taking some courses and thinking about my future. Not sure where it's going to be yet, but I'm happy,' Shea said.

'I'm happy, too. Looking forward to my new job.'

'Thanks, Ro. Are you okay with being by yourself at the station? It's been a while since you've lived at home.' Shea was the most intuitive of the five sisters and always cut straight to the chase.

'I'll be okay. I'm a big girl now, although I will admit I did get a bit shaky when I saw the defibrillator on the ground in the shed.'

'Hard to believe the accident was this morning, and it's not even five o'clock, and he's already been admitted to Royal North Shore Hospital,' Shea said.

'It's restored my faith in the health system.' Róisín stared through the kitchen window and frowned. She thought she noticed a swirl of smoke to the west, but whatever it was dissipated quickly.

'Don't get too excited; there's still a long way to go,' Shea said.

'Stay in touch, Shea. I still have to call Erin and Bridget. Okay? Love you.'

'Okay, I'll let you go; I've got a yapping dog calling from the waiting room for me. Love you back. See you soon, I hope.'

As Róisín pressed the speed dial for Erin's number, regret clung to her. Regret that she had left it so long between calls to her sisters. When Greg lived with her, life had been one hectic rush from work to dinner, to social outings, drinks at bars in the city after work and the inevitable trip to the races every couple of weeks. Until she'd come home for Christmas, months had passed since she'd found the time to speak to her sisters.

She frowned when she spoke to Erin; her sister sounded strange, and her reaction had been subdued. Even before Róisín had told her why she was ringing, she had been quiet, which was totally out of Erin's usual outgoing character.

Róisín repeated what had happened.

'Okay,' Erin said quietly, and then there was silence. Róisín waited and finally spoke.

'Are you still there, Erin?'

'I'm here.'

'Look, we're pretty sure Dad is going to be fine, and I promise I'll keep in touch. We're going to put his number on the family chat group.'

'I'll call you in a few days,' Erin said.

'Are you okay? Is Jack there? I don't want you to be worried there by yourself. Where are you now?'

'In Wagga, so I haven't got far to come home. Where will

you be? How long are you staying at *Ceann Mara*?'

'I'm not sure. I have to go to Wilcannia sometime this week. I'm just about to make a call to my new boss and find out when they want me to start now that I'm back in the district.'

Silence again.

'Erin, are you there?'

'I'm here.' Her voice seemed detached, as though she was doing something else.

'What are you doing? Are you sure you're alright?' Róisín knew her voice held concern.

'Not really,' Erin said, 'but that's not something I'm going to go into now. It doesn't matter now, with Dad being so sick.'

'Are you well?' Róisín jumped in quickly.

'Oh yes, physically, I'm fine,' she said. 'Don't worry about me. I'm coming home.'

'What's happened? Is Jack there?'

'No. Look, it's a long story, and I don't want to go into it at the moment,' Erin said. 'When I come home, we'll grab a bottle of wine and go sit down by the billabong.'

'Sounds good to me,' Róisín said. Erin's voice held a bitterness that was totally out of character, and her younger sister sounded as though she was on the verge of tears. Róisín suspected it was more than the news about Dad that had upset her.

'Any time you need to talk before then, you make sure you give me a call, okay? You've got me worried.'

'Don't worry about me. I'm a big girl now. Love you, Ro.'

'Love you too.'

Bridget, the baby of the family, was at summer school taking an additional graphic design course. She wanted to pack up and come home immediately, but Róisín convinced her that there was no point doing that since no one would be there.

'Cat and Logan are still in Dubbo, and I will be in Wilcannia some of this week. And I don't know how long it will be before Dad and Mum are home. Leave it until you finish your course.'

'I don't care,' Bridget said. 'I'd rather be at home. This school sucks. I'm not going back after the holidays. I can stay home and help Mum look after Dad.'

'But you're not even in Year 12 yet,' Róisín said. 'You have to get your HSC.'

'No, I don't. There's no need for it because I'm not going to uni. I'm ready to start my own business,' Bridget said. 'I want to get out of this hell-hole now. Look at Cat, she wasted all that time at uni and then came home.'

'Not the right time to talk about it,' Róisín said, 'but we will have a chat when you get home. Promise me you won't do anything silly. Mum and Dad don't need any more worry at the moment.'

When she first started boarding school, Bridget tried to run away a couple of times, but a good talking-to from Dad had convinced her to stay. Being the baby of the family had seen Bridget spoiled by all of them.

'I suppose. Alright, I promise. Ring me as soon as you hear anything. Do you promise?'

'I do,' Róisín said. 'Love you—'

Bridget hung up before she could say, 'Love you, bub.'

Róisín's last call was to Wilcannia, where the Water Integrity Review Authority's office was temporarily based. Seth Brodie mentioned in her interview that it was still uncertain where the office would be established.

'May I speak with Seth Brodie?' she asked when the phone picked up.

'Just one moment. May I ask who's calling?'

'It's Róisín O'Byrne.'

'Oh, hello, Róisín. My name's Debra. I'm the receptionist here. I actually got your office ready for you this morning.'

Róisín laughed. 'Well, that answers one of my questions. I was wondering whether I was still going to be at the office there.'

'Sometimes,' Debra said. 'But look, I'll put Seth on and let him tell you all about it.'

'I'm looking forward to meeting you.'

'You too. See you soon.'

Róisín waited for Seth Brodie to come onto the line; she'd been impressed with his efficiency and manner when he interviewed her for the position. His questions were concise and relevant to the position advertised. She had a few questions to ask him because she was still trying to get her head around the position.

However, after her experience with Greg, she was going to be very careful in the workplace. She was supposedly an intelligent woman and knew she was a damn fine lawyer—how had Greg Henderson sucked her in? She pushed the thoughts away as Seth's voice came through the phone.

'Good afternoon. It's good to speak with you again, Róisín.'

'Seth, hello. I just wanted to let you know that I'm in the district now. I can come down to Wilcannia anytime over the next two or three days if that suits you.'

'No chance of you coming down tomorrow?' he asked.

She hesitated. 'I'm not quite sure, but I'll check and let you know first thing in the morning.'

'Okay, I'll leave it with you. Text me on this number. I'll be in the office all day.'

'Thank you. Is there a specific reason you wanted me to come a little bit earlier?' she asked.

'Well, we're having some issues with the location of the offices, and I was hoping to talk to you about a potential move, but that discussion can wait.'

'I will. It will be good to meet you at the office and rest assured, I'm willing to be flexible as to where I'm based if that helps,' she said.

'Thank you,' he said. 'We'll talk when you get here.'

Chapter 11

Ceann Mara - Tuesday evening, mid-January.

Róisín was tidying up the kitchen after the cheese toastie she'd prepared for dinner when her phone buzzed in her pocket. She'd unpacked the car and taken everything she'd brought with her up to her room. She tensed, and her smile faded until she checked and saw it was Mum calling.

'Hi, Mum. Everything okay still?'

'Hi, sweetheart. I'm sorry I wasn't there when you arrived today.'

'I probably just missed you by a bit. I had to pull over for a break; I would've passed you otherwise.'

'No worries,' Laura said. 'We were in a rush to get to Dubbo and make sure Dad was okay.'

'It's okay. You and Dad will be home before we know it. I'm just glad you were all able to help Dad.'

'As we all are,' Laura replied. 'I'm still in shock. I don't think I'll sleep very well tonight.'

'Are you still with Dad at the hospital?'

'No. I just got back to the motel. It's not too far from the hospital.'

'You be careful in Sydney, Mum.'

'I will. There's a taxi rank at the door, and even though I could walk the distance, I was sensible.'

'How is he tonight? He'll be exhausted.'

'He is, but he was a bit down. That's why I'm ringing. I thought I'd get you first, and you can pass it on. I'd say Cat will be asleep by now. She was really tired when she and Logan took me to the airport.'

'Why was he down? Everything's okay, isn't it?' Unease skittered down Róisín's nerves.

'The specialist looked at the scans and came to see him before I left. I was pleased I was still there.'

'And? What did he say?'

'The good news is that even though the main vessels to his foot were blocked, collateral circulation ensured that enough blood was getting to his foot, so there was no tissue damage.'

'What does that mean? Collateral circulation, I mean.'

'I learned a lot today. It means that when your collateral circulation takes over, smaller blood vessels get larger to accommodate the increased blood flow. And that saved his foot.'

'That is good news. So why was Dad down?'

'The specialist said because of the disruption, they're going to have to put a cast on his leg while everything heals. To keep it in the right position.'

'Sounds okay.'

'Yes, but they want him there for at least ten days to make sure everything is okay.'

'He's in the best place.'

'Yes, but . . .'

'But . . . what?' Róisín's voice rose with concern.

'Well,' Laura continued. 'There's a bit of an issue with the heart specialist. He's still not one hundred percent sure everything is as it should be. They're going to run some more tests tomorrow, probably an angiogram, to check for blockages.'

'He's in the best place if anything happens. I'm sure he's hooked up to machines and monitors, Mum.'

'He certainly is, and you can imagine how he hates that. But you know your father. If he's away from *Ceann Mara,* he's not happy. He was hoping to be home in a few days, and he didn't take the ten-day news well.'

Róisín sighed. 'Mum, just remind him he's in the best place, and we're all thinking of him.' Then, with a spark of an idea, she brightened. 'Wait—what if I send him something to cheer him up? Is he up to reading?'

Laura hesitated. 'I'm sure he is . . . but whether he's interested is another matter.'

'I found the mail in the shed. Cat mentioned it to me on the phone before. The photocopies Dad was waiting for from the National Library. Cat said something about them being a letter to a Samuel. If you think Dad's up to it, and it's not too much for him, I'll photograph the pages and send them to you, and he can read them on your phone, and see it's our Samuel.'

'Better than that,' Laura said. 'I've got my iPad here. It's bigger and easier for him to read. I think that's a great idea. Once he has the heart tests done tomorrow, it would keep his mind off everything. I'll only show him if I think he's up to it.'

'Excellent! I'll send that to you in a while by text.'

Her mum's voice softened. 'And what about you, sweetheart? How are you?'

'I'm good. I was actually going to call you in the morning. Do you think Dad would mind if I took the Cessna to Wilcannia?'

'Of course, he won't; it's the family plane—it's as much yours as it is his. You just haven't flown for ages,' Laura said. 'Will you be okay?'

'That's great, thank you. And yes, it's like driving a car,

you don't forget. I'm going down to have a meeting with my new boss before I start next week.'

'Do you know how wonderful it is to have you home? Even though I'm not at home, I can visualise you there,' her mother said. 'We've missed you, Ro.'

'I know, Mum. You don't have to say it. I'm back now. In all ways.' Róisín smiled. 'And the job is sounding really exciting. I start next week, and my boss mentioned there'll be a lot of opportunities for remote work. I should be able to work from home or on the road when I'm travelling to different properties. I'm not going to be stuck in an office all day, and I'm not going to be listening to spoiled rich women trying to fleece their ex-husbands.'

Her mother chuckled, and it was good to hear. 'It's going to be so good having two of my girls back home. Though I guess I'm being a bit selfish, wishing all my girls were home. I know that's not realistic.'

'We're all grown up now, Mum. Almost all of us, anyway.' Róisín laughed softly. 'You take care of Dad and give him our love, okay?'

'Will do, darling. Love you, Róisín.'

'Love you too, Mum.'

As soon as she tidied the kitchen, Róisín went to Dad's

study, where she'd put the package from the shed onto his desk. She picked up a pair of scissors and opened it carefully. There were six sheets of paper in plastic sleeves, with a covering letter on top.

She pulled out her phone and quickly took photos of each page, including the letter.

Even though Róisín wasn't as interested in the family history as Dad and Cat, her excitement quickened as she read the first page that she photographed. If this was the right Samuel, Catriona and Dad were going to be ecstatic.

Kilgarvan Vicarage - December 1852

My dearest Samuel,

It has been more than five years since you left for the Antipodes, and though the ache of your absence grows deeper by the day, I write this with love still in my heart. How could I not? Each moment I spend thinking of you keeps my spirit alive despite the hardship here in our country.

Things are still difficult here, as I am sure you can imagine. The famine still tightens its grip on the land, and we've had to make do with so little. We live day by day, and I am overwhelmed each day by the generosity of the parish, who always ensure that we have enough food and peat to keep us fed and warm.

It is so wonderful to have an address to reply to. I will place all of the letters I have written since you left me in one parcel and ask James to take me to Kenmare Post Office as soon as he can.

I pray each day that one day soon, you will find your way back to me.

Yours in hope and love,

Breda

Blinking away tears, Róisín attached the images to a text to her mother's phone and pressed send.

She checked that the downstairs doors were locked, turned the lights off, and made her way up the dark staircase to her room.

Chapter 12

Kilgarvan Churchyard, Country Kerry, Ireland - spring 1846.

Samuel O'Byrne knelt beside his grandmother's weathered gravestone in the mist-cloaked churchyard of Kilgarvan in County Kerry, the earth damp beneath his knees. The soft wind sighed through the trees, carrying with it the sweet, melodic song of a nearby robin. The lonely, warbling melody rose and fell gently in the quiet of the Sunday afternoon. A light drizzle, typical of County Kerry, began to fall, mingling with the scent of moss and wet stone. His fingers brushed the engraving on the stone, tracing the worn name of his maternal grandmother, Catherine O'Connor. He had tended to her resting place each Sunday since she had passed ten years ago. *Mamó* had been the one who had understood him the most—his drive to be successful in his own right and not take advantage of the family wealth and living in what the tenants called 'the big house'.

As Samuel rose to his feet, his horse whinnied, and then

another sound broke the silence. He tilted his head, listening, and then turned slowly.

A young woman in a grey dress huddled beside a grave in the row behind his grandmother's stone. Her dark hair was damp, sticking to cheeks wet with tears, and her shoulders trembled with grief.

Samuel rose and approached quietly through the long, soft grass. As he drew closer, the young woman didn't notice him, and he glanced at the gravestone, recognising the name engraved on the stone: Mary Atkins, the vicar's mother, who had died last year.

He now realised that the young woman was Breda, the vicar's young sister. She was kneeling at the gravestone, weeping quietly.

Samuel had rarely attended the services at St Peter's over the past months; he went to very few places where he mixed with local people. These were troubled times, and no one could be trusted. While many in the community gathered each Sunday for solace and reassurance, Samuel and his younger brother Thomas focused their efforts on supporting those suffering in more direct ways. Their absence from community gatherings and church avoided drawing unwanted attention to themselves. They discreetly interfered with the bailiffs' work, quietly sabotaging their efforts to seize land and belongings from struggling families.

He coughed quietly. 'Miss, I don't mean to intrude, but are you alright?' Samuel kept his voice low, careful not to startle her.

Breda Atkins looked up, her hazel eyes shimmering with tears. 'Ah, for sure, I'm grand . . .' Her voice cracked, and she glanced at the gravestone. 'It's been a year today since'—she gestured to the grave— 'but it feels like yesterday.'

Samuel nodded, empathising with her grief. 'I know that feeling all too well. My grandmother has rested over there for ten years now.' He nodded to the grave he had been tending. 'And sadly, the pain never really leaves us, but hopefully, it will ease a little more for you each year as it has for me.'

She shook her head, wiping her face with the hem of her apron. 'Perhaps.'

After a moment of silence, she introduced herself. 'Thank you for your concern, sir. I'm Breda Atkins. I reside at the vicarage now that our mother has passed. I am the housekeeper for my brother, John, the vicar. And unless he finds himself a wife, I fear I will be doing scullery duties for the rest of my life.'

He offered her a kind smile. 'I remember you as a child, Breda. You have grown up. I am Samuel O'Byrne from *Ceann Mara*,' he said, bowing slightly.

'I know who you are.' Her gaze was direct. 'I haven't seen you in the church for a long time.' She stood, and as her eyes stayed on his, Samuel found it hard to look away. The fair skin that contrasted with her dark hair was unblemished, and her cheeks held a pink rosiness; Breda Atkins had grown into a beautiful young woman.

'I have been busy with the estate. I assist my father with the accounts,' he said. 'But I do find myself here often. It's quiet and gives me a measure of peace in these times.'

'It is peaceful,' she agreed. 'But there's little else to hold onto, isn't there? With the famine . . . everything is so bleak. In one way, I am pleased that Mother didn't live to see such sorrow.'

Life in County Kerry had been unforgiving these past years, and the hardship of the famine was stripping families of their dignity, leaving them with empty fields and relentless hunger as crop after crop failed. It wasn't just the hunger that consumed them—it was their loss of hope, as each crop failure meant no food, as well as eviction and the threat of death or jail if farmers refused to leave their land. Many families had already left for America and the Antipodes as violence escalated.

Samuel looked around the graveyard; the trees surrounding it stood bare and tall in the chill of early spring. Beyond them, the woods stretched out, a place where time seemed to slow. The underbrush was tangled with wild brambles, and moss covered the trunks in lush green despite the harsh winter that had just passed. It was sometimes hard to believe the hunger and hardship caused by the famine that surrounded them.

'I was about to take a walk,' he said, glancing toward the narrow leaf-strewn path that wound through the woods and then out into the open countryside. 'Perhaps you'd like to join me? Get away from the graves for a while.' He smiled down at her as she stepped closer, brushing the leaves from the front of her apron. 'And your chores?'

Breda hesitated, then smiled again. 'I'd like that. I have already prepared John's dinner.'

They walked slowly at first, their footsteps crunching the leaves until the path widened. The trees stood tall, and the underbrush was thick, muffling the sounds of the outside world.

As they walked side-by-side, Breda spoke of her sadness, the monotony of the days at the vicarage, and the drudgery of tending to her brother's needs.

'I know I should be thankful,' she said. 'We have a roof over our heads and food on the table—the congregation and the churchwardens are very kind to us—and I do know how much suffering there is out there, but I yearn for more, for something outside the vicarage. Something away from County Kerry.'

Samuel listened intently, his worries fading as her lilting voice held his attention.

'You have a strong spirit,' he said quietly, pleasantly surprised by her honesty and her need for more. 'It's a hard time for all, but you seem to carry it with strength. It is not wrong to want to improve your life.'

'I don't feel strong. I feel trapped, as though the walls themselves are closing in on me. I want to be anywhere but here, but there's nowhere for me to go. No escape. Many families are leaving for New York, but I cannot do that alone. And I cannot leave John.' Her voice held a trace of mirth for once. 'I fear he would starve to death and be found eventually beneath a pile of sermons.'

As they reached the fork in the road, Samuel stopped and turned to face her. 'Remember, Miss Atkins, you're not alone. We all feel that in these difficult times. But there are moments, like this one, where the world doesn't seem so miserable. We have to hold on to those.'

'Thank you for walking with me, Master O'Byrne.' Her smile was sweet, and a sudden warmth suffused Samuel's chest.

'Would you walk with me again next Sunday afternoon?' he asked. 'And please, call me Samuel.'

Breda lowered her eyes, and her dark lashes fanned her

cheeks as she nodded. 'I would like that very much. It will give me something to look forward to, Samuel. And I am Breda.'

Chapter 13

Ceann Mara - Wednesday, mid-January, four a.m.

Róisín woke with a start just before dawn, her heart thudding. She had been dreaming about Greg, but as she woke, she was certain she'd heard a car outside the house and seen headlights sweep across the veranda. She blinked as she came fully awake and then sat up. That couldn't be right—her room was upstairs on the opposite side of the house, away from the driveway and any headlights.

In her dream, Greg was in the sports car he'd sold a couple of months ago, driving up the front road of *Ceann Mara,* revving the engine as he swept around the curves. He always wanted to be the best and fastest, showing off his superior driving—or the driving *he* believed to be superior. Róisín hated being a passenger and was pleased when he sold the car. The only problem then was that Greg considered Róisín's SUV to be equally his, and she lost count of the number of times she'd gone to the basement car park, only to find that Greg had taken her car.

'But sweetheart, what's mine is yours, so it works in reverse too,' he'd justified when she complained one night.

It must have been the dream that awakened her, but it still felt real and was hard to shake off.

Even though she knew it was only a dream, Róisín couldn't shake the feeling someone was out there. She got out of bed, opened her bedroom door, and walked to the end of the hallway. She reached the small window that overlooked the back garden and driveway and hesitated for a moment before pushing it open. She opened it slowly so it didn't creak.

There was nothing out there. No sign of any vehicle, no sound of an engine. Just silence. A blissful silence that she hadn't experienced for a long time

Róisín exhaled slowly, resting her elbows on the windowsill, gazing out over the station. The moon was bright enough to illuminate the trees at the edge of the runway across to the south, casting long, soft shadows. She closed her eyes and let the sounds of the Darling River night wash over her.

It felt wonderful to be home. Already, the problems she'd faced in Brisbane were receding.

Hearing directly from Mum this afternoon had been

wonderful. Dad had undergone his surgery, and the vascular surgeon was extremely pleased with the result. The heart specialist still needed to get back to him, and if they got the all-clear as they were hoping, it looked like he would be home within a week or two.

As she'd settled into bed last night, she'd tensed as her phone dinged with an incoming text.

Surely not Greg again? She reached over to the bedside table, and her tension fled as Dad's name appeared in Messenger.

She clicked on the message and smiled as Dad got straight to the point as he always did.

Ro love, you are a champion. Thanks a heap for sending those attachments. Don't tell your mother but seeing she kindly left me her iPad, I've already read the letters you sent.

Róisín smiled at the three smiley emoticons in the middle of the message. Looked like the letters had given Dad a boost. As long as he didn't overdo it.

I've messaged Cat, but she said they're heading home tomorrow and she'll look in our records when she gets home late afternoon. We now have another name to research. Cat will check the files to see if there is a mention of a Breda.

She's also going to log onto the National Library of Ireland site as they travel to look at Kilgarvan Vicarage and see if she can

establish the last name of the woman who wrote the letter—maybe to our Samuel!

Róisín texted straight back to him.

Hey, Dad, don't get overexcited. I'm going to bed now. YOU go to sleep too! Love you.

Her phone dinged immediately.

Too hard in this noisy ward. Wish I was home. Miss you all xxx

She texted back. **Won't be long** and hoped that would be the case.

Chapter 14

County Kerry - Winter 1847.

Late at night, the fire crackled in the drawing room at *Ceann Mara*. Samuel swirled the glass of port in his hand, his eyes fixed on the deep, rich, red liquid. Across the room, his father stood rigid by the hearth, his face set in anger, while his cousin Richard sat back, his fingers drumming on the armrest of the leather Chesterfield.

'We're blessed,' Samuel murmured, his voice low but carrying in the stillness of the room. 'Food, drink, shelter. All of it while the country is starving. How long can we sit here, untouched by the famine, while everything around us crumbles?'

Last week, an eviction had gone awry, resulting in the death of a bailiff fifteen miles away from *Ceann Mara*. Samuel and Thomas had managed to leave without being apprehended, but it was only a matter of time before the bailiffs arrived at the estate. They would have been recognised; he did not doubt that.

Thomas sat beside him, quieter than usual. His brother's face was drawn, their lucky escape hanging over him. Samuel glanced at him, then back at his father, whose scowl deepened with every word Richard spoke.

'I'm telling you,' Richard said, leaning forwards, his eyes sharp with urgency, 'the Antipodes offer your best chance. I have vast tracts of land, more than I can manage. You could leave this godforsaken place, come with me, help me stock the land with sheep. There's a future there, not this . . . decay.'

Their father slammed his hand down on the mantel, rattling the decanter of port. 'Leave?' he spat, his face red and the veins standing out on his forehead. 'You think my sons can abandon their birthright just like that? Run off to the ends of the earth while our tenants starve? How can you even suggest it, Richard? I will say that they were both home with me that day. And that will be the end of it.'

Richard's expression didn't waver. 'You cannot save everyone, Michael. The famine is killing the land, and soon enough, it will come for you. And Samuel and Thomas . . . they are hunted men. Do you think they can hide forever after what happened?'

A sharp pang pierced Samuel's chest. The memory of the bailiff collapsing in the dirt, Thomas' wide-eyed horror as he held the revolver—it haunted his days and filled his dreams at night. He looked at his brother, who sat staring into the fire, his jaw clenched. Thomas had flung the gun into the woods a few miles closer to home and hadn't said much since that day, but Samuel could tell by his expression that he was considering Richard's offer.

Father turned to them now, his voice thick with bitterness. 'Is that what you want, then? To run away? To leave me behind with your mother and Sean to face the ruin?'

Samuel shifted in his chair, uncomfortable at his father's words, but his thoughts drifted, unbidden, to Breda Atkins. He could see her clearly in his mind—her clear skin, her steadfast gaze as she had walked with him this afternoon. The promise of a walk again next Sunday. If he were to leave, he wouldn't see her again. A flicker of guilt tore through him. How could he think of that now, with so much on his shoulders? A pretty girl he had walked with each Sunday for a year.

But still, Breda's image lingered.

'I don't want to run,' Samuel said, his voice firmer now, struggling to focus on Richard's suggestion. 'But we cannot stay here and pretend nothing is wrong. The famine will claim everything. We have to consider this, Father. And the situation we have got ourselves into. I do not want to spend the rest of my life in prison.'

Thomas turned to their father, his voice slow and heavy. 'Samuel is right. We . . . I . . . cannot undo what has been done. That bailiff—' He paused, the words catching in his throat. 'We didn't mean for it to happen, but no one would believe it was an accident. And now . . . now there's no going back. Father, we have no choice. You would not be believed. We must do as Cousin Richard suggests.'

Richard eyes were fixed on them. 'You could have a new start. Samuel, Thomas—there's opportunity in the Antipodes. You could build something far from here without fear of prison. The new country needs men like you on the land, men who know how to work and succeed.'

Samuel's thoughts flashed to Breda. If they left, it would be soon. How many times would he see her again? He set down his glass, looking up at his father, his heart torn between common sense and the painful longing to stay in the country he loved. 'We need to think of the future,' he said, trying to keep his voice steady. 'There's nothing for us here anymore. We can't save this land. But maybe we can save ourselves.'

Their father stared at him for a long moment, the anger in his eyes giving way to something deeper, something Samuel couldn't quite name. Disgust perhaps. Or sorrow.

'And what of Sean?' Father asked, his voice quieter now.

'He and Lydia were going to live at her father's estate in Berkshire, as she has no brothers. Will I now be handing this estate to my youngest son? Samuel, I have spent many months showing you the estate management. You disappoint me.'

'Sean can handle the estate,' Thomas said. 'He'll do well by it, and after his marriage . . . he will be more settled.' Samuel glanced his way, thinking that their younger brother would undoubtedly have to change his ways once he married. 'But as for us . . . it is time to leave.' He turned to Samuel. 'If we stay, we will either be hanged or transported to the colonies anyway. We have no choice. We will go as Cousin Richard suggests. As free settlers.'

The room fell into a tense silence. Samuel's thoughts drifted again back to Breda, to her soft voice as she told him of her longing to get away.

Maybe Thomas was right. Maybe it was time to leave before everything they knew turned to dust. But as the fire crackled and the dark shadows danced on the walls, all Samuel could think of was the woman he would leave.

Chapter 15

Ceann Mara - Wednesday, mid-January, 9.00 a.m.

Early the next morning, Róisín smiled as she leaned against the wing of the Cessna, the soft outback breeze rustling through her hair. The familiar scent of the red earth and eucalyptus trees filled the air, a world away from the smog and constant hum of the city. She felt energised here—grounded. After the bustle of Brisbane, standing on the family land at *Ceann Mara* was balm to her soul. She'd fallen back into a deep sleep when she'd gone back to bed after her night had been disturbed.

As soon as she'd had her coffee, she reached for her phone and texted Seth Brodie, figuring she might as well go today to meet him because Cat and Logan wouldn't be home until late afternoon.

I'll be there today around ten-thirty. Róisín O'Byrne.

She glanced up at the endless blue sky—perfect flying weather.

With a deep breath, she began her pre-flight checks, moving around the Cessna as the routine came back to her. Fuel levels: good. Oil: topped up. Propeller: flawless. She ran her fingers along the smooth metal of the fuselage, feeling the warmth of the morning sun beneath her skin. This was her element—nothing but her and the open sky beckoning.

Róisín climbed into the cockpit, settling in with a sense of anticipation. She closed the door with a firm click and buckled in, feeling the familiar snugness of the seatbelt. A smile tugged at her lips. The city had its moments, sure, but nothing compared to this—the quiet of the bush and the expanse of open blue sky waiting for her to carve a path through it.

She ran through her cockpit checks, flipping switches, adjusting dials, and listening to the engine roar to life with a deep, satisfying purr. The sound vibrated through her, grounding her in the present. Checking the altimeter and radios, she set the fuel selector and then gave the throttle a gentle push. The plane surged into life, and she couldn't help the laugh that bubbled up. God, she'd missed this.

As she taxied to the dusty strip that served as a runway, Róisín absorbed the country of her family home. It was at times like this that she could understand Dad and Cat's fascination with where *Ceann Mara* had all begun. She'd been too involved in being a city lawyer to appreciate the value of what they were doing. Now that she was going to be home more, she might get involved, too.

If she had time. No, she'd make time.

Mr Haydn, the young teacher at their local primary school, had taught them the history of their region even before it was a compulsory part of the New South Wales curriculum. They'd learned of the Indigenous people who had lived around the Darling River for tens of thousands of years, with evidence suggesting settlement dated back at least 40,000 years. She remembered going home and asking Dad how long that would take to pass.

He'd smiled at her and said, 'Forty thousand years.'

Cat had interrupted and asked if that was longer than it took for Christmas to come every year.

Róisín smiled; she could still hear Dad's chuckle. Tears pricked in her eyes; she was looking forwards to hearing it again soon.

One of her enduring memories of primary school at Louth was when Mr Haydn had taken all the pupils on an excursion to look at the fish traps at Brewarrina, which were on the Barwon River, a tributary of the Darling.

Róisín reached the end of the makeshift runway and turned the Cessna, took a deep breath, and ran through her final checks.

Everything was in order—time to get into the air.

She pushed the throttle to full, feeling the Cessna's engine respond instantly, its power surging through her as the wheels bumped along the strip. She tightened her grip on the yoke, the wind rushing against the windshield. Fifty knots . . . fifty-five . . . sixty.

And then, with a gentle pull, the plane lifted from the earth, effortlessly rising into the vast sky. It was so open, so peaceful. How could anyone prefer crowded city streets over this? She glanced down at the mailbox that had become a family landmark, and she thought about how Dad's heart attack could have changed everything. But for now, Dad was recovering in the best place, and the family could breathe again.

And so could she.

As she banked the plane over the southern end of *Ceann Mara*, Róisín spotted something unexpected. A red ute with a dog box on the back sat near the billabong where the kayaks were. Someone had set up camp there. Her brow furrowed as she looked down. She'd locked the front gate near the mailbox and all the gates to the campground. No one was going to be here to check in any campers until she got back this afternoon or when Cat and Logan arrived.

The only way someone could have entered was through the

back gate along the river, the one that was clearly signed: **PRIVATE PROPERTY, DO NOT ENTER.**

Later this afternoon, if they were still there when she flew over, she'd drive over and tell them they had to leave. *Ceann Mara* shrank below her as she climbed higher, the familiar yellow and brown patchwork of farmland and scrub rolling out beneath her like a living map. The paddocks stretched endlessly in every direction, the Darling River a shimmering ribbon snaking toward Wilcannia.

As she followed the river south, her thoughts turned to her new job. After talking to Seth yesterday, she was really keen to get started.

Out on the Darling, everything was connected. The land, the water, and the property owners who depended on it. She knew you couldn't separate one from the other. Without the Darling, there'd be no crops, no cattle or sheep, no station life. She knew that in her bones, just as every property owner out here did. As she'd grown up at *Ceann Mara*, she—and her sisters—had seen the river at its strongest and its most fragile.

But it wasn't just about their property—it was about fairness, about making sure everyone, from the stations upriver to the smallholdings further down, got what they needed. The water had to be managed, protected, and shared. Otherwise, the river would suffer, and so would everyone along its banks. She was proud to be starting work with an authority that would ensure that happened.

Up here in the cockpit, the world below seemed distant—as though she'd left all the worries and stresses of life on the ground. Her heart soared as she leaned back in her seat, relaxing into the smooth rhythm of the flight. The Cessna hummed softly, the only sound interrupting the serene quiet of the sky. This was freedom—with no stress. She glanced at the horizon, a deep blue line stretching as far as the eye could see. As she levelled off at her cruising altitude, Róisín let out a breath she didn't realise she'd been holding. She was home. Really home. And up here, with nothing but the endless outback below and the bright Australian sky above, she was exactly where she belonged.

It was such a vast land; she wondered how the first settlers would have survived. The more she thought about it, the more she wanted to know what Dad and Cat had discovered.

Chapter 16

County Kerry - late Winter 1847.

Breda stood patiently in the quiet graveyard, the wind cool against her cheeks. If she closed her eyes, she could sense a hint of the scent of warming earth and new grass. Perhaps it was wishful thinking as she longed for spring to arrive. The sky was pale blue, the occasional wispy cloud scudding across the sun that bathed everything in a watery light, making even the worn, weathered gravestones seem less sombre. Her heart felt less troubled today, lighter than it had since her mother had passed on two years ago.

As she waited for Samuel to arrive, she couldn't help the smile that spread across her face. She wondered if he remembered it was a year today since they had first met by her mother's gravestone on the last Sunday of winter last year. Over the past year, when the weather was favourable, they had walked in the woods each Sunday. Their friendship had grown and strengthened as they shared their hopes and dreams. It was purely friendship, no matter how much she longed for more. Samuel O'Byrne was from *Ceann Mara* and would one day be the master of the estate, and she was simply the vicar's sister.

As Breda waited for him, her thoughts drifted, turning over the feelings she had been pushing aside for the past few months.

Why was she so drawn to Samuel? Was it simply because he had been kind to her when few others had? Or was it something more? Maybe it was because he was the only man who had ever truly paid her attention. For so long, she had been invisible—the girl who kept to herself, her only real value found in caring for her mother, her brother, and the vicarage. But Samuel—he had *seen* her. And he listened to her.

Her stomach fluttered at the thought of the fine-looking man who walked with her. Tall and broad-shouldered, with dark hair that curled at the nape of his neck. She knew his reputation well enough; everyone in County Kerry did. Samuel was known to be a rake, charming and reckless in equal measure, his name often whispered by girls at the market or in church, usually with a mixture of longing and disdain. She had heard it all before she'd met him—the stories of his dalliances, the broken hearts he left behind. And yet, despite knowing this, she couldn't shake the feeling that there was something different in the way he treated her. He wasn't just walking with her out of some fleeting fancy or to pass the time.

Since she'd met him, Breda wondered if him being a rake was purely jealous gossip. And yet, beneath her excitement, a small voice still whispered doubts. What if she was just another one of those girls to him? What if this was just a game?

But Samuel had never been anything but circumspect in his behaviour to her. On the occasion that he would hold out his hand to help her over a stile or a muddy patch after rain, he would let go as soon as they had passed through.

There was respect in the way he smiled when they met, in the way his eyes softened when he looked at her, as though there was something in her that he saw, something others had always overlooked. He wasn't trying to impress her with grand gestures or false promises. He was just there, steady and sure like the pure sunlight filtering through the clouds today.

When he held her eyes with his, she saw something that made her believe this was different. His gaze was always sincere, and her trust gradually strengthened, and she sometimes hoped for things she hadn't dared dream of before.

As Breda stood there, waiting for Samuel to walk along the road, a soft warmth spread through her chest, starting low in her belly and slowly rising, filling her with a mixture of excitement and nerves. Her heart fluttered, and a gentle heat warmed her cheeks despite the cool wind. She smiled; Samuel had told her last Sunday how pretty her rosy cheeks were. A pleasant shiver ran down her spine, her fingertips tingling as if her body sensed his presence before she even saw him.

Her hands trembled slightly; she clasped them together, trying to calm herself. There was a faint, almost exquisite tension in her stomach that left her feeling light-headed; her legs were just the tiniest bit weak, as if she might sway if she didn't keep steady.

As she heard his footsteps behind her, she swung around, unclasping her hands. The warmth bloomed through her chest and down her arms, her breath catching.

Was she foolish to let these feelings take hold? But when he was near, all those doubts seemed to fall away. He wasn't just the rake people gossiped about. He was Samuel, the man who had been patient with her, who had asked about her thoughts and dreams as if they truly mattered. As he had told her of his dreams, his despair had shown, and she knew that the famine was making him doubt his future, too.

Her heart fluttered again. Maybe this *was* real. Perhaps she could make him happy?

'Hello, Samuel,' she said.

He smiled back, though it didn't quite reach his eyes this

afternoon. 'Hello, Breda.'

'Is everything alright?' she asked gently.

For a moment, she thought he was going to tell her why he looked worried, but he shook his head and smiled again. This time, his eyes were brighter.

'Everything will be wonderful while I walk with you this afternoon.' He reached out and tilted his head to the side. 'May I take your hand today, Breda?'

'You may,' she said, looking down, not wanting him to see the love that she knew would be apparent in her eyes. More warmth suffused her as he took her hand, and his ungloved hand curled around her bare fingers. They left the graves behind and walked along the path that led to the woods.

'I never thought I'd feel this happy again,' Breda said as they reached the point where the path narrowed. She glanced up at him. 'After Mother died . . . I thought the grief would stay forever. But you have helped me through it very much this past year.'

Samuel's gaze softened, and he squeezed her hand a little tighter. 'You are strong, Breda. I'm just pleased I could be here with you.'

'I never told you,' she continued, her voice catching slightly as her thoughts turned to her late mother. 'For so long, I'd come every Sunday to tend the grave, but I couldn't make peace with it. I'd just cry and feel so… lost. And then you came.' She paused, her chest tightening with the thought of the confession she'd never shared before. 'You made me see that life doesn't have to be all sorrow, even with the hard times we live in. You brought me back to myself.'

The wind rustled through the trees as they walked, but it was the intensity of the moment that filled Breda's chest. The birdsong, the rustling grass—it was all a backdrop to the sense of contentment that had taken root in her heart this past year. She looked up at Samuel, expecting to see the same happiness mirrored in his eyes, but instead, there was something else—something sad.

'Breda,' he said, his voice low and serious now, and her heart skipped a beat. 'There's something I must tell you.'

Her lightness started to ebb away, replaced with a growing sense of unease. 'What is it? What is wrong?'

Samuel stopped walking and turned to face her fully, his hand still holding hers but not as firmly. Her stomach twisted with dread as he looked at her. 'Thomas, Caitríona, and I . . . we're leaving. For the Antipodes.'

'Caitríona? Caitríona Lowe?'

'Yes, she is marrying Thomas.'

The words hung in the air between them, heavy and

disorienting. Breda blinked, trying to grasp their meaning. 'And you are leaving? But . . . when?'

'In two weeks. We're sailing from Liverpool.' His voice was laced with regret, as though the words hurt him as much as they hurt her.

'Two weeks?' Her heart dropped, and her legs felt suddenly weak. 'You're leaving in two weeks?' She pulled her hand away, her fingers trembling. 'Why didn't you tell me before? You surely must have known. This must have been in the planning.' She had been a fool, dreaming of love; if Samuel had cared for her in any way, he would have told her.

'I didn't know how,' he said, anguish creeping into his tone. 'I didn't want to lose you, but I . . . I cannot stay.'

Her heart leapt at his words. 'You didn't want to lose me? Then why are you leaving? You will inherit the estate. You are the oldest son. You can't go.'

He shook his head. 'I have no choice. Something has happened, Breda. Something I did not tell you because I was ashamed.'

She swallowed hard, her mind racing, trying to understand. 'What happened?'

'Thomas and I were responsible for the death of a man at Lissyclearig,' Samuel whispered, his voice barely audible. 'The place where the bailiffs killed two farmers last month. A bailiff during one of the evictions. It was not our intent . . . but he died. All I can think of is that even though Seamus Kelly was responsible for the evictions, he was still a man with a wife and children. A man simply doing his job.'

He had taken a life.

As Samuel's words sank in, Breda's breath hitched in her throat, and instinctively, she took a step back, her hands pressing to her chest as if that could steady the disbelief swirling inside her. The man she had begun to care for, the man she thought she knew, had done something so unimaginable, so utterly against everything she believed in.

She blinked rapidly. Her heart pounded in her ears and drowned out the quiet of the graveyard. How could this be true? How could this kind and gentle man she had spent these quiet Sunday afternoons with, the one who made her heart sing with every glance, confess to something so terrible? *A life, taken . . .* the words hung heavily, almost suffocating her.

A sickening chill crept through Breda's veins and she clasped her hands tighter, trying to steady herself. Everything she knew, everything she had been taught—the sanctity of life, the commandment that *thou shalt not kill*—echoed in her mind. And yet, Samuel stood, telling her he had broken that most sacred law.

Her lips parted, but no words came at first. Tears welled up in her eyes, blurring Samuel standing before her. 'How?' she whispered, her voice trembling as much as her body. 'How could you do such a thing?'

All she could think of was the sermons she had listened to her whole life, her brother's voice preaching forgiveness, mercy, and the immensity of sin.

Thou shalt not kill.

All she could do was stare at Samuel, her heart breaking, not just for the man who had been killed, but for him— and what this meant for him. She knew he was a good man.

Her faith demanded forgiveness, and yet, how could she offer it? The very idea of taking a life was unimaginable to her. Every instinct told her this was wrong, so deeply wrong, and yet how could she reconcile what she felt for Samuel and his action in taking a man's life?

Tears spilled down her cheeks, but she let them stay there. 'You must leave.'

'Yes, I have to go, Breda. I was going to ask you, and of course, seek your brother's permission, if you would come with us, but that was a foolish thought. I would marry you.'

Bitterness laced her voice. 'What sort of man would preface a proposal with the announcement that he had taken a life?' She shook her head, trying to hold on to the joy she'd felt only moments before.

Samuel's jaw was set. 'I will pray for your forgiveness, and I swear to you that when you can see your way to forgiving me, I will come back. I need time to make things right.'

'You need time to seek forgiveness for what you have done.' She nodded slowly as she turned away from him. 'I must go home now.'

'May I say goodbye to you before we leave?' His voice shook with emotion.

'I will give it some thought.'

As she turned and left him, Breda's heart shattered.

Chapter 17

County Kerry - early Spring 1847.

'When I have gone away, *Mamo*, I shall think of you often from wherever I am.' Samuel's voice shook as he crouched beside her grave; he knew this would be the last time he would visit his grandmother's grave. He would see the vicar and ensure that it was kept neat and tidy. Perhaps Breda would come to the door when he called.

As Samuel rose, the despair of the past few days pressed heavily on his chest. His father's sudden death last week had been a shock for all of them. He was numb; it was as if part of him had been buried in the grave with Father. Even though the burial was at the family graveyard at *Ceann Mara*, and the vicar of the Church of Ireland in Kenmare, Reverend Godfrey, had conducted the service, John Atkins had attended and extended his sympathies to the O'Byrne family. There had been no sign of Breda, and it would have been inappropriate to ask after her.

None of his family knew that he had been walking with her each Sunday, and it was better to leave it that way. He didn't want any gossip to circulate about her; even though the local tenants were immersed in the hardship of the famine, gossip still festered like a sore.

Shock and grief remained with Samuel, but what troubled him most was his guilt. He knew, deep down, that the bailiff's death was a burden he would always carry, even though he hadn't fired the gun. His father had collapsed the day after the constabulary widened the investigation of what they called murder—the shooting of the bailiff at Lissyclearig. The constant fear of discovery seemed to seep into every corner of their lives. The famine had taken his father's strength, but it was the consequences of his son's actions that had taken his life.

What weighed on Samuel just as heavily was the grief his mother carried. Samuel felt that her silent suffering was as much his doing as the bailiff's death. The guilt stayed with him day and night, intensified by the knowledge that he had caused not only the loss of his father but also the breaking of his mother's heart. She would not talk of their imminent departure and spent most of her days in her bed.

On top of that was the knowledge that he was leaving Breda. No matter how hard he had tried to push the thought to the back of his mind, in the dark of sleepless nights, it had been nigh impossible.

He had known when he told her the truth that her strong faith would have made it impossible for her to understand the situation. There was no point telling her that Thomas had fired the shot that had killed Seamus Kelly. It could just as easily have been him.

Now, with Thomas and Caitríona married and their departure for Liverpool just days away, this would be his last chance to see Breda. Would she be there, as she had been all those Sunday afternoons for the past year? Had she found a place in her heart to forgive him? Even if she had, it was too late to ask her to accompany them to the colonies; so many of their fellow countrymen were leaving for America and the Antipodes, the passages were booked months ahead.

Samuel slowly pushed open the gate, the rusty creak breaking the silence of the graveyard. His heart quickened with the familiar sense of anticipation, but it was tempered by dread.

As he stepped through the gate, his gaze fell on the figure kneeling by her mother's grave, her head bowed in quiet reflection. A wave of emotion hit him like a dam breaking, overwhelming him, and for a moment, he couldn't move. Breda looked so peaceful, so pure, kneeling there in the soft sunlight, and her presence was both a comfort and a deep ache in his heart.

His feelings for her had grown as they had walked and talked since last spring. Samuel had known for a while that he loved Breda Atkins. Leaving her would be like leaving a part of himself behind.

He took a deep breath and walked toward her, his footsteps soundless on the wet leaf litter, yet he knew Breda was aware of his approach. She stood and turned to face him. The moment their eyes met, his doubt lifted. Her eyes were soft, without a trace of the judgment he had feared.

'I heard about your father,' she said gently, stepping toward him. 'I'm so sorry, Samuel. I prayed for you and your family.'

He nodded, swallowing hard, trying to find his voice. 'It has been . . . hard. Sean is taking over the estate now. Thomas and Caitríona will marry the day after tomorrow, and then we will leave for Liverpool. I had to see you to say goodbye. I am hoping that you would walk with me one last time.'

Breda's gaze held his, full of compassion. 'I've forgiven you, Samuel,' she said softly. 'John told me more . . . about what's happening with the bailiffs and the evictions. I didn't know it all. He tries to protect me from the worst of it.' She glanced down at the ground, her brow furrowing. 'So much suffering . . . I've been sheltered. It's not right, what's happening.'

'I am so happy that you came today.' The knot in Samuel's chest loosened; Breda had forgiven him. He hadn't expected that, but he should have known; she had demonstrated her kindness and understanding often over the past year. It was one of the many things he loved about her.

They began to walk together, leaving the graveyard behind. The air was cool, but the wind was gentle, and there was a faint hint of spring, the promise of new life after the bleakness of winter. They wandered towards the stream, the running water over the stones like a distant, comforting whisper.

Samuel paused by a fallen log, removed his coat, and spread it on the soft grass in front of the log. 'Shall we sit for a while this afternoon?' He wanted to linger; the time with Breda would go quickly. All that was waiting for him at the house were his mother's sobs and the final packing of his trunk.

He let out a long, shaky breath as she nodded. The strain of the past days—the grief, the trepidation of what lay ahead—was catching up to him. The thought of leaving Breda behind and worrying about her happiness and her very survival was almost enough to make him break his word to Cousin Richard.

'I don't know if I can do this,' he confessed, his voice breaking as he sat beside her. 'My father's gone . . . Sean will run the estate now, and I—I don't know if leaving is the right thing to do. I feel like I'm abandoning everything. Including you.'

'You must. I understand now.' Breda reached out, wrapping her arms around him in a gentle embrace. The warmth of her touch broke something in him, and for the first time since his father's death, Samuel let the tears come. His shoulders shook, and he buried his face against her neck, overwhelmed by the grief he had held back.

'I'm so sorry,' Breda whispered as she lifted one hand to stroke his hair. 'I'm sorry I was so harsh with you before. You've been carrying enough without my mean-spiritedness.'

Her words comforted him, and he pulled back slightly, wiping at his eyes.

'This is our last walk,' he said, his voice hoarse with emotion. 'I don't know when . . . I'll come back. It may be a very long time.'

Breda nodded, her gaze steady, but her eyes welled with tears. 'I know,' she said, her voice barely a whisper, the sadness in her eyes mirroring his own. He reached up and, with his thumb, gently caught the first tear as it fell. 'Why does life have to be like this?' Breda's voice broke. 'It makes me doubt my faith. What sort of God could make our country suffer so much? What sort of God would take your father so suddenly? What sort of God would—'

'Hush, my love,' he said. 'Let's not spend our last hours with tears. I want to remember your happy, smiling face and your laughter.'

They leaned toward each other, and Samuel could not help himself. His arms went around her, and he lowered his head, his lips tenderly meeting Breda's. As the reality of his imminent departure filled their thoughts, their kiss deepened. Breda moaned softly as she lifted Samuel's shirt, and her hands caressed his back.

The afternoon passed in a blur, a whirlwind of emotions as they discovered each other and their mutual love. Afterwards, as they lay together, the beautiful, melodious song of a thrush broke the silence of the late afternoon.

Breda's fingers lingered on his chest as Samuel rested his hand on her bare skin. There were no regrets —just a quiet acceptance of what had passed and what was ahead.

'I love you, Breda.'

Her eyes were wide as she looked up at him and nodded. 'And I you, Samuel O'Byrne.'

They lingered until the evening began to draw in, and they knew that they had to say a final goodbye. As they walked back to the church, Samuel kept his arm around her the whole way. When it was time to leave each other, Samuel reached for her hand as they stood together at the gate.

'I'll come back for you,' he promised, though even as the words left his lips, he saw the sad smile that tugged at the corners of her mouth.

She nodded, but the sadness in her eyes told him the truth. She didn't believe him.

'Trust me, Breda. You have my word.'

He would return as soon as he could and ask her brother for Breda's hand in marriage. 'I will write to you so that you can share my journey until I can return.'

***

Breda looked into Samuel's eyes, allowing herself to hope—just for a moment—that he would keep his promise. That somehow, despite the distance, despite everything that hung over him, he would come back.

'You promise you will write?'

'I will,' Samuel said, brushing her hair from her face and leaning down to kiss her forehead. 'The moment we arrive in Liverpool, and then from wherever we land next. You will always know where I am.'

'I will reply to each letter you write, but I will hold them until you can tell me where to send them.' Breda looked into his eyes, searching for the certainty she so desperately needed. The warmth of the day had disappeared, and the promise of spring was overshadowed by the fear of what was to come. But as Samuel pulled her close, holding her tightly against him, she allowed herself to hope—just for a moment—that his promise would hold. That somehow, despite the distance, despite everything, he would come back.

He kissed her again gently and, with one final, lingering look, turned and started walking away, his figure disappearing into the woods. The wind whispered through the trees, carrying his steps away until there was nothing left but the faint rustle of leaves and the ache in Breda's heart.

She would wait. No matter how far, no matter how long. She would wait for Samuel to return from the other side of the world.

Chapter 18

Wilcannia - Wednesday, mid-January, 10.45 a.m.

Róisín's nerves were humming as she switched her sneakers for low heels, smoothing down the navy skirt she'd chosen with care that morning. It was a small detail, but she wanted to be prepared and in control. This would be her first face-to-face with Seth Brodie, and after everything that had gone wrong with Greg, she couldn't afford to misjudge him. Not this time.

Her thoughts lingered on her first meeting with Greg. It had been a strange interview; he'd actually interviewed a group of five law graduates in one meeting. He had been charismatic, and most of the time, the group had been laughing and having social conversations.

He told her later that he was able to sense her keen intelligence by her demeanour, and she'd fallen for it. She'd been blind to so many signs, misreading his charm for sincerity, his confidence for integrity. It wasn't just that she'd been fooled—she should have known better. Was there something about her, some blind spot when it came to reading people? That nagging doubt had crept in since Brisbane and been magnified with Linda's story.

Today, she'd be different. She'd pay attention to the little things, the ones that people often missed—his tone of voice, the way he carried himself, how his eyes moved during their conversation. Body language could speak volumes, and she needed to listen. Seth Brodie had a reputation for being both professional and personable—she'd Googled him—but she wouldn't rely on hearsay. She'd see for herself and take her time.

It was nine kilometres from the airstrip to the business area of Wilcannia, and she'd called the community centre and organised a lift into town. Her driver, a longtime local, was waiting near the small shed when she landed. He wanted to chat, asking many questions about why she'd flown into town, and she was pleased it was a short trip.

'Are you here to go to the school?' he asked.

'No, just a meeting in town,' she said.

He was persistent in his questioning, but she managed to remain vague.

'Are you available to pick me up and drop me off at the

aerodrome around three-thirty?' she asked the elderly man as he pulled up outside the historic building.

'I'll pick you up here at three-thirty, lass,' he said as she paid him.

'Thank you.' As she stepped out of the small sedan, Róisín admired the sandstone buildings that lined the streets leading to the bridge. She was pleased to see that some of the old buildings were being restored. The town, a former port on the banks of the Darling River, was rich in heritage and held an undeniable charm. Cat and Dad would love it, she thought. Victorian sandstone buildings told of bustling bygone days when the locality was rich and the paddle steamers were running the river.

The temporary office of the Water Integrity Review Authority was situated on the corner just off the street by the river. She smoothed down her skirt, patted her hair as she approached the front steps, and pushed open the double timber doors.

'Good morning.' The young woman behind the reception desk smiled at her.

'Hi, I've got an appointment to see Seth Brodie this morning.'

'Ah, you must be Róisín O'Byrne! Lovely to meet you. Seth just stepped out to grab a coffee. He wasn't expecting you for another half-hour or so.'

Róisín hid a smile. This was going to be very different to the office situated in a mecca of coffee shops.

'Do you want to wait in the foyer, or would you like to see your office?' The young woman jumped up from behind the desk and held out her hand. 'I'm Debra, the receptionist, Girl Friday, and jack-of-all-trades. Seth even had me fixing a broken chair yesterday!'

Róisín shook her hand with a smile. 'Good to meet you, Debra. You sound talented.'

'Come on, I'll show you. Not the chair, I mean. Your office.' She giggled, and Róisín instantly warmed to her. 'It's good to have something to do. We're just starting up, and to be honest, I've been a bit bored the month we've been here.' The young woman chatted as she led Róisín down a corridor past three empty offices.

'How many people work here?' Róisín asked.

'Right now, just you, me, and Seth,' Debra replied with a grin. 'It'll be nice to have another woman around. He's a great boss but not the most talkative. He's all about work—no after-hours drinks or anything like that.'

'To be honest, I'm much the same,' Róisín said but tempered her words with a smile.

Her office was simple, with a large desk and a desktop

computer. Her smile widened as she saw the vase of fresh flowers at the side of her desk.

Debra pointed to them. 'I thought it would make it a bit more welcoming for you. My oldies own the caravan park across the river, and Mum loves her flowers. Her garden is really pretty.'

'Thank you; that was a lovely gesture.' Róisín felt at ease and hoped that Seth Brodie would be as easy to get along with as Debra.

'We're fully connected.' Debra gestured to the computer and printer. 'Seth had the tech guys in from Broken Hill last week, so everything's working. There's a folder in the tray on your desk with your login and password. Anyway, come back out whenever you're ready. You can keep me company while we wait for Seth.' She left Róisín to check out her office. She sat in the brand-new swivel chair and touched the computer keyboard. The twenty-seven-inch curved screen on the desk was an unexpected bonus. She was used to working on a laptop.

She walked back out to the foyer, and soon Debra had her laughing over a story about the fellow who had picked her up at the airport.

'Pluto could talk the leg off a chair,' Debra said with a grin.

'Pluto?' Róisín shook her head. 'That's his name?'

'Yep, and no one knows why. That's the only thing he won't ever talk about.'

The door opened, and as Róisín turned, a tall man walked in, balancing a cardboard tray with three coffees.

'Hello,' he said with a smile. 'I'm assuming you're Ms O'Byrne?'

'Yes, please call me Róisín,' she replied.

'Ah, Róisín,' he said, repeating her name with a smile that didn't quite reach his eyes. 'I'll admit, I wasn't sure how to pronounce your name when I first saw your file. I intended calling you Ms O'Byrne until you said it.'

He put the coffee tray on the desk in front of Debra and shook Róisín's hand, his grip firm but his expression unreadable.

'It's good to have you here,' he said. 'Shall we step into my office? I got you a coffee—flat white. I hope that's okay?'

'That's perfect, thank you, Seth,' Róisín replied, following him down the hallway. His office was spacious, with large windows overlooking a paddock at the back of the building.

He gestured to a chair at the side of the desk and she sat down, placing her coffee on the edge of the desk.

'I'm sorry I wasn't here when you arrived,' he said, settling into his chair.

'No worries, the wind was with me,' Róisín replied casually.

His brow lifted. 'You flew in?'

'Yes.' She nodded.

He gave a faint smile, but she could discern criticism in his tone. 'Not everyone has the luxury of their own plane.'

She shrugged. 'It's handy. My *father's* Cessna saved me an eight-hour return drive while he's away. Flying down and back this afternoon suited me. But I will be driving from next week when I start work.'

Seth leaned forwards. 'I wasn't expecting that. I thought you were from Brisbane.'

Róisín held his gaze, her expression cool. 'You assumed I was. Yes, I've spent time in Brisbane, but I grew up at a station four hours from here on the Darling River Run.

Seth's eyes narrowed; he seemed intrigued, but she was unsure if he was pleased or not. 'So, you're a country girl. Almost local.'

'Local to the Darling, yes. That was one of the attractions of this position,' she said firmly.

'Interesting,' Seth mused. 'I did wonder why a lawyer used to dealing with celebrities and high-end city clients, would want to come west.'

Róisín forced a polite smile. 'I spent my childhood in the outback. Trust me, I know how to handle more than city life and celebrity divorces.' She knew her tone was sharp, but she didn't appreciate his implied criticism.

'Well, I guess I may have misjudged you.' Seth studied her. 'But time will tell. I was very impressed with your philosophies at the interview.'

'Perhaps you did,' she replied. 'But let's just make sure neither of us make any more assumptions, shall we?'

With that, Seth nodded. 'Fair enough. Let's get started then.'

Chapter 19

Wilcannia - Wednesday, mid-January, 11.00 a.m.

Seth put his coffee cup down and observed Róisín for a long few seconds before speaking. She had an air of quiet confidence, although he could sense some nervousness in the way she held herself. Her hands were clasped in her lap when she wasn't holding her coffee. Still, there was something about her that reassured him—maybe it was the fact that she was a local, born and raised along the Darling. That tempered his initial reservations a bit.

They hadn't had many applicants for this role, and the two others had been entirely unsuitable. Now, it was down to Róisín. He wondered, though, how someone who had spent her time post-graduation career practising divorce law would make the leap to something as complex as water integrity.

Róisín lifted her chin and held his gaze steadily, and for a moment, Seth was struck by the honesty in her direct look. Maybe he had underestimated her. She had an appealing clarity about her.

'First up, thanks for coming down today,' he began, shaking off the thought. 'I'm happy to tell you more about the position and answer any questions you've got. But I'm sure I don't have to remind you of the confidentiality of this?'

'Of course.' Her eyes left his and drifted over the map of the river spread across his desk, looking interested in the map and what he had to say. He nodded.

'Alright,' Seth continued. 'Here's where we step in. The Darling River—the heart of agriculture in New South Wales—is also ground zero for some serious criminal activity. Water theft, manipulation of rights, illegal sales . . . it's been a mess for a few years.'

'As the position was advertised by a recruitment agency and with the lack of signage here on the building and no logos on the documents'—she gestured to the folder in front of her—'I'm not quite clear whose jurisdiction we're under.'

'Good question.' His opinion went up a notch. 'A simple one, but with a multi-layered answer.'

Her eyebrows rose.

Seth paused for a moment as he gathered his thoughts. 'The recruitment agency is new to this sector, and we've had a limited response. Two unsuitable candidates, and now you're here. The lack of branding reflects the urgency of the situation—this role is crucial, but we've struggled to attract the right talent.'

Róisín nodded slowly, absorbing his words. 'So, you're saying the agency's involvement might not have been the best decision?'

'It's complicated,' he replied. 'We're trying to tackle a pressing issue, but the right fit is essential. You being a local definitely softens my reservations. I hope you'll bring the understanding we need for this challenge.'

Róisín's brow furrowed in curiosity. 'But I'm still in the dark. You still haven't told me whose jurisdiction this authority falls under.'

Seth nodded, pleased that she wanted to know the whole structure. 'Right. The primary jurisdiction is the state government of New South Wales. They manage water resources here, so the authority will operate under the NSW Department of Planning and Environment. Our role will involve investigating water rights and usage, ensuring compliance with regulations, and tackling any illegal activities.'

He paused to make sure she was following. 'If we discover anything untoward—like water theft or manipulation of licenses—we'll need to communicate directly with local law enforcement, particularly the NSW Police's specialised units focused on environmental crimes. They'll help us enforce the laws and take necessary action.'

'That's good.'

'We'll also keep federal agencies in the loop, like the Australian Federal Police or the Department of Agriculture, Water, and the Environment, especially for serious breaches. Collaboration is key; we'll share findings and evidence to ensure a coordinated response to any criminal activity.'

Róisín's gaze remained fixed on the map as Seth leaned back slightly, studying her. 'I've heard many stories over the years. I thought a lot of them were just local gossip, but it really is that bad?' she asked.

'Worse than most people know. Farmers and irrigators have been siphoning off water for years tampering with meters, bypassing them altogether. And it wasn't just small-time operators. Some of the biggest players were in on it. Communities downstream were left to dry out, and ecosystems suffered.'

He watched as the furrow in Róisín's brow deepened. 'So, this isn't just landowners taking a little extra on the side?'

'Not even close,' Seth replied, his voice hardening. 'We're talking large-scale theft—diverting entire river systems for cotton crops. Stealing water, on-selling water licenses for money laundering. There are even some international players involved.'

Róisín looked up from the map, thoughtful. 'And nobody noticed?'

'It was known,' Seth said with a sigh. 'But enforcement was weak. Loopholes were exploited, and some of these players had connections—deep ones. The 2019 Royal Commission exposed a lot, but by then, much of the damage was already done.'

She nodded slowly, considering his words. 'So now we're in clean-up mode?'

'Exactly,' Seth said. He hesitated for a second. 'You've got a strong legal background, but I've got to ask—how do you see your skills in family law translating to this work? Water rights are a whole different beast.'

Róisín didn't flinch. 'True. But in my experience, whether it's a marriage or a water license, it's all about understanding relationships. People's interests, their motives. In divorce law, you have to read people—their body language, the way they communicate. I imagine it's similar here. If you can understand when someone's trying to hide something, you can catch them out. And contracts . . . I've dealt with enough of those to know how to spot the fine print.'

Seth was impressed by her calm, considered response. 'Fair

enough. What was your process when handling difficult cases—ones where the stakes were high?'

Róisín thought for a moment. 'I always focused on the facts first. Emotion can cloud judgment, but facts, evidence—that's where you build a case. I made sure everything was airtight, with no room for slip-ups and no grey areas. I'll apply the same approach here—no matter how complex or entrenched the water rights are, there's always a way through.'

Seth nodded slowly, feeling his earlier scepticism begin to ease. Maybe she would work out after all. She wasn't just giving him standard answers; there was depth in her thinking, a steadiness that he could appreciate. 'Good to hear. You're going to need that mindset because out here, it's not just about legalities. You're going to be facing pressure from all sides—political, economic, personal.'

Róisín lifted her chin a little higher. 'I've faced pressure before. I know how to handle it.'

Seth studied her a moment longer. 'Alright, then. Let's see what you can do.'

Chapter 20

Wilcannia - Wednesday, mid-January, 2.00 p.m.

As Seth and Róisín continued to discuss the intricacies of the position, the afternoon passed quickly, each topic flowing seamlessly into the next. Seth's enthusiasm was infectious, and Róisín found herself getting lost in the conversation, ideas sparking between them as they headed off on tangents. She was surprised at the difference in the actual role from what had been advertised. Seth summed it up well—we do the investigating, provide the evidence, and then the law takes over.

She admired his passion and commitment; it was clear he wasn't just looking for a team member—he wanted someone who could work closely with him. They would be the team.

As he spoke, she noted the confidence in his voice and the way he carried himself. He was a very attractive man, good-looking, but the real attraction was in his passion for what he was talking about. His face lit up, and his enthusiasm shone from his hazel eyes.

He's not just a boss, she thought, but a man who genuinely cares about the work and the people involved. It was such a change; she kicked herself. If she'd chosen wisely when she graduated, she could have been involved in something like this since then.

It seemed it was going to be a big change from working for Greg, whose selfishness and self-serving ambitions had now left a bitter taste in her mouth. Seth's words and demeanour held a refreshing honesty. He was approachable and down-to-earth, and she felt she had gained his trust after this one meeting. Not at all what she'd expected from today's meeting, his professionalism far exceeded any expectations she'd had.

But she pulled herself up. Don't be gullible, she reminded herself. Greg, at first, seemed charming and genuine, but he revealed his true nature later. By that time, he had held a form of coercive control over her, and she had stayed with him much longer than she should have. She couldn't bear to think how long she would have stayed if Linda hadn't sought her out. Róisín knew she had to remain vigilant, keeping her guard up just enough to protect herself while still being open to this new opportunity.

They continued their conversation, digging into the

complexities of water management, the laws they'd need to navigate, and the work ahead. Time passed quickly until Róisín's stomach growled loudly as they discussed the schedule for the next couple of weeks.

'Oops, sorry,' she muttered with a self-conscious smile.

'Not a problem at all.' Seth glanced at his watch. 'Time's flown by. I didn't realise it was after two. Sorry, I get carried away,' he said, chuckling softly. 'It's well past lunchtime.'

'So did I,' she replied, smiling at him. 'I've been digesting everything you've said.'

'I need to digest some food.' His eyes crinkled in an appealing smile. 'What time do you need to leave?' he asked.

'I can fly in the dark, but I would prefer to be at home before sunset, so, if possible, I'd like to leave by three-thirty,' she replied. She'd like to be there when Cat and Logan arrived home, but she wasn't giving away any personal information yet, if ever. This was a professional position, and that's how her conversation would stay.

'How long have you been flying?'

'A few years. Since I was seventeen,' she said. Seth raised his eyebrows in surprise, and her stomach emitted another grumble.

'How about we finish our conversation over lunch, and

then I'll drop you back at the aerodrome. We can take a break from all the heavy-duty stuff, maybe work out a bit of a schedule for you, and get you back in the air by three-thirty. Would that work for you?'

'That would be fine, thank you.' Róisín hesitated for a moment. Lunch felt too personal, but her stomach had made it impossible to refuse without seeming ungrateful. 'I've already organised a lift from here to the aerodrome.'

'Pluto?'

She nodded, unable to stop her grin. 'Yes.'

'I'll get Debra to give him a call on our way out. Oh, and Róisín, just one more thing before we go. I want to be totally upfront with you. Give you the opportunity to change your mind.' He leaned back in his chair, growing more serious. 'I want to make sure you know exactly what your role will be. You're not just here for the legal advice. You're going to be right at the centre of this investigation, making sure we don't make any missteps.'

Róisín met his gaze. 'Of course. I'm ready for whatever comes.'

'Good. This isn't just about paperwork and courtroom appearances. The Darling's been a playground for years— farmers, brokers, big corporations—they've been bending and breaking the rules to make millions. We're here to stop that.

You're the one who's going to make sure we do it by the book.'

Róisín frowned slightly, focusing. 'So, I'll be guiding on legal compliance? Making sure the evidence is collected properly?'

'Yes,' Seth said. 'But more than that. You'll be overseeing how we gather evidence, ensuring every step is airtight. One misstep and any decent lawyer will rip us apart in court. You'll need to make sure we've got solid cases—warrants, handling of evidence, the works.'

'Understood,' Róisín said, nodding. 'I'll work closely with the team on building airtight cases. What about closing loopholes?'

'That's where you'll come in strong,' Seth replied. 'You'll be combing through contracts, water licenses, trading records—everything. Find the violations, analyse the breaches, and work with prosecutors to build strong cases after charges are laid. And there will be charges laid; I've already come across some inconsistencies in the month since I started in the role. And we'll need your advice to tighten the regulations where loopholes still exist.'

'So, I'm the watchdog for every legal angle.'

'Exactly,' Seth said with a grim nod. 'But don't forget—some of these people have powerful connections. Once we start digging, they'll know. They might try to intimidate us.'

Róisín raised an eyebrow. 'Intimidate? You mean threats?'

Seth's forehead furrowed deeply, and as she stared at him, the corners of his mouth turned slightly downward, drawing her attention to a slight tension in his jaw. 'Possibly worse. These aren't small-time players. They've got deep ties to politics and business. Cutting off their cash flow could make them dangerous. You'll be in the crosshairs like the rest of us.'

Róisín met his gaze, steady. 'I'm not afraid. I knew what I was getting into. If they want a fight, we'll fight back—legally, of course.'

Seth couldn't help but smile. 'So that doesn't dissuade you?'

'No, I'm in.'

'Good. Just stay sharp. This is going to be tough; I'm confident we'll get the results we're after. Now, let's go eat!'

Seth stood, and then Róisín followed suit and stretched. The only time she'd left the office since she'd arrived was for a quick trip to the ladies' room.

'Is there somewhere we can eat here?' she asked.

'Yeah, the café at the golf club will be open for a light lunch—it's Wednesday. They've got toasties and Reuben sandwiches, nothing deep-fried.'

'Suits me. Do they have good coffee?' she asked.

'They make a decent one; that was the one you had earlier.'

'Okay, sounds good,' Róisín agreed, still feeling cautious but not wanting to appear rude.

She knew that Seth had picked up her hesitation, but it wouldn't hurt. 'What about Debra?' Róisín asked.

Seth laughed, the sound of it catching Róisín off guard. She found herself noticing, for the second or third time, just how attractive he was—and immediately, her defences went up.

'Gosh, no,' Seth said with another chuckle. 'Deb eats at eleven-thirty sharp. She's always starving by then. She finishes her day at three.'

Róisín said goodbye to Debra after Seth asked her to cancel Pluto. 'I'll see you next week,' she said.

'Nice to have another girl on board,' Deb said with a grinning glance at Seth.

He pulled a face at her, and it made him seem even more approachable to Róisín.

They walked the short distance to the club, the air hot and dry, typical of a summer afternoon in the west. Dust clung to the buildings, and the stark beauty of the sunbaked landscape stretched out beyond the town, across the paddocks and to the river.

Seth held the door open for her, and she stepped inside,

escaping the oppressive heat.

'Thank you,' Róisín said quietly as they approached the bistro counter, where a woman sat looking at her phone. She looked up and smiled.

'Hello, Seth. Back for more coffee?'

'Lunch please, Maureen,' he replied, offering Róisín a private moment to collect herself, respecting her earlier request to keep their meeting confidential.

'What would you like?' Seth asked, pulling out his card. 'My shout—it's the least I can do since you flew down today.'

'No, it's fine,' Róisín said, holding her purse. But as he looked at her with curiosity, she reconsidered. There was no need to be so guarded.

'Okay, thank you. I appreciate it.'

They both ordered, and Róisín was surprised when their toasted wraps and coffee arrived quickly.

Her eyes must have widened at the quality of the food because Seth remarked, 'Maureen had her own café in Brisbane.'

'It's wonderful,' Róisín said, impressed. She glanced down at her ham, beetroot relish, and sour cream wrap, savouring the mix of flavours. 'I wonder what kind of cheese this is.'

Seth called out, 'Maureen, what cheese is in the wrap?'

'*Grana Padano*,' Maureen replied from the kitchen.

'Well, I'm impressed,' Róisín said, smiling. 'I've never

had it before.'

They ate in companionable silence for a while, Maureen bringing over two coffees in delicate yellow cups adorned with white daisies, entirely unexpected in the rugged, deserted town of Wilcannia.

'Thank you,' Róisín said. 'Pretty cups. Seth said you had a café in Brisbane?' she asked Maureen.

'Yes, love. Sold it when I moved back here. My kids are here now, and with my husband gone, the farm needed someone to look after it.'

'I'm glad you did. The food is absolutely delicious,' Róisín said warmly.

As they finished their meal, Róisín caught Seth pouring three packets of sugar into his coffee. She raised her eyebrows in amusement, and he caught her look.

'I only have sugar in the middle of the day—it gets me through the afternoon,' he said, smiling.

'My dad's the same. Loves his coffee but loads it with sugar.' Róisín found herself relaxing, surprised at how easily the conversation flowed.

When their coffee was finished, Seth called out. 'Thanks, Maureen. I'll see you next week.' He turned to Róisín. 'I'm driving back to Sydney for a couple of meetings tomorrow.

That's one of the reasons I really appreciate you coming today.'

'One?' she asked as they walked back to the office.

'The other is that it was a pleasure to talk to you and realise that I have the right person on the team. I think we're going to work well together.' This time, his smile was wide. 'I apologise for assuming that a divorce lawyer wouldn't suit.'

Heat ran up Róisín's neck, but she ignored it. 'Thank you. I'm feeling good about the job, too.'

Chapter 21

Wilcannia aerodrome - Wednesday, mid-January, 3.45 p.m.

Seth stood by the car, waiting for Róisín as she gathered her bag and files from the back seat. The late afternoon sun bathed the barren landscape in a warm, golden light, the hot earth stretching endlessly toward the horizon. The airstrip felt like a remote outpost, with not one person in sight; the leaves of the scattered gum trees rustled in the wind, breaking the otherwise silent expanse.

He cleared his throat, turning his attention back to Róisín as she walked around the front of the four-wheel drive to stand beside him. 'Thanks again for coming down today. I'll see you on Monday. I'll be back in town on Sunday, and then the week after that, we'll have interviews to conduct further up the river. I'll confirm the locations by the end of the week. I'll stay in touch by email. Or do you prefer text messages?'

'Email is fine.' Róisín's expression was thoughtful, yet he sensed a hint of excitement beneath her calm words. The anticipation in the subtle smile she tried to suppress, as if she was already thinking about the work ahead, didn't go unnoticed by him.

'That all sounds great,' Róisín said, her eyes gleaming with renewed enthusiasm. 'The work will be far more interesting than anything I've done in the past few years.'

Seth raised an eyebrow, intrigued. 'Yeah, I was surprised to read about your background online after I received your application. You've had some excellent feedback from some well-connected people. I even recognised some names.'

Róisín's response was steady, her tone measured. 'I have, but it's my past now. It wasn't the work I imagined doing when I studied law. The city, the corporate side it wasn't fulfilling.'

He saw the shift in her demeanour, and he knew she wasn't here for the salary; she was here to make a difference, and that made him confident in his decision to bring her on board.

'There is one more thing I neglected to mention,' Seth said, his voice taking on a more serious tone. He hesitated for a moment, not wanting to cause her any discomfort, but he had to ask. 'I need to check something with you. Don't take it the wrong way, but we've already got a list of properties that are going to get our attention first. I'd appreciate it if you could tell me the name of your family's station. It's best to avoid conflicts of interest before we start investigating.'

Róisín straightened, meeting his gaze head-on. Seth admired the way she handled herself—no defensiveness, just clear professionalism. 'I understand. My family's property is *Ceann Mara*, and my father's name is Thomas O'Byrne. It's been in our family since the nineteenth century. Don't worry about any conflict of interest. My father is as keen to protect the river as I am.'

'I wasn't implying anything about your family,' he clarified, though a part of him was relieved to get this out of the way early. 'Just checking we won't strike any problems.' He recalled the list that he'd been studying over the past month. 'Where's it located?'

'Louth,' Róisín replied, her tone tightening just a little.

Seth's frown deepened.

'Don't tell me my father's name is on this list.' Her voice was tight.

'I recall two properties around that area that interest us— one called *Guntana* and another about fifteen kilometres downstream. *Dunleavy*.'

Róisín's face remained calm, but Seth caught a flicker of tension in her glance down. '*Guntana* was sold last year. The new owner is my sister's partner. You need to know that. Logan hasn't worked on the land long. He's a former policeman from Queensland.'

That doesn't necessarily mean he's honest, Seth thought. He studied her face, wondering if there was something left unsaid, but he didn't push. Still, she was upfront, and that earned her a further measure of respect in his eyes.

They shook hands, a firm, professional exchange, though his grip lingered slightly longer than usual.

'I'll see you Monday,' Róisín said, her voice softer now.

Seth allowed himself a small grin. 'Are you going to be flying down to work every day?'

Róisín shook her head. 'As much as I'd love to, it's not exactly practical. I'll be staying at home until you decide where I'll be based. I'll overnight in Wilcannia until then and go home on the weekends.'

'Sounds like a good plan. I can recommend the local motel. They do meals too.'

'I'll make a note of that. Well, I'll see you next Monday, Seth. Thanks again for today. If you haven't picked it up already, I am very excited about this position. It'll be challenging, but I'll be working with something that's very close to my heart.'

As she walked toward the small plane, Seth watched her go, her quiet enthusiasm softening his worry about the challenges they were about to face.

Chapter 22

Ceann Mara - Wednesday, mid-January, 5.30 p.m.

As Róisín turned to the Cessna, the smell of rain reached her, the distant clouds on the horizon hinting at a storm. It made her think of *Ceann Mara*, of the droughts they'd endured, and how welcome was every drop of rain that might fall.

Róisín deliberately hadn't shared much of her personal life with Seth; she kept that part of herself guarded. None of his business, she reminded herself. She planned to keep her personal life and her new job entirely separate. However, she had to admit that working in such a small office with only two others might make it difficult to remain so detached. But she'd managed so far. All Seth knew was that she was flying the family plane, where their property was, and that Logan, who was connected to her, owned *Guntana*. She hadn't missed his flicker of interest when she'd mentioned her connection to *Guntana*. She held no doubts about Logan, but *Dunleavy* was another matter entirely.

That was the McGillvray's station, and she wouldn't trust Reg McGillvray one bit.

'Good to know,' she thought, but she tried to contain her excitement as her mind went back to all they'd talked about. Most of her thoughts were preoccupied with everything Seth had told her. This job was going to be amazing; she knew she had to brush up her legal knowledge and do a lot of reading about current water use legislation. She glanced at the bulging folder on the seat beside her; Seth had asked Debra to print out the Water Act, the Basin Plan and the latest updates, as well as including a hyperlink to the server that contained the Water Entitlement Registers, as well as her login and password details.

The next Basin Plan was due in 2026, and Seth said he did not doubt that their investigation, findings, and subsequent charges would impact its content.

Róisín's grin was wide as the flight home passed quickly; it would certainly be different to dealing with the A-listers in Brisbane. Before she knew it, she was soaring over the stations close to *Ceann Mara*. She pulled a face at the sight of Old Reg McGillvray's land. *Wouldn't put it past him to sell water,* she thought bitterly. She'd never liked that family.

She'd gone to primary school with the McGillvray boys, and they'd been as dishonest as anyone she'd ever met. Time will tell, she mused as the plane began to descend toward *Ceann Mara.*

She frowned when she spotted the red ute from this morning along the billabong, almost at the southern boundary of their property. If the setting sun hadn't glinted on the windscreen, she would have missed it. The vehicle was parked in a dense clump of saltbush. She peered down and spotted a swag set up next to another clump.

What's he doing all the way out there, she wondered, her brow furrowing. She made a mental note to mention it to Logan later. It looked like they wanted a free camp, hiding the vehicle like that.

Flying over the homestead, her mood lightened as she spotted her parents' Land Cruiser driving in from the main road. Seeing Cat and Logan would be great, and she was looking forwards to hearing firsthand how Dad was really doing and how Mum was coping.

A few minutes later, she was taxiing the Cessna towards the shed from the north, keeping an eye out. There was no sign of Logan in the shed. They're probably inside, she thought, or maybe they've rowed over the river to their place.

Once the plane was secure, Róisín grabbed her bag, shoes and the armful of files and walked over to the house. The back door was open, so she tapped lightly before stepping inside.

'Anyone here? Cat? Logan? It's me,' she called out.

Footsteps thudded on the timber stairs down the staircase at the end of the back hallway, and soon Cat burst into view, her eyes wide with excitement.

'Róisín! It's good to see you!' she cried, rushing to embrace her. 'I can't believe you're here. And to stay home too!'

Róisín laughed. 'It's good to be home, but I won't be staying long. I'll be on the road a fair bit.' she said, stepping back and looking at Cat. 'You look tired.'

Cat nodded, and her eyes swam with tears. 'I'll never forget yesterday, Ro. That shitty morning in the shed will stay with me forever. I felt so powerless, watching Dad on the ground. I honestly thought he was going to die in his shed.'

'I know. It'll be hard to shake that memory, but you have to move forward. We all have to stay strong for Dad—and Mum. How is she?'

'Strong, now, but she was a mess in the shed, too.' Cat looked up, brushing the tears away. 'I just want everything to be okay for him. How did the girls take it?'

'They were worried, of course, but we all accepted he was in the best place. So long as he stays there as long as he's supposed to!'

'I wonder how long it'll be before they all come home.

Mum and Dad are going to regret ever offering that we could all stay here whenever we wanted.'

'I'm sure they won't mind their routine being interrupted if everyone's here when they arrive home. I told them we'd keep in touch. I'm sure Erin, Shea and Bridget will come home to make sure Dad's okay. And if he has to be in Sydney a while, we'll get down there to see him.' Róisín didn't elaborate on her worries about Erin, sensing that what Erin had told her was not to be shared.

'I think Dad's recovery is going to take a while, though,' Cat said, concern etching lines on her forehead. 'Something to do with the fracture and the plaster and the circulation in his leg—it could keep him in Sydney for a while. The doctor in Dubbo was fabulous. He explained to all of us the leg injury could complicate his heart condition and that they would monitor him closely. It's frustrating because he's not the type to sit still for long.'

Róisín's brow furrowed. 'He'll be going stir-crazy.'

'Exactly,' Cat replied, a sigh escaping her lips. 'He's already restless. I can't blame him. I mean, he's always been the one to work with his hands, to be out in the paddocks. Being cooped up in a hospital room is going to drive him mad. Plus, they'll need to do physical therapy once the plaster comes off, and he won't like that either.'

Róisín nodded, understanding the implications. 'Yeah, but it's for his own good. I hope it doesn't affect his ability to move around the property too much.'

'Me too,' Cat said. 'But we need to make sure we're ready when he does come home. He'll need us to help him adjust, not just to the injury, but to everything he's been through.'

'We'll all be there for him, Cat. No matter what it takes.'

'We've just got to be thankful that it happened when it did. He could have had the heart attack out at the mailbox.'

'It seems to be the medical opinion that it was the accident on the bike that caused the heart attack because of his leg injury. His heart seems to be getting the all-clear. They're just waiting for the final results from the specialist now.'

'That's great news. But I think it gave Mum and Dad a bit of a fright.'

'Yes, I think Dad's going to focus on different things now. He was even talking to me on the phone today about taking Mum on a big holiday overseas when he's better.'

'Bloody hell,' Róisín said. 'This is from the man who doesn't even have a passport!'

'He was talking about going back to Ireland, so I guess it has something to do with the family history as well.'

Cat shrugged. 'We'll have to wait and see.' She turned with

a smile as Logan came in through the back door.

'I thought I heard the plane come in!' Logan grinned, walking over to hug Róisín.

'Hi Logan. It's good to be here. Listen, before I forget, I think there's someone camped way up the southern end. I saw his setup when I flew out this morning, but now he's moved right up to the boundary line.'

'Not many people come this time of year,' Logan said. 'We've only had a couple of tourists in a van recently, and they left the day Tom had his accident. Before that, no one's been here for a couple of months.'

'Well, this guy seems settled,' Róisín remarked. 'He's got his swag out and a fire set.'

Logan's smile disappeared. 'There's a fire warning in place right now. I thought I noticed a puff of smoke when I was in the punt. I went over to feed our dogs,' he explained. 'But when I looked again, it was gone, and I thought I'd imagined it.'

'I don't know how he got in.' Róisín frowned. 'I locked all the gates after feeding the dogs yesterday. I didn't want to be dealing with randoms showing up.'

'I'll go down now,' Logan said. 'Just a friendly warning, and ask them to move on in the morning.'

'There's plenty of free camps further along,' Cat suggested.

'I'll come with you, Logan. It'll be good to stretch my legs, and I'll tell him about the free camp on Gentle Nellie's Road.'

'Sounds good to me,' Cat agreed. 'I'll get dinner on. I'm starving. It was a big drive from Dubbo.'

Róisín looked at her sister quizzically. 'You're not heading back across the river tonight?'

'No.' Cat shook her head. 'We talked it over on the way home. It's better to stay here to help Dad. He's got so many jobs lined up that it doesn't make sense for us to keep going back and forth every day. We'll just stay in my old room.'

'That doesn't sound like your usual style,' Róisín teased. 'I'm not going to be here much anyway,' she said. 'I start my new job on Monday. I was down in Wilcannia today meeting my new boss.'

'How was it?' Cat asked, curiosity gleaming in her eyes.

Róisín smiled. 'It went really well. I'm excited—I think it's going to be everything I hoped for.'

'And with us staying here, I can get into Dad's study and keep his research going. The more I can get done, the more he'll have to do back here when he gets home.'

'Speaking of that,' Róisín said, suddenly remembering. 'Have you been talking to Dad about the last letters I sent him?'

Cat nodded. 'Yeah, he's itching to get home and compare

the dates and content—especially Samuel's letters—with the rest of the family history we've pieced together. He's particularly interested in seeing if Samuel's trips to England and Ireland match up with the timeline in the letters from the National Library. I'm fairly hopeful,' Cat added.

'Are you going to look into it?' Róisín asked.

'I could, but I'm leaving that bit for Dad. There are other bits I can work on. Like the woman who wrote the letters. If it is the same Samuel it's going to be such a big step forward. I want Dad to have that moment.'

Chapter 23

Cape of Good Hope - early July 1847.

Samuel O'Byrne stood on the deck of the *Avoca*, his hands gripping the railing as the wind howled around him. The stormy sea churned violently beneath the ship as they rounded the Cape of Good Hope, the southernmost tip of the Cape Peninsula. Since they had left Cape Town, the waves had crashed against the hull in a relentless rhythm. The ship groaned with every lurch, the dark clouds overhead mirroring his turmoil. Salt spray stung his face, but he welcomed the cold—it was a distraction from the thoughts that had been gnawing at him since he had left Breda at the gate of the vicarage in Kilgarvan. He had written her from Liverpool and again from Cape Town and now had another letter ready to post once they docked in Fremantle on the west coast of their new country.

Thomas joined him on the deck, his face glowing from the

cold wind, his eyes bright despite the storm.

'A bit rough tonight, eh?' his younger brother said, leaning beside him and surveying the wild sea with a grin. 'The captain says we are making good progress. It'll be calmer once we're past the Cape.'

Samuel said nothing, his gaze fixed on the horizon, though he saw nothing but endless grey. It was hard to see where the sea and the sky met, such was the depressing expanse of grey. Thomas had embraced the journey and was often speaking with the captain; Samuel had been morose, and his thoughts were full of what he had left behind.

'Come on, brother,' Thomas said, slapping him lightly on the shoulder. 'Why so glum? I thought you'd be in better spirits now that we're on our way. Think of what lies ahead. A new land, new opportunities. We'll be free of everything that held us back.'

A bitter taste filled Samuel's mouth as he glanced at his brother. Thomas looked so full of hope, so sure of their decision. But Samuel couldn't share it, not anymore. His thoughts kept pulling him back to the last day he'd seen Breda, the tears in her eyes as he left her in that graveyard.

'I don't know if we're doing the right thing,' Samuel finally muttered, the words nearly lost in the roar of the wind. His chest tightened, the confession squeezing his heart.

Thomas frowned, turning to him. 'What are you talking about? We had no choice, you know that.'

Samuel shook his head, struggling to put his feelings into words. 'It's just . . . this life we're running towards, this new start. Are we really doing it for the right reasons? Can we believe everything that Cousin Richard promised?'

Thomas looked at him and shook his head. 'We're starting over, Samuel. There's a difference.'

'For you, maybe,' Samuel muttered. 'You have Caitríona and a family on the way. A future. But me...' He trailed off, unable to voice the true source of his despair. He wouldn't tell Thomas about Breda. Not now, not when the distance grew between them with every day they sailed.

Thomas clapped a hand on Samuel's shoulder again, this time with more force, his grip reassuring. 'We will make a good life, Samuel. But there's no going back. You know that as well as I do. Seamus Kelly's death set us on our path, and our life will not be in Ireland. We can never go back.'

Samuel's stomach twisted at the mention of the bailiff's name. As Thomas spoke of never going back, Samuel remained silent, his thoughts turning to Breda and the promise that he would return for her.

Thomas smiled, his voice softening. 'This is a new

beginning for us. We'll build a good life in the colonies. I know we will. Caitríona's carrying our first child. A whole new life is waiting for us.'

Samuel forced a weak smile in return, though the joy Thomas spoke of felt distant, unreachable. But Samuel's heart rebelled against that truth. Someday, somehow, he would return.

As the storm raged on around them, Samuel stood in silence, his brother's words fading into the wind. His heart was no longer on the *Avoca*—it was still in Ireland, with Breda, and he knew it always would be.

Chapter 24

Kilgarvan Vicarage - late September 1847.

Breda stood at the kitchen window, her hands idly twisting the hem of her apron as she gazed out at the road. The soda bread was almost ready to take from the bake pot over the open hearth. John was visiting the tenant farmers and wouldn't be back for lunch, so she had time on her hands this morning. Her hand went to her stomach, and she smiled as she smoothed her fingers over the firm bump. She was preparing herself to speak to John. She knew he suspected something was wrong. He had asked her to come to his study when he returned.

The late morning sun bathed the fields in a soft glow, but Breda's mind was far away. She thought of the places she had never seen but felt she almost knew them; it was almost as though she was making the journey with them as she read Samuel's descriptions.

She would write to Samuel again soon, and when—if—he told her where he was, she would send the other letters she had written since he had left. She had not written of her condition as she didn't want him to worry. Her letters were chatty and contained snippets of information about the local parishioners, the weather, and her prayers that he was well and happy.

Breda knew that if she told him she was carrying his child, that would force him back to Ireland, and she would always wonder if that was the only reason he came back. If Samuel did come back one day, he would learn then. If he did not return, she would depend on John for support. Goose bumps ran up her arms at the thought of delivering a child with no one to tell her what to expect. Her future and well-being depended on her brother's reaction.

Suddenly, the familiar clip-clop of hooves echoed down the road, interrupting her thoughts. Her heart skipped, and she darted to the door, throwing it open before stepping onto the gravel. It was the mail delivery.

Her pulse quickened as she watched the postman approach, his horse trotting steadily up the lane. Samuel's last letter, posted from Madeira, had arrived six weeks ago. He had described the sea journey, the strange birds, and his anticipation of joining their Cousin Richard in Port Melbourne. Breda had clung to every word, imagining the sea voyage, the endless blue horizon, and the distant promise of the new land.

She smiled at Patrick O'Riordan as he dug into his satchel and pulled out three letters.

'Two for the vicar and another one for you,' he said. 'Is that soda bread I can smell, Miss Atkins?' Patrick sounded hopeful, but Breda was not to be swayed from opening her letter.

'It is, but it is not ready yet, Patrick. Perhaps if you stop on your way back to the village, there will be some for you.'

'That I will.'

She hurried back inside, lifted the bake pot from the fire, and put it on the stone flagstones before reaching into her apron pocket and opening the letter. Samuel's familiar writing made her heart sing as her eyes eagerly scanned his beautiful writing.

My Dearest Breda,

It has been some weeks since I last wrote en route from Liverpool to Madeira, and I hope this letter finds you in good health and spirit, as always. I miss you every day, though the wonders and trials of this voyage often provide a distraction from my loneliness. Thomas and Caitríona have been occupied; their son, James, was born as we crossed the equator off the west coast of Africa. Young James is a healthy baby by all accounts, not that I have ever had experience with children. It pains us that our mother will not see her grandson, but Thomas has written to Mother and Sean. Hopefully, she will receive it as you receive mine.

We left Madeira behind nearly a month ago, and the change from that lively island to the wide, open sea has been profound. Madeira itself was a marvel—a paradise of green hills and white-walled houses perched above the ocean. I couldn't help but wonder what life might be like in such an isolated place, but I am sure we will know that for ourselves when we reach our destination.

Soon enough, we set our sights southward. We anchored there just long enough to take on fresh water and supplies and post my last letter to you, which I hope you have received. It amazes me that this letter will then be aboard a ship back to Ireland on its way to you. Many new experiences are shaping my view of the world; even though we lived on the big estate at home, Thomas and I have discussed how little we knew of the wider world.

The journey from Madeira to Cape Town has been eventful. The ship is sturdy, but the sea can be a harsh mistress. As well as the birth of James, we have had days of calm, where the ship glided over glassy waters, and then days and nights of ferocious storms, where we clung to our beds. Luckily, as we are travelling as a family, we were able to book a passage for a larger sleeping area, which gives us more privacy and better ventilation. My heart goes out to those in the cramped accommodation below deck.

The crew is a hardy bunch, though many of the passengers, especially the children, have suffered from the constant motion of the sea. We have all managed to stay healthy, thank God.

As we neared the southern tip of Africa, the wind turned colder. When we finally sighted Cape Town, it felt as if we had reached the very edge of the world. The city lies beneath the imposing Table Mountain, and it is as busy a port as I've ever seen, full of ships from every corner of the globe. The people here—both the sailors and the locals—have been very kind, and I must tell you, our captain is a man of true honour. He knew the journey was beginning to wear on many of the passengers and allowed an extended stay at port. He even arranged for Thomas and I to visit the town.

Cape Town itself is a wonderful place. The markets are full of sights and smells I've never imagined—spices from India, silks from the East, and fruits I'd never tasted before. The air here feels warm and free, a brief respite from the sea's endless swell. But it is the captain's steady hand and good judgment that has kept us all in good spirits. He is a fair man, often seen speaking with the passengers, ensuring their well-being, and treating the crew with respect, which I believe is not always the way of things at sea.

We leave for the final leg of our journey tomorrow—rounding the Cape of Good Hope and heading across the Indian Ocean. The captain says the seas will be rough, but with luck and a steady wind, we should be in Port Melbourne before the end of the southern winter. Autumn will be closing in at home for you.

I think of you every day, my love, and I pray this journey brings me ever closer to the day I can see you again. I will write to you again as soon as we are across the Indian Ocean.

I hold onto the hope of a future where we will be together.

Yours always,

Samuel

Two hours later, Breda stood nervously at the door to her brother's study, shifting her weight from one foot to the other. The heavy oak door was ajar, and she could see inside—the usual chaos. Books were piled high on every available surface, and scattered papers lay across the floor. The scent of old paper and ink mingled with the faint whiff of candle wax. Her brother, who had returned from his visits, now sat at his desk, head bent over his sermon notes, lips moving silently in prayer or perhaps lost in thought.

He rarely called her in here. She had learned from a young age to stay out of the study. Yet today, he had summoned her.

'Breda, you'll only move things! I don't mind a bit of dust,' John would say, a long lock of fair hair falling over his forehead as he waved his hand, his absent-minded nature often leading to him misplacing important documents. As she hesitated in the doorway, John looked up.

'Come in, Breda. I won't keep you long.'

She stepped inside, careful not to disturb anything. Her heart pounded, knowing that something had been noticed.

Her brother's kind face was creased with concern. He gestured to a chair across from him. 'Sit, dear sister,' he said, smiling gently. 'You've been distant lately, Breda. I've noticed. Not that you speak of anything wrong, but I see it in your eyes. The way you put your embroidery aside each night and stare into the fire.'

She swallowed hard and sat down, her hands folded tightly in her lap. Her eyes darted to the mess of papers on his desk, looking for anything to focus on except her brother's questioning gaze. She had sinned, and she must tell him about the consequences.

John leaned forwards, his voice kind but insistent. 'I know Mother's passing weighed heavily on you, but for a time, you seemed happy again. I thought you had found some peace. But now . . . now I sense something troubles you. Are you well, Breda?'

Breda's breath hitched, and her throat closed. She tried to steady herself, but the burden she had been carrying for weeks was too heavy to bear alone. 'I … I'm well, really. There's nothing to worry about, brother.'

'Perhaps well in your body, but you are troubled.' He shook his head gently, not willing to let it go. 'Please, Breda, you can tell me anything. I've prayed for guidance every night for you. But I cannot help if I do not know what weighs on your heart.'

His words broke through her resolve, and suddenly, the secret she had held inside felt unbearable to keep. She lowered her gaze to the floor, her hands trembling in her lap. 'I have sinned . . . I'm with child.'

The silence that followed filled her with fear. Her brother, who always had something to say—a kind word, a prayer, a gentle reprimand—was suddenly quiet. She dared not look at him, but she could sense his shock in his silence. The ticking of the grandfather clock in the corner seemed to grow louder, marking each second of his silence.

Finally, John spoke, his voice hoarse with emotion. 'Breda…' His chair scraped the floor as he stood, moving around the desk to kneel beside her. His hands gently took hers, his grip warm, but his hands shook. 'How long have you carried this burden alone?'

Tears welled in her eyes, and Breda shook her head, unable to speak for a moment. When she finally did, her voice was thick with emotion. 'Since late spring. I didn't want to disappoint you . . . or want anyone to know. It will be a scandal—the vicar's sister carrying a child out of wedlock. I didn't know what to do. I still don't know what to do.'

He squeezed her hands gently, his eyes filled with sorrow. 'You should have come to me. You must know that I would never abandon you, never cast you out. You're my sister. I love you.'

Breda blinked, letting the tears slip down her cheek. 'I have been so afraid.'

He stood up and pulled her into an embrace, holding her tightly. His voice was steady. 'You have nothing to fear. I'll care for you, for the child. This is our family now, and we will face this together.'

For a moment, she let herself relax into his arms, feeling safe for the first time since Samuel had said goodbye. But her relief was short-lived. John gently pulled back, his eyes searching hers. 'Who is the father, Breda? Will he not support you?'

Breda froze. She couldn't tell him, couldn't mention Samuel.

'I cannot say,' she whispered, her voice barely audible.

He frowned, confused. 'Cannot say? Breda, you must tell me. I need to know so I can help.'

She shook her head. 'No. It's . . . too difficult a situation.'

Her brother looked at her, his forehead wrinkled in a deep frown. His absent-mindedness faded in that moment, replaced by the sharpness of a man who had given his life to understanding human nature. 'I don't understand, Breda. You've been with no one, as far as I know. You hardly leave the house except on Sundays to tend to the graves. Who could it be?'

She shook her head and stayed silent; her lips pressed together. She would not betray Samuel, not now. Her brother's frown deepened, but after a long pause, he sighed and pulled her into another embrace.

'Whoever it is,' he murmured into her hair, 'we will get through this. I won't press you further. You're safe here, and I'll stand by you.'

As her brother held her close, Breda let the tears come. She sobbed in John's arms, all her fear and uncertainty spilling out as he held her close. As he murmured reassurance, his fingers gently smoothed her hair until she settled.

In the quiet of his study, as the fire crackled in the hearth, Breda made a vow to herself. She would be a good mother, no matter what the future held. She would hold fast to the hope that Samuel would return, just as he had promised. She knew the journey to Australia of over a hundred days would soon be complete, but it would take many months for Samuel to settle, stock a farm and build a house, and then another one hundred days for him to sail back, but she would wait.

She would begin a diary to capture everything—how she felt, how she longed for Samuel, how she grew as their child grew within her. When Samuel came, through these words, they would share their lives, even from the far corners of the earth.

As she left her brother's study that evening, her heart felt heavy but steadier, the future uncertain but not as hopeless as it had seemed. She had faith that somehow, some way, she and Samuel would be together again.

Chapter 25

Ceann Mara - Wednesday, mid-January, 6.00 p.m.

Logan and Róisín climbed into the quad runner and headed toward the river along the road leading to the airstrip. Once they passed the airstrip road, they turned right, following the big loop that wound around all the billabong campsites.

'You reckon you saw him at the last one, near the southern boundary?' Logan asked.

'Yeah, he was definitely there when I flew in, just as you guys were driving home.'

'So, what's that? About two hours ago?' Logan slowed the quad runner when the track narrowed.

'Yeah. I can't see any lights ahead. He had a fire going, which I thought was a bit strange at that time of the afternoon. It's not cold.'

'Probably cooking,' Logan said. 'We've had to watch that. I know Tom and Laura have been careful with it being so hot now. After all the rain over the past nine months, the grass has grown like crazy. But now summer's hit, and with the strong winds, it's just waiting to ignite.'

'How about we stop here and walk the rest of the way?' Róisín suggested.

The sun was hovering low, just above the horizon, and the sky was fading into a pale apricot hue.

They parked the quad runner at the second-to-last campsite, near the drop toilet on the left, and walked along the road before turning down the short track to the last site. Sure enough, at the end of the site, beneath a big river gum, sat a red ute and a swag.

'Still here,' Logan muttered.

'Let's see what he says before we start accusing him of anything,' Róisín replied.

As they approached the campsite, a huge man with a long white beard appeared over the river bank, carrying a fishing reel in hand.

'G'day, mate,' Logan called out. 'How's it going?'

'G'day,' the man replied. 'Okay, no fishin' luck, though.'

'Wrong time of year for yabbies,' Róisín said as she checked him out.

They stood there in silence for a moment, sizing each other

up. Logan finally broke the tension. 'So, mate, what's the deal with camping here?'

The man shrugged, his small eyes steady. 'I'm campin' here, mate. That a problem?'

'Actually, it is. We run a registered campsite here with powered sites, and the property is closed for a couple of weeks,' Logan explained. 'How'd you get in?'

The man puffed out his chest and folded his arms. 'Through the gate. Didn't see no sign sayin' it was closed.'

'Perhaps you missed the one that said it was private property?' Logan asked.

'Nope. Didn't see that either,' the man said, defiantly.

'Well, we're going to ask you to move on,' Logan continued. 'The campgrounds are closed. We've had some family illness, and we're not taking bookings at the moment. There's a free camp about ten kilometres north at the end of Gentle Nellie's Road.'

'Been there. Not as good as here,' the man grunted. 'I'll stay here, thanks.'

'Sorry, mate. You can't,' Logan said firmly. 'So, get yourself packed up and move on.'

The man took a step toward Logan. 'And what if I say no?'

'Well,' Logan said, his tone calm but firm, 'then you'll be breaking the law. This is private property, and I'm pretty sure you *did* see the sign because it's hard to miss at that back gate where you came in.'

'Didn't see it,' the man growled. 'And I don't think you've got the right to move me on. You're not Tom O'Byrne. Who are you?'

'How do you know Tom?' Róisín asked, keeping her voice steady. She didn't let on that Tom was her father.

'Everyone knows who owns this place. And he always lets me stay here. And I'll listen to someone with the right to tell me to go.'

'What's your name?' Logan asked, stepping closer.

'None of your business,' the man said, his posture challenging.

Róisín and Logan exchanged a glance, and Logan made his move. He stepped even closer, lifting a single finger as a warning. 'Well, Mr. No-Name, you've got half an hour to get off this property, or you'll find yourself in a lot more trouble.'

'And if I don't?'

'If you don't,' Logan said calmly, 'you'll face the consequences.'

Róisín's gaze flicked to the back of the ute, where she noticed a large rifle sitting on the roof. She nudged Logan subtly and gestured with her head when the guy turned away from them.

'Mate, we don't want any trouble,' Logan continued, his tone measured. 'Like I said, the place is closed. So, move on. Thank you.'

They turned and walked away, with Róisín's back tingling at the thought of that rifle back there. She'd lived out here long enough to know the types of people and drifters that could hang around. If there was trouble, they could disappear further west or cross state lines before anyone could catch them.

Finally, they reached the quad runner and Logan started it up.

'Do you think he'll go?' Róisín asked as they headed back towards the house.

'No,' Logan replied. 'I don't think he will. I'm pretty sure we'll need a Plan B. I'll ring the station at Louth and see what they say, maybe check if they've seen him around.'

'Actually,' Róisín said with a frown. 'I'm pretty sure I saw him in Louth when I came through yesterday. He was behind me most of the way from Bourke, then overtook me to get to the fuel bowser first. I'd forgotten about it, but I'm pretty sure it was him. It was a red ute; I was talking to a mate there and didn't take much notice.' Róisín's frown deepened as she recalled something. 'I thought I was dreaming last night, but I thought I'd heard a car driving around outside the house. I wonder if it was him sussing the place out.'

'Did you have any lights on?'

'No, but my sedan was parked out front, near the gate.'

'Then he probably knew someone was here.'

'I wonder if he recognised my car from Louth?'

'White SUVs are pretty common out here,' Logan said with a glance at her.

'Still, it doesn't give me a good feeling,' Róisín muttered.

'Same. I'll do some digging. I got his number plate, so I'll check with a few people.'

'But let's make sure we lock up well tonight,' Róisín said. 'I'm glad you and Cat are back.' She forced a chuckle. 'I've turned into a city girl, haven't I?'

'Doesn't hurt to be careful wherever you live.' Logan's expression was tight as he swung the quad runner into Dad's shed. It still felt strange not to have Mum and Dad there. 'Tell Cat I'll be in soon. I'll feed the dogs, and I've got some tools to take off the battery chargers. I'd hate to burn down your dad's shed while he's away.'

Chapter 26

Ceann Mara - Wednesday, mid-January, 6.30 p.m.

'Yum,' Róisín said when she walked into the kitchen. 'Do I smell sausages and onion gravy?'

'You do,' Cat replied, grinning. 'With mashed potato and Grandma's peas.'

'Oh, yum! You know, one of the things about living in the city and going out to restaurants all the time is that silly thing they call—'

Cat waved her hand. '*Nouvelle cuisine.*'

'Not even that,' Róisín said, laughing. 'You never get enough to fill your stomach! And it's always sprinkled with black sesame seeds or some kind of special mushroom because Greg didn't want to eat something I cooked. I've barely had a home-cooked meal in the last twelve months. That smells divine and extra yum, Grandma's pea recipe.'

'I knew it was your favourite meal. It was what you always

chose for your birthday meal when we were growing up.'

Róisín laughed. 'We certainly liked our *haute cuisine*. I remember yours was curried sausages.'

Cat grinned. 'So, I took some sausages out of the freezer and thawed them in the microwave. I cheated a bit—Mum had a batch of caramelised onion gravy in the freezer, so all I had to do was thaw it and zap it in the microwave, too. How did you go with the guy at the camp?'

'He was a bit difficult. I'm not sure if he'll go or not.'

'Last thing we need at the moment,' Cat said.

Róisín walked over and placed her hand on Cat's shoulder as she stirred the gravy. 'I appreciate you cooking, Cat. You know, it's so good to be home. We've grown apart since I moved to Brisbane and you moved to Sydney. Want a wine?'

'Please. Yeah, I got caught up with all my friends,' Cat said softly, her smile fading slightly, a hint of the past year's pain creeping into her expression. What had happened to Cat last year when someone she thought was a friend almost killed her wasn't talked about much. It was all over now, and Róisín knew Cat had been to counselling a few times.

'Red or white?' Róisín asked, opening the fridge.

Cat laughed. 'White, please. There's a bottle of Sav at the back—it's Mum's favourite. Dad keeps the fridge well stocked.'

Cat shook her head as she put the spoon on the benchtop. 'You should have seen Logan's face the first time Dad showed him the cellar and his wine collection.'

'Impressed?'

'He was, but more with the fact that the cellar is part of the original nineteenth-century structure than the wine. He's not much of a wine drinker; he'll most likely have a beer when he gets back.'

Róisín poured two glasses of wine and handed one to her sister. 'You've done well, Cat. He's a lovely guy. You seem really happy.'

Cat's eyes were dreamy. 'He is, isn't he? Who'd have thought, a year ago, that I'd be back here, not doing my honours and actually loving being home?'

'Must've been meant to be,' Róisín said with a smile.

'Grandma used to say that.'

They both sat at the table as the sausages simmered in gravy and the vegetables cooked on the huge gas cooktop.

'So, tell me about Greg. I'll be honest. I never thought much of him. Even though he was the boss and obviously wealthy, he seemed to be using you,' Cat said, picking up her wine and taking a sip. 'What brought on the breakup? You've never said much. Mum and I didn't like to ask in case you got upset with us.'

'I was really stupid.' Róisín sighed. 'I suppose it wasn't so much about Greg, but more about me being stupid . . . not seeing him for what he really was. I guess I got sucked in by the glamour of working at one of the top firms in Brisbane, rubbing shoulders with celebrities. You know, we even went to a party once where both Hemsworth brothers were.'

'Get out!' Cat gasped. 'You *were* mixing with the big-time!'

Róisín smiled. 'I didn't get to speak to them, though. Greg did, of course. He was quick to hand them his card—he always had a way of pushing himself forward.'

Cat frowned. 'Bit of a tool. What happened between you, exactly?'

Róisín sighed deeply. 'Well, you remember how he moved into my apartment?'

'Yeah, I remember. He'd just moved in that weekend I came up from Sydney to see you. I didn't like him then, but I didn't tell you.'

'Your instincts were right,' Róisín admitted. 'He started to . . . how can I put it? Take over my life. I sort of lost myself for a while. He'd buy my clothes and pick which shoes I should wear with a dress when we went out. He always insisted on choosing what I wore even to work.'

'Why?' Cat asked, her eyes narrowing.

'"To keep up the firm's reputation," he used to say,' Róisín scoffed. 'Not that I could see how my wardrobe choices affected that. Then, there were the little things. He started making changes in the apartment. He sold my car, bought a new one, and I ended up paying for it. I couldn't really afford it because I'd been putting everything into the apartment, trying to pay it off without touching the money Grandma left me.'

'Are you renting it out now that you've moved back here?' Cat asked.

'No, as soon as I got the new job, I drew out the money, and I paid the mortgage off,' Róisín said, taking a sip of wine. 'But I'm thinking about letting someone live there.'

'So, what actually happened?' Cat pressed.

Over the next fifteen minutes, Róisín explained the events of that fateful afternoon—and how she'd withdrawn three thousand dollars from Greg's account and given it to Linda.

'For goodness' sake!' Cat exclaimed when Róisín finished. 'I can't believe anyone would do that!'

'I'm ashamed I let him do it,' Róisín admitted quietly. 'Linda wants to get a job when her daughter starts school at the end of the month, and I was thinking of offering her my apartment. It all depends on where she goes to school because Linda doesn't have a car. Petrie Terrace State School isn't far away from where I live.'

'He sounds like a right bastard.' Cat had stopped smiling as Róisín told her story. 'Did you enjoy the work?'

Róisín shook her head. 'No, not after the first six months. Once I got into the big cases, it was horrible. I saw just how nasty people could be—people who'd been married for years, had children together, and they'd tear each other apart. Some of the things husbands did as a payback to make sure their wives didn't have a decent life were disgusting. And if I was representing them, I had to do as they requested. Within reason, anyway. One of them—and you'd know who it was, but I can't say—leaked personal videos to the media to tarnish his ex's reputation. Her career was destroyed.' She paused, and when she spoke, her voice was thick with emotion. 'It was depressing. And then, that afternoon, when Linda showed up . . . it all hit me. I hated what I was doing. I didn't want to live in the apartment anymore; I didn't want to live in the city. I sent off my resignation that very night, and I told him to stay away as I had COVID.'

'Wow,' Cat whispered. 'It sounds like a movie.'

'Not one I'd want to watch, 'Róisín pulled a face. 'I didn't deal with Greg. I spoke to the HR person at the agency, but she emailed me later saying I couldn't just leave. I emailed her back, and I was really rude.'

'What did you do after that?'

'After I met Linda, I found the job, applied for it, had an interview the next day, came here for Christmas and put on a happy front—'

'You sure did,' Cat interrupted. 'You had us all fooled. Academy award goes to Róisín O'Byrne this year!'

'Then, when I went back, I sorted out the apartment and then went down to the Gold Coast to get *me* sorted. Now I'm excited about the job. At first, I wasn't even sure if I wanted it, but after visiting Wilcannia and meeting up with the boss and finding out what's involved, it's going to be fantastic.'

'God, you've been through a lot,' Cat said, reaching for her hand. 'Coming home will do you a world of good.'

Róisín nodded, her eyes softening. 'Logan mentioned I could stay at your place for a while until Dad comes home. Is that okay with you?'

'Of course it is.'

Cat soon had dinner ready to serve, and when Logan came back from the shed, they sat down to the simple meal of sausages, Mum's gravy, and mashed potatoes, with Róisín's favourite peas.

The clouds that Róisín had noticed at Wilcannia had moved north and delivered; rain drummed lightly on the roof in a soothing rhythm. They'd finished eating when Cat's phone buzzed on the table.

'It's Dad,' she said as she switched to speakerphone so Róisín and Logan could join the call.

'Dad, how are you? Everything okay?' she asked, a knot of worry tightening in her chest. 'Róisín and Logan are here, too. We've just had dinner.'

'I'm good, love. Got some news for you all,' he replied. 'The doctors said my heart's looking much better. No need for that surgery after all.'

Róisín let out a breath she didn't realise she'd been holding. 'That's such good news, Dad. I'm so relieved.'

They talked for a few more minutes before Dad said, 'Mum's still here. She wants a chat, too. Love you, girls.' He chuckled. 'And you, too, big fella.'

'Hurry up and get well soon, mate,' Logan said with a grin.

'Itching to get home already. We've got a wedding to plan.' They could hear the smile in Dad's voice, and Cat and Róisín smiled at each other. 'Here's your mum.'

Hearing Mum's happy voice cheered them even further. 'Hello there. It's funny not to be home with you, but I'm getting used to being here.'

'At least you're with Dad,' Cat chimed in.

'I am, and I'm pleased to be able to tell you he's doing

everything he's supposed to. They even got him out of bed this afternoon.'

Róisín mouthed to Cat. 'Don't mention the letters.'

Her sister grinned and gave her a thumbs up.

'Is everything okay at home?' Mum asked.

Cat leaned closer to the phone on the table. 'Yeah, everything's fine. I cooked tea for Ro and Logan. I hope it was okay—I used some of your onion gravy from the freezer, and those sausages Dad made a few weeks ago.'

'Of course, it's alright, sweetheart. You don't have to ask. *Ceann Mara* is still your home, too.'

Cat hesitated, then spoke. 'Mum, Logan and I have decided to stay over here until you come home. That way, we can keep an eye on things. Do you want us to reopen the campground?'

'It's up to you, sweetie. It won't be too busy at this time of the year. Has anyone come by?'

Cat glanced at Logan. 'Just one guest.'

'Well, if you're up for it, go ahead. Just as long as you don't mind cleaning the amenities and emptying the bins. But don't stress about it—it's a lot to handle with everything else that has to be done.'

'Mum, it's fine. Ro's here, too. She doesn't start work until next week, so we'll pitch in. Every little bit helps these days.'

'Thanks, sweetie.' Her mum paused. 'Can you put Logan

on for a minute?'

'All good, Laura. I can hear you. I'm happy to do the bins and the amenities if anyone comes through.'

'Thanks, love. Look, we have to go now. They've just brought Dad's cup of tea, and I'm going back to the motel.'

'Bye,' they all called out.

'Talk tomorrow.' Róisín disconnected the call and pushed Cat's phone across the table to her sister.

'Cup of tea sounds good,' Cat said. 'Who else wants one? There's some cake for dessert, too. Or do you want another wine, Ro?'

'No, a cuppa, please. I've got work to do.'

Logan stood. 'Make me one too, please. I'll just go down and see if that bloke's moved on.'

'Do you want me to come with you?' Cat asked, her voice laced with concern. 'I'm not happy about you going down there by yourself.'

Róisín stood. 'I'll come, too.'

Logan waved his hand, but he seemed distracted. 'No, it's fine. I'll be careful. I won't do anything silly. If he's still there, I won't confront him. When I get back, I'll call Louth police and get them to run the number plate for me.'

Cat stood and walked Logan to the door, wrapping her arms

around him. 'You be careful, okay?'

'I will, don't worry,' Logan reassured her. 'I've been in worse situations many times.'

He turned to Róisín. We'll take you over to *Guntana* tomorrow in the punt to see if you're happy to stay there. Then, if that suits you, take your car around and head to Wilcannia from there next week.'

'Sounds good to me.' she said.

***

Logan went to Tom's gun safe at the back of the shed and took out a rifle. He left the quad runner in the shed and walked to the campsite. He approached quietly, his steps deliberate. The bloke glanced up from his folding chair, eyes narrowing as he spotted the rifle by Logan's side.

'You've got no business here,' Logan said, his voice calm but firm. 'This is private land.'

The man straightened up, glanced across at his ute and folded his arms across his chest. 'I'm not going anywhere. What's it to you?'

Logan didn't move. 'I told you before; you're camping illegally. Last warning—pack up.'

The man's defiance hardened. 'You think you can just tell

me what to do? I'm not scared of you, even with your piddly rifle.'

Logan stared at him for a moment, then said quietly, 'Perhaps you should be more careful where you choose to camp, Colin Wilson.'

The man's face shifted. 'How the hell do you know who I am?'

Logan's lips twitched into a cold smile. 'You're quite distinctive, Col. I remember when you did time for that bank robbery at Noosa.'

He took a step back. 'Who the fuck are you?'

Logan leaned in slightly, his tone low and unyielding. 'No need for you to know. But this is your last warning. Get off this property, and don't come back.'

He watched thoughtfully as the criminal stood and moved across to his swag.

'Alright, I'm outta here. It's a dump anyway.'

***

Cat and Róisín sat waiting for Logan to come back over a cup of tea with one of Mum's cakes in the middle of the table.

'Mum would be proud of us having a cuppa and cake

instead of drinking wine,' Cat said.

'I knew if I had another glass, I wouldn't even be able to have a conversation with you. I'm exhausted, too,' Róisín replied. 'It's been a stressful time for all of us.'

'But Dad sounded great tonight,' Cat said.

'He did. You know he texted me last night. Don't tell Mum, but he's already read those files I sent him.'

Cat's lips curled into a smile. 'I know. He texted me, too.'

'He said he was going to get you to do some research on the way home. I was worried he'd be stuck in hospital, just watching the news and bored.'

'He seems okay for now, at least.' Cat reached for a second piece of cake. 'He needs to keep busy.'

'Did you do what he wanted when you were travelling?'

'I did,' Cat said, her excitement bubbling to the surface. 'And I've found Breda already! We just have to figure out where she fits in with the family—or if she even does. Dad will have plenty to do in the study when he gets home.'

'So, tell me about this Breda. I read a bit of one letter.'

Cat's face lit up. 'Don't tell me you're finally getting interested in the family history.'

Róisín grinned back at her. 'A bit.'

'Well, I've found her in the ancestry records, including when she was born and who her parents were. She had one brother, as far as I can see, but I'm not sure whether she married the vicar at Kilgarvan, and that's why she's living there.'

'But that doesn't explain why she's writing to Samuel.'

Cat laughed. 'You *are* hooked!'

'I'm interested,' Róisín admitted.

'I still have to look at the marriage records,' Cat said. 'Do you want to come into Dad's study and have a look at our progress?'

Róisín shook her head. 'Love to, but I have a stack of documents to read. Speaking of which, I'll head up now and get to work. I can hear Logan coming. Say goodnight for me.'

They hugged, and Róisín headed up to her room.

Chapter 27

Kilgarvan Vicarage - Christmas Eve 1847.

'Breda, have you heard anything of Sean O'Byrne during your visits to the village?' John leaned against the doorway, watching Breda as she cradled her belly, her eyes locked on the envelope he had just handed her. She suspected that John had worked out who the father of her child was, but he had said nothing. He also watched her as she paused and lifted her head when the clip-clop of Patrick Riordan's horse sounded in the laneway.

'No, should I have?' She kept her voice even as she lifted her head.

Her brother's gaze lingered for a moment longer before he spoke, his voice gentle.

'It seems he's not as present at *Ceann Mara* as he ought to be,' John began, his tone measured. 'Spending more time in Hertfordshire with his wife while the estate here needs his attention. It's rather concerning, do you think?'

Breda looked up, startled by the mention of Samuel's family estate, and laid the envelope in her lap. 'I didn't know that,' she replied, her brow furrowing. 'I only know that things seem to be changing. Who is living there with Mrs O'Byrne?'

'Only a few staff remain with her.' John stepped closer; his concern evident. 'It's important for Sean to be there, especially with his mother in poor health. The poor woman has not recovered from the sudden death of her husband and the departure of her two sons only a week after.'

Breda bit her lip as a knot tightened in her chest. She sensed John's growing interest in the O'Byrne family, and she swallowed hard, trying to keep her composure.

'I hope she is well looked after,' she said softly, keeping her voice steady despite the fluttering in her heart.

John's gaze softened. 'I understand your concern for Mrs O'Byrne, Breda. We all want the best for those we care about.'

'I have never met her.' Breda shifted in her seat cautiously.

'Perhaps you will visit her after the child is born.' John's gaze was steady, and his voice held an expectation.

At that moment, she knew that her brother suspected the truth. She held her hands protectively over her belly, her mind on Samuel, hoping John wouldn't press further, but he held her eyes until she answered.

'Perhaps I will,' was all she said.

He nodded and went to his study.

Breda closed her eyes, calming herself as the fire crackled and comforting, familiar sounds came from the kitchen. She sat by the warmth of the hearth, her swollen belly stretching as she shifted to find comfort in the frayed chair. At eight months pregnant, every movement seemed to require effort, and she felt her baby shift within her as she reached for the letter that John had given her.

She shivered as she carefully opened the envelope, the paper trembling slightly in her hand. She was eager for reassurance that Samuel had arrived safely. The cold wind blew from the north, but inside the vicarage, the smell of baking filled the parlour. Mrs O'Donoghue was in the kitchen, insisting that Breda rest. The parish believed their visitor was a cousin from County Cork who had come to stay with them over Christmas, but John had made the arrangements discreetly—he was preparing for what was to come.

Though this year—already known as Black '47— had been particularly brutal for the county, and indeed all of Ireland, the kindness of the local folk remaining had meant there was enough flour and dried fruits to make a simple cake for Christmas. As the death toll increased, many fled the country, emigrating in search of survival.

Thoughts of the famine fled as she read Samuel's words.

Dearest Breda,

I am writing to you from the shores of our new country. We have docked in Fremantle after many long weeks at sea, and I scarcely know how to describe this place that will be our new home. My first glimpse of the land filled me with wonder and a strange sense of relief—it was a relief to stand on solid ground again, with a true sense of a new life beginning.

We are all well, and baby James is thriving; his lusty cries when he is hungry can sometimes be heard up on deck.

Breda's breath caught. If only he knew, but she would not tell him.

The air here is dry and hot, carrying the scent of eucalyptus, which is sharp and earthy, nothing like the woods back home. Fremantle itself is a rough settlement, with sandy streets and buildings of limestone that seem to glow in the sun. I've seen men working the docks, their skin weathered by the heat, and women bustling through the markets, their faces a mix of hope and weariness. It is a far cry from the green hills of Kilgarvan, but there is something free about it.

I can't say yet that I will ever feel as though I belong to this land. There's an emptiness here that the open sky can't quite fill. I think of you, Breda, every waking hour. More than once, I have imagined you beside me as we stepped ashore, as if you could somehow share this new world with me.

The journey isn't over—we still must make our way to Port Melbourne to meet Cousin Richard. He was fortunate to get an earlier passage while we waited for eight weeks in Liverpool. So many times in those weeks, I wanted to come back to you, but common sense prevailed.

Did I ever tell you about how Richard made his fortune here? My cousin left Ireland before the famine in search of adventure. His luck held, and he was in the southern parts of the colonies when gold was discovered at a place called Bendigo. His engineering knowledge and his wealth assisted him greatly, and he quickly amassed a fortune, which he has used to purchase large tracts of land to run sheep.

However, as an engineer, Richard knows little about farming and sheep. He anticipates that our knowledge will help him establish the flocks. We can only hope and pray that we will succeed.

I've heard that the land there is fertile, with many rivers, and that there is great promise for settlers. I pray it is true. But no matter what this land holds, it will never feel complete until I can bring you here, as I promised. I dream of the day I see your face again, and I beg you to hold on to that hope, too.

Breda, I love you more than my words can ever express. Each day away from you has only made that clearer to me. As I write this, I carry our dreams, and I promise you I will make good on them. I will build a fine home for us here, and when the time comes, I will come back for you.

Until then, please keep faith in me as I do in you. I will send you an address as soon as I am able, but it may be a very long time until then. Life is an unknown.

Yours forever,

Samuel

As Breda finished reading, a sharp pain knifed through her, taking her breath away. The pain was sudden and unexpected, cutting through the warmth and cosiness of the room. When she groaned, John came from the study, his face drawn into a frown at the sight of her distress.

Chapter 28

Ceann Mara - Wednesday, mid-January, 11.00 p.m.

Róisín jumped as her phone buzzed in her pocket. She'd forgotten to take it out when she came up from the kitchen. She glanced at the time on her bedside clock as she answered the call. She'd been immersed in legislative files for two hours.

Who could be calling at this time of night? Surely not Greg. She hadn't given him one thought since she'd flown home this afternoon. She pulled the phone out and stared at the screen.

She hesitated before pressing the answer button. 'Hello?' she said cautiously.

'Oh my God, Róisín, please listen to me!'

'Who is this?'

'It's Linda.' Her voice sounded shaky, almost frantic.

'Take a deep breath. What's wrong?'

'Oh, God, Róisín. I'm scared.'

'Linda, listen to me! Take a deep breath. It's okay, tell me what's going on.'

'I'm sort of okay now . . . but—'

'What do you mean "sort of okay"?' Róisín's voice tightened. 'What's happened?'

'Greg's been to the refuge. He was here when we got home, and he was in my room. He's not supposed to be here, but he told them he was my divorce lawyer. They're pretty useless here.' Linda's voice hitched. 'He stayed in our room until we got home. I took Aurora to McDonalds for tea. He waited for an hour, he said. He was swearing. He was talking—talking about you.'

'Talking about me? What did he say?'

'He said he knows where you live. He was ranting about some three thousand dollars you stole from him.'

Róisín's stomach twisted. 'Did you tell him we'd met?'

'No, I didn't. But, somehow, he must know we did.'

Róisín gripped the phone tightly 'I don't want you to worry. I'm going to get someone to come and get you. I have a friend, another lawyer, and she can help you. Are you still at the refuge?'

'No.' Her voice trembled. 'Please help us.'

'Where are you, Linda?'

'Oh, God, thank you for believing me. You should have seen the way he looked at Aurora. He . . . he told me . . . that we would both end up in a place where I couldn't get any of his money off him. He sneered at our room. He is an evil man.'

'Where are you now, Linda?' Róisín kept her voice even. She ignored the sickness roiling in her stomach, thinking that this was the man she had worked with, lived with, slept with, and trusted.

'We left. I threw all of our things into a couple of bags and we got out. I won't be going back there ever, not now that he knows where we were living. I can't believe it, Róisín. It's been four years, and he didn't find me. How did he find me now?'

Sympathy mixed with fear and anger, flooded through Róisín and she forced her voice to stay even. 'Linda, you'll be okay. Trust me. Tell me exactly where you are right now.'

'We got the train from the Valley, crossed the river. I got off at the station at Coopers Plains, but I don't know where to go. We've walked a little way along the main road.'

'Is there a café or anywhere nearby where you can wait?'

'I don't know,' came the shaky response.

'Listen, how about you and Aurora keep walking a little bit more. Stay on the main road and you'll come to a garage or something eventually. Maybe a café? Promise me you'll ring me straight back when you do. Is the road well lit?'

'Yes, and there's lots of cars. Oh wait, there's a big shopping centre on the other side of the road ahead. It looks like there's a McDonalds at the front.'

'Perfect. Go there and call me as soon as you're inside. I guarantee that my friend Meg will be there within an hour. She lives out near Ipswich, so it won't take her too long to get to you. She's got a big house, and she'll be happy to have you stay for a while. Do you trust me?'

'I do,' Linda answered, calmer now.

'You're going to be okay. I'm with you every step of the way.'

'Thank you, Róisín. I knew you'd help me. I owe you so much.'

'I'm just pleased that you did call me. Now, here's what's going to happen. As soon as I hang up, I'll call Meg, and she will come and get you. Are you okay with that?'

'Yes. Thank you. We'll go over there, call you again, and then wait for your friend.'

'Just stay calm. Meg is lovely, and she will make sure you're safe. I'll get to Brisbane as soon as I can, and we'll figure this out together. What Greg's doing is harassment and intimidation. He could go to jail for this. Have you ever taken out an AVO on him?'

'No . . . I haven't. I've always been scared of what he'd do. I have Aurora to think about.'

'Listen to me,' Róisín said gently. 'Take a deep breath, and close your eyes if you need to. You can trust me. You know that, right?'

'Yes, I know that.' In the background, Róisín could hear crying.

'What's wrong with Aurora?'

'She's scared. She knows we've left, and she's upset because she's left her friends behind.'

'Linda, I'm hanging up now. Text me as soon as you're over there.'

'Okay.'

Róisín disconnected, and her hands were shaking as she found her friend Megan in her contacts. To her relief, Megan picked up the call immediately.

'Ro, hi! It's been ages since I've talked to you. How are you?' Meg's usual cheerful voice brought a brief smile to Róisín's face, but it quickly faded.

'Hi, Megs. I feel terrible. It has been ages, hasn't it? Listen, I've got a huge favour to ask you . . .' Her voice shook, and her worry finally affected her physically.

'What's going on? You don't sound good at all.'

'Look, I'm fine. Well . . . no, I'm not.' She swallowed hard, her words rushing out now. 'I'm actually back home in *Ceann Mara*. I've got a job out here now, and I was going to email you about it, but everything's happened so fast. I've barely had time to breathe. There was. . . a bit of a nasty situation when I left Brisbane. It's my ex . . . Greg . . . I don't know what to do. I didn't even know his ex-wife existed until recently, and now he's threatening her. She's in hiding, Meg. She's got a little girl, and they're homeless.' Her voice cracked.

'What?' Meg's voice rose, alarmed. 'What kind of bloke does that?'

'I know . . . I know.' Her chest tightened, the guilt and disbelief flooding back. 'I can't believe I was so blind. He was my partner, for God's sake, Meg! I thought I knew him. But that's not even the worst of it. His ex, Linda Henderson, called me to warn me. He threatened her, and she thinks he's after me too.' Her breath hitched, panic rising. 'She called from a train station. Coopers Plains. She's near a shopping centre now. She's scared, Meg. She's got very little, and she's running out of options. She needs somewhere to stay, just for a couple of days, until I can figure something out. I didn't know who else to call . . . I don't want to involve the police if I can help it. That would have upset her more. I know it's a huge ask, but can you pick her up and take her to your place?'

There was a pause, and for a moment, Róisín's heart pounded, fearing the worst, maybe Megan wasn't even in town.

'Of course, I'll do it. Do you know exactly where she is right now? I'm in the city anyway, about to head back to Ipswich. I've got room for them.'

Relief washed over Róisín, but the anxiety still buzzed in the background. 'She's at the shopping centre. Hold on, I just got a text.' She fumbled with her phone, her hands shaking as she checked the message. 'She's sent her location. She's at a coffee shop near McDonalds, actually in the shopping centre—I'll send it to you now. I'll text her and let her know you're on your way. Megs, I owe you so much.'

'You owe me a good visit, that's all,' Megan said lightly. 'I'll head over straight away.'

'It's been a crazy time here at home, too—Dad's in hospital after a heart attack, and I'm starting a new job on Monday.'

'And on top of that, this bastard's threatening her and possibly you? It's a lot to take on, Ro. Just . . . take care of yourself.'

'I will. Let me know when you've got them safe, okay? And we'll FaceTime when things calm down.'

'I'll text you as soon as I have her, promise. Trust me, Ro. I've got this.'

'I do. Thanks, Meg. I'll talk to you soon.' She hung up, her hands trembling as Greg's threats hit her. 'Call me when you're at home.'

It wasn't long before Róisín's mobile buzzed on the bedside table. She reached for it and let out a sigh of relief when she saw it was Megan already. She answered quickly.

'Hey, Ro, it's Megan.' There was a slight pause on the other end, and the sound of cars was in the background. 'I've got Linda and her little girl with me. They're safe. She looks dreadful, Ro . . . worn out.'

Róisín let out the breath she was holding, relief mixed with concern. 'I'm so glad you've got them. Is she talking?'

'Not much,' Megan said, her voice softening. 'But that's okay for now. I'll take them back to my place and make sure they're settled. I don't want to rush her.'

'You're a good friend, Megs,' Róisín said, her gratitude genuine. 'Thank you. Really.'

'Of course. I'll give you a call in the morning and let you know how they're doing.'

They disconnected, leaving Róisín staring at her phone for a moment, her thoughts swirling. Her mind was too full of Linda's situation to do any work that night, so she shut down her computer and took a quick shower before climbing into bed.

She lay there for hours, thinking about the situation and coming to the logical and sensible conclusion that she couldn't represent Linda.

Megan had always been dependable, especially for women like Linda—those needing refuge, protection, and guidance through the legal maze. As a fellow lawyer, Megan had done incredible work with refugees and women escaping dangerous situations. Róisín trusted her judgment; Linda was in good hands. Now that she was thinking more clearly, she knew it wouldn't be right for her to take on Linda's case, but she knew that Megan would be willing to handle it. She'd ask her when she called tomorrow.

And to be fair to Linda, once she started work at the Water Review Integrity Authority, she'd be busy with that and not able to go to Brisbane often enough to give Linda a fair hearing.

##

Róisín was still in a deep sleep when her phone rang at eight o'clock the next morning. She jumped, disoriented by the crazy dreams she'd had all night, not knowing for a moment where she was. Her heart settled as she recognised the pale green curtains blowing gently at the window of her bedroom at *Ceann Mara*.

'Hi Ro, it's me, again.' Megan's voice was bright as Róisín pushed herself up in the bed and pulled her hair back from her face with her free hand.

'Morning, Megs. Thanks again for last night. How are they today?'

'Not too bad. Linda's sitting out on the veranda, having a coffee, and Aurora's playing with my cat.'

'It's such a tangled situation,' Róisín said. 'I've been thinking about it most of the night.'

'It is. We talked for a couple of hours last night. The poor love tried to give me money, but I reassured her that this was part of my work. Speaking of which,' Megan continued, 'she told me that she had asked you to represent her in the divorce. I'm not comfortable with that considering the situation with you and Greg, are you?'

'No, I was going to ask you if you would take her on as a client.'

'And I was going to offer.'

Róisín's shoulders relaxed as the tension left her. 'Thank you.'

'This is what I've picked up from our conversation,' Megan said. 'Let me know if I've understood her correctly. She was pretty upset at first. And frightened. He sounds like a proper bastard.'

'He is. Right, I'm listening,' Róisín said.

'Okay, so Linda's still technically married to Greg and has never had a cent of support or her entitlements. She's been in and out of refuges since Aurora was born. From what she's said, most of their assets were her financial contribution to the marriage.'

'Yes, including the proceeds of the sale of her parents' property,' Róisín replied, her heart aching for Linda. 'What's your plan?'

'Well, I need to file for a formal separation first and start building Linda's case to claim her share of the marital assets,' Megan said, determination evident in her voice. 'But I'm thinking the first step is to apply for an AVO to keep Greg away from them. It'll give her some immediate protection, especially given his threats.'

'Absolutely, that's essential. I can only imagine how he'll react to the legal action, but it's everything he deserves,' Róisín agreed, feeling a surge of anger on Linda's behalf. When she thought about how gullible she'd been and how he'd manipulated her, she felt ill.

She brought her attention back to Megan as she kept talking. 'The next steps will likely involve financial orders to compel Greg to provide for Linda's living expenses while the case moves on. He can't cut her off completely, not without legal repercussions.'

'Exactly. And you'll need to push for interim spousal maintenance since Linda has no income,' Róisín added, knowing the road ahead was going to be hard.

'I know it'll be a slow process,' Megan said, and Róisín could imagine the determination in her friend's expression. 'But Linda needs to know what her options are. First, I'll file the necessary forms to begin divorce proceedings if that's what she decides to do. Then, with evidence of Greg's refusal to settle fairly, we can seek court orders for property settlement and support.'

'It won't be easy, that's for sure,' Róisín cautioned, staring out the window. 'Greg will fight you on this. I know he invests in quite a few companies as well as the legal firm.'

'I'm ready for him,' Megan assured her, confidence shining through. 'I've dealt with situations like this before. I'm sure you would have, too, when you worked for his firm. One thing you could help me with is a bit of insider knowledge. What sort of businesses was he involved in?'

'Would you believe he never shared that side of his life with me? All I know about now is a pub and a restaurant, and Linda told me about them the day she came to see me.'

'Okay, leave it with me, and I'll call if I need anything.'

Róisín felt a burden lift, knowing that her friend would get Linda through this. 'Thank you, Megan. She's lucky to have you in her corner.'

'And you too, Ro. Just do me one favour.'

'What's that?'

'Look after yourself and don't have anything to do with the scumbag.'

'There's no fear of that. I don't think I'll ever trust another man as long as I live.'

'There are some good ones out there. Don't be jaded by one bad experience, love. We'll talk soon.'

Róisín put the phone down on the bedside table and flopped back on her pillows, surprised when she felt a tear roll down her cheek.

Chapter 29

Henderson and Associates, Brisbane - Friday mid-January, 5.30 p.m.

Greg Henderson paced the length of the balcony outside his office; his jaw clenched as he pressed his phone harder to his ear. The expensive office space he had carved out above the bustling Brisbane city was supposed to be a haven, but today, it felt like a trap. Below him, the Millennial crowd stood on the footpath, overflowing from the trendy bar he often drank at. The laughter and the clinking of glasses of craft beers and cocktails rang out like an irritating soundtrack to his building anxiety.

'Bloody woman,' Greg muttered under his breath, nearly shaking with frustration. He'd just had a call from Wilson. 'She's flying. Flying, for God's sake! I didn't even know she had a pilot's license.'

At the other end of the call, John Carpenter, the Bulimba

hotel's licensee and partner in his other business operations, sounded calm. Too calm for Greg's current state of mind.

'What do you mean flying?'

'Wilson tracked her all the way to the boondocks where she grew up, and then she bloody flew out in a plane.' Greg slammed his fist down on the polished desk, rattling the glass of whisky that sat next to his laptop. 'You don't get it, John! Róisín could have been watching me the whole time. She cuts ties with the firm suddenly, disappears, and now she's got her hands in water management. How the hell didn't I see this coming? Was she sniffing around our business the entire time? Maybe she was a plant.'

'I recall asking you about her background.' John's voice sent a chill down Greg's spine. 'You told me you were sure she wasn't involved.'

He paused, staring out the window at the Brisbane River, brown yet glittering under the late afternoon sun. 'Yeah, I *was* sure. But can you trust anyone these days? She got out too fast. I have no idea what she's found. And if she knows what we've been doing out there where she is . . .' His voice trailed off, but the threat hung over him like a dark cloud.

'You'll have to get rid of her. You can't afford to stuff up again, Greg.'

'When Wilson finds her, he can bring her here. We need to

find out how much she knows and who she's told before we do anything.' Greg leaned against his desk, running his hand through his hair. 'But we do need to cover our tracks fast. We should never have bought into Scaramouche. It felt like easy money at the time, but now it's hanging around our necks like a noose.'

'*My* money. *Your* neck.' John's voice was cold. 'You created this mess, Greg. *You* sort it out.'

Jesus. Greg ran his hand over his face and was angry when he felt the perspiration trickling down towards his collar. He'd dealt with his stupid ex-wife today, and now John was playing the heavy. At least he'd sorted Linda out.

From downstairs, the laughter of pub patrons drifted up again. Greg glanced down to see a group of twenty-somethings in their designer clothes sipping cocktails without a care in the world. The sleek, modern decor of the bar—clean lines, minimalist art, neon signs—felt worlds apart from the mess he was in. It built his anger even more, and he kicked the bin beneath the desk, sending it flying to the wall.

He forced himself to calm down. 'What do you suggest?'

John's reply fuelled Greg's rising panic. 'Get rid of her. In the meantime, I'll shift some assets and create a few shell companies to distance my companies.'

Greg took a long swig of whisky, trying to steady himself. 'I'll see if—'

'Do it. If she's got even an inch of proof, we're screwed.'

Greg nodded, though his stomach churned with a mix of anger and unease. He didn't mention that he was certain Róisín had been in contact with Linda—two stupid bitches. The problem was that Linda knew too much. Way too much. And he knew that Róisín was involved somehow, no matter how much Linda denied knowing her. He'd seen Róisín's business card on the table in her room in that dive. When he'd found it, his rage had been vicious.

If Róisín had stuck her interfering nose into any of his business, she was dead, and Linda wouldn't be far behind.

It was sheer luck he'd seen his ex-wife. During a meeting with a client at Woolloongabba, he'd spotted her coming out of that refuge with the kid. As soon as the deal was done, he'd walked in, flashed a card, and claimed to be Linda's lawyer. The dumb woman at the front desk had barely blinked before letting him into Linda's room. He had time to rifle through her things and found the business card.

When she came back, he put the fear of God into her—threatened her with enough to make sure she wouldn't dare cause trouble. She'd always been spineless, so easy to control. She'd believe anything he told her.

It was Róisín he was worried about. She was the one who could bring him down, and she was bloody smart enough. She was too sharp and calculating. She was in cahoots with his ex, and now she had her fingers in his business interests. Now, he was scrambling to cover his tracks, unsure if he was too late. John's patience was gone, and if that source of income dried up, Greg knew he was in deep shit. Róisín O'Byrne was the cause of all his problems, and he'd get Col Wilson to deal with her.

After he found out how much she knew.

Chapter 30

Wilcannia – Monday, late January, 8.30 a.m.

Seth concentrated as Anthony Branzini's voice crackled slightly through the phone.

'So, Róisín O'Byrne? She starts today? You said she's excellent. Smart. Committed. Local knowledge. She sounds perfect for what we need.'

Seth leaned back in his chair, phone pressed to his ear, staring at the papers on his desk without really seeing them. His boss from the Authority—who had also been a friend since boarding school in Canberra— had called to see how Róisín was shaping up, believing that she had commenced last week.

'I'm sure she will be,' he said, his tone more thoughtful than certain. 'She's everything you'd want for this kind of work. But . . .' Seth let out a quiet sigh, glancing at the untouched coffee beside him. 'I'm slightly unsettled about the people she's conncctcd to.'

There was a brief pause on the other end, and then Anthony asked, 'What do you mean?'

Seth rubbed his forehead as he spoke, tension weighing down his words. 'She grew up in the area. Knows practically everyone there. Families and properties are all under scrutiny now. Even her sister's partner is on our list of potential suspects.'

A low whistle came through the line. 'That's a bit close,' Anthony said, his tone shifting.

'Exactly,' Seth replied, sitting up straighter in his chair. 'I've got no reason to doubt her professionalism so far, but her ties to the place run deep. It's making me second-guess if I made the right call bringing her onto the team.'

Anthony's voice was thoughtful now. 'You think she might . . . cover for them? Her own? Or have deeper motives?'

'I don't know.' Seth's fingers tapped lightly on the desk as he considered the question. 'My gut says no—she's sharp, committed, and really wants to fix this water mess. But personal relationships can complicate things. I've seen it before. People get protective, sometimes without even realising it.'

A pause stretched over the line before Anthony spoke again, his voice quieter this time. 'And you've got your own baggage. That could be influencing your reputation.'

Seth managed a humourless smile, though Anthony

couldn't see it. 'Yeah . . . I do.' He leaned back, looking out the window at the morning sun bathing the sandstone building across the road. The street was quiet as usual. Wilcannia, like many other towns in western New South Wales, was grappling with significant economic decline and the closure of local businesses. Prolonged drought, frequent unseasonal flooding, the impacts of climate change, and shifting economic conditions in the region had resulted in a population decline.

'That last relationship was a work one, and you know how that turned out. It's hard for me to trust easily now, especially when the stakes are this high. I can't afford to be wrong again.'

Anthony's reply was measured. 'She sounds like she's worth it. And remember it's not a relationship; it's a professional association. You just need to have that conversation. Make sure she knows what's at stake.'

Seth nodded to himself, his grip tightening slightly on the phone. 'I will. I'll talk to her today. I need to know she'll stay objective, even when it's personal.' His voice grew firm as he spoke the last words. 'Trust is everything in this.'

After talking to Anthony, Seth sat at his desk, the low hum of the computer filling the quiet space as data streamed across his screen. He had been in the office since early that morning, downloading reports on water usage. The radar metering system, implemented on many of the properties they were monitoring, provided near real-time data. These meters used radar technology to measure water flow with precision, bouncing signals off the water's surface to gauge the volume passing through irrigation channels. It was a vast improvement over manual readings—efficient, accurate, and hard to tamper with— but Seth knew even the best systems could be fooled if someone was determined enough.

As he scrolled through the figures, his eyes flicked up to the window. Róisín hadn't come in yet, but he expected her at any moment. He leaned back in his chair, taking a moment to stretch, just as the door swung open.

'Morning, Seth.' Debra smiled at him as she breezed in, takeaway coffee in hand, cheery-voiced and dressed in her usual brightly-coloured clothes. Without missing a beat, she placed the cup on his desk. 'Thought you might be ready for this.'

'Thanks, Deb,' Seth said, smiling as he reached for the cup. He could already smell the rich scent of freshly brewed coffee. 'You're a lifesaver.'

His receptionist hovered near his desk, arms crossed, her tone casual but curious. 'So, Róisín's on board today, huh? You think she'll fit in?'

Seth took a sip of the coffee, glancing at the door, half-expecting to see Róisín behind her. 'I am. She's smart. Knows the region, knows the law, especially when it comes to water rights. She's exactly what we need.'

'I liked her too.' Debra nodded, sitting on the edge of his desk, her expression thoughtful. 'She's known around here, too. Grew up right on the Darling, didn't she?'

'Yeah,' Seth replied, setting the coffee down. 'She's got roots here.'

'I was friends with her sister, Shea. She worked at the vet's here for a while last year. Nice girl. Good family. Well respected.'

'Yes, she knows practically everyone along the river from here to Bourke. It's why I brought her on board. Local knowledge can be a real asset.'

Seth shrugged, the concern of his earlier conversation with Anthony creeping back in, but he wasn't going to express his concern to Debra. 'She's the right person for the job. I'm looking forward to working with her.'

Deborah studied him for a moment before speaking again. 'Well, from what I've heard, Róisín's no pushover. She can handle herself. Sounds like you've made the right call.'

Seth nodded slowly, though his mind was still working through the potential conflicts. 'Yeah, I'm sure I have.' He took another sip of coffee, savouring its warmth as he mulled over the next steps.

Time to get to work.

***

Róisín drove down from *Guntana Station* to Wilcannia on Sunday afternoon. The journey from *Ceann Mara* was slightly shorter than it would have been. She'd driven up to Louth, crossed the river and driven down to Logan's place on Saturday afternoon. Cat had gone with her and picked up their car so that they would have both Mum and Dad's Land Cruiser and their own twin-cab ute until Dad came home.

Róisín hadn't been over to the property since Uncle Gary, Dad's brother, had lived there for a few years before the fire that destroyed it. Logan had built a new home when he bought the land; it was small but comfortable and would suit her fine for the short term until she got settled in her new job.

'It'll be a good help if you're here some of the time,' Cat said as they drove in. 'We could take Molly over to *Ceann Mara*, but she really doesn't get on with Dad's dogs.'

'It'll be easier for you, too, not having to come over and feed her every day. I'll let you know when I'm back from Wilcannia,' Róisín replied with a smile. 'And it'll be nice for me to have some company. Excellent watchdog—she knows me, that's why she's not barking now.'

'If a stranger or a strange car comes in, she'll let you know,' Cat said.

Now, here she was, about to start her first day. Róisín took a deep breath and pushed open the door to the office.

##

Wilcannia – Friday, late January, 8.30 a.m.

As Róisín sat at her cluttered desk at the end of her first week in the office, the morning sun streamed through the office window, heating the room quickly and glaring on the paperwork spread out before her. She tapped her pen against the notepad, her eyes skimming the data they'd gathered over the week.

'So, it looks like we have a pretty solid plan for the three days next week,' she said, glancing over at Seth, who was hunched over his laptop on the small table next to her desk. They'd been extracting data for three hours, and it was easier to be in the same room, rather than running in and out of each other's office when something of significance came up.

'Yep, we'll hit the properties along the river, one a day, maybe two if there are a couple close together. That'll give us enough time to assess water usage and meet the owners,' he replied, glancing up from the screen.

'Accommodation's on you then,' she teased, her eyes dancing with mischief. 'Not a lot around some of those properties unless you want to take a swag and camp.'

The look of horror that appeared on Seth's face made her laugh. 'I take it you're not an outdoors person?' she asked, raising an eyebrow.

He scoffed, shaking his head. 'I've done enough camping to last a lifetime. I was in the army for eight years. Trust me, I prefer my creature comforts now.'

Róisín's eyebrows shot up, surprised by the personal insight he'd just shared. Until now, their conversations had remained strictly professional. She had thought back to her first day when Seth had quizzed her about her ability to remain objective in their work and how that question had hung over her all week.

Shutting her eyes, she let the focus on the job slip away for a moment. The work had kept her busy, but her thoughts often drifted back to Linda and the situation with Greg. She could still hear Cat's words echoing in her mind about how helpful the clinical psychologist in Broken Hill had been for her after her trauma last year. Maybe it was time to consider seeking some help herself.

'Róisín? You still with me?' Seth's voice broke into her thoughts. 'We've got a job to do next week, and it sounds like it'll be quite the adventure. Although the camping idea didn't excite me.'

She nodded, appreciating his attempt to lighten the mood. 'I'll make sure to have a proper plan for accommodation, just in case,' she replied, focusing on Seth. 'And maybe I'll throw in a bit of a camping lesson for you, just to make the experience memorable.' She couldn't help teasing him, and she realised what a good working relationship they'd settled into already.

He chuckled, shaking his head. 'I'll stick to hotels, thanks.'

'You might get a shock.' As Róisín settled back into her chair, she glanced over the data they'd compiled throughout the week, eager to discuss their approach. 'So, looking at these figures, which properties do you think we should prioritise? I've set out a possible route. I'll share it with your screen.'

Seth leaned close to his computer, examining the map on the screen. 'Looks good. Starting with the properties that show the highest water usage. The data indicates that *Dunleavy* and *Twin Trees* are drawing significantly more than average from the river.'

Róisín nodded, her brow furrowing slightly. 'That makes sense. We need to understand why their usage is so high. Do we know if they've been complying with their licences?'

'Not yet, but that's what we'll find out during our visits. We can dig into their records and see if they have valid reasons for the excess use and see if that aligns with what they say,' Seth replied. 'After those two, I suggest we visit the Thompson and Hughes properties next. They're not far from each other, and the data shows some irregularities in their reporting. And then *Guntana* will be the last stop,'

'Right,' she agreed, jotting down notes. 'We should also ask about their irrigation practices. It's possible they're not aware of how much water they're actually using or misreporting it out of habit.'

'Exactly,' Seth said, a smile creeping onto his face. 'It'll give us a good picture of what's happening along the river. Plus, visiting these properties will help us build rapport with the owners, which will be crucial if we need their cooperation down the line.'

Róisín leaned back in her chair, satisfaction washing over her. 'I appreciate that you agree. I was worried we might be going too broad early, but it feels like we're on the right track.'

Seth shrugged modestly. 'I just want to make sure we're effective. We've got a lot of ground to cover, especially since we have to fit it all in before my meeting at head office.'

'Yeah, and if we can show them that we're not just

collecting data but also actively engaging with the community, it'll reflect well on our team,' she added, feeling more confident about their upcoming visits.

'Definitely. Let's make it a point to gather as much evidence as we can. I think these initial visits will set the tone for the rest of our investigation,' Seth said, closing his laptop. 'And if anything seems off, we'll address it on the spot.'

With the plan solidified, Róisín nodded. 'Sounds good.'

'Okay, let's make sure we have everything ready by Monday. I want to hit the ground running.'

Chapter 31

Two hours later

Seth looked up from his computer; he was back in his office. A grin stretched across his face as Róisín handed over the rest of the data she'd downloaded for their upcoming visits since they had spoken earlier. He felt more at ease with her now, his earlier concerns melting away. She had proven herself capable, and the more they worked together, the more he appreciated her insights. Yet, at times, he caught glimpses of worry etched on her face, making him wonder what she carried beneath her professional demeanour.

'So, looking at these figures, are you still happy with that route?' she asked, her focus intense.

Seth flicked through the figures and then leaned closer to the screen to look at the distances on the map. 'Spot on.' He chuckled. 'Well, you have to admit, the drama of potential overuse is practically edge-of-your-seat material. Plus, if we find out they're breaking the rules, I get to feel like a water vigilante.' He grinned at her. 'I see you've had Debra booking the accommodation.'

Rolling her eyes playfully, she replied, 'Yes, and the bad news is there are two nights when we'll have to camp out.'

'If I must.' He rolled his eyes.

'I was teasing.'

'I know. I saw the list Debra made.'

Róisín grinned back at him, caught out.

Still, Seth couldn't shake the feeling that something weighed on her mind. He decided to push a little further. 'You seem a bit distracted today. Everything okay?'

She hesitated, and he saw her defences flicker. 'It's just family stuff,' she finally admitted, her voice softening. 'My dad had a heart attack when I was travelling down here a couple of weeks ago, and I'm still worried about him.'

Seth's expression shifted from playful to serious in an instant. 'I'm sorry to hear that. Is he doing okay?'

'Sort of,' she said, her eyes clouding with concern. 'He's still in hospital in Sydney. My sister and I have been sending him information about our family history research. It keeps him focused and engaged. We think if he gets too anxious without something to do, it could be harder for him.'

He nodded, pleased that she had shared with him. 'That

sounds like a good idea. Keeping his mind busy should help.'

'Yeah, it's just tough. I wish I could be there more,' she confessed, her voice tinged with sadness. 'But I also know he needs something positive to latch onto. I want him to be okay.'

'You're doing what you can, and it sounds like he appreciates that. Just don't hesitate to reach out if you need to talk,' he said, meaning it. 'Or ask if you need time off.'

'Thanks, Seth. It helps to share it. And there's no way I'd ask for time off unless—' She cut herself off. 'I won't need time off until I'm due for it.'

A pleasant warmth built in Seth as they spoke, the boundary between personal and professional blurring again. At that moment, he realised he had accepted her fully; beneath Róisín's strong exterior lay vulnerabilities that she acknowledged. Her honesty and closeness stirred something in him, something unfamiliar.

He instinctively pushed back against the growing attraction, reminding himself of the past—the scars from his relationship in the army that still lingered. He didn't want to complicate their working relationship. 'So, how far back does this family history go?' he asked, attempting to steer the conversation back to safer ground.

Róisín looked up and met his gaze, and for a brief moment,

the air between them crackled with an undeniable pull. Time seemed to stretch, and the world around them faded into a blur. 'The 1850s,' she replied, her voice soft yet filled with a sense of pride.

Chapter 32

Kilgarvan Vicarage - May 1849.

Breda sat at the scrubbed wooden table in the warm kitchen, sunlight streaming through the small window, casting a gentle glow on the room. Catherine, her sweet little girl, now almost two years old, played happily at her feet. She busied herself with a handful of colourful wooden blocks, stacking them with great concentration, her chubby fingers working diligently.

Breda's diary lay open in front of her, and she added to the record she was keeping of Catherine's developments—her first words, the way she clapped her hands with delight when she spotted a bird outside the window, the way she tried to mimic her mother's soft humming. Writing in the diary had become a cherished routine, a way to document each precious moment of Catherine's childhood until the time that Samuel came to get them.

'There has been no letter from Samuel for over a year since his short missive to me arrived in March last year. He told me they had arrived safely in Port Melbourne and were heading north of the river. Yet, I remain positive. Catherine is a delightful child. She has my dark hair and complexion but her father's eyes, and as she grows older, she tilts her head and looks at me intently the same way he used to.'

Breda looked up as John entered the kitchen, his face lighting up in a smile as he crouched down beside the table.

'Look at you, my little builder! Can you make the tower even taller?' he asked. Catherine giggled as she added another block to her precarious tower. A smile spread across John's face, and Breda's heart swelled with love for her brother. He had been a wonderful support to them.

'What a fine job you're doing, Catherine! That tower looks like it could reach the sky!'

'She is determined when she discovers something new,' Breda said. 'She lights up like the sun.'

John leaned closer to Catherine, his eyes sparkling. 'You're keeping a wonderful record for her, Breda.'

For Samuel.

But her thoughts and trust that Samuel would return remained unspoken.

Breda smiled, her worries momentarily forgotten as she

watched her brother lift her child and tickle her. Screams of laughter filled the kitchen. It was a small joy amid the challenges they faced. 1849 had been another difficult year with severe food shortages, widespread disease, and a staggering death toll, but she wrote none of that in her diary.

##

Later that evening, as the fire crackled and sent shadows dancing along the walls, Breda sat quietly with John. Catherine was asleep in the next room, her soft breaths barely audible. Breda stared into the flames, trying to keep her thoughts at bay, but she could feel John watching her, his unspoken questions hanging in the air between them.

Finally, John broke the silence, his voice soft but steady. 'Breda . . . is Catherine Samuel O'Byrne's child?'

Breda stiffened at his words; she knew her brother had suspected the truth. She had been waiting for this moment, knowing it was only a matter of time before he asked. She kept her eyes on the fire, her fingers curling into her lap.

'I remember seeing him with you once,' John continued, his voice gentle. 'In the graveyard. Just before he left for the colonies, I didn't think much of it at the time, but now . . . I see him in Catherine. There's a resemblance.'

Breda's breath caught in her throat, and the tears she had been holding back as she had worried about the lack of a letter from Samuel finally spilled over. She lowered her head, her hands trembling as she wiped her eyes.

'Yes,' she whispered, her voice barely above a breath. 'Samuel is Catherine's father. But he doesn't know that he is a father.'

John's head flew up. 'He does not know?' The firelight flickered across his face as he leaned closer, his elbows resting on his knees.

'He left before I knew. And now I do not have a return address.'

'So… the letters you've been getting. That's him, then?'

Breda nodded, her heart aching as she spoke. 'Yes, it's Samuel. He writes . . . or he did. I will not tell him about Catherine. I do not want to put pressure on him or make his life harder. He will meet her when he comes back for me.' Her voice cracked, and she swallowed hard. 'But it's been almost a year since he last wrote to me.'

John's eyes softened as he watched her, but his mouth drew into a thin line. 'And you're sure he's coming back for you?' he asked gently, though his tone hinted at a quiet doubt.

Breda's lips trembled as she tried to hold herself together.

'He promised me, John. He promised he'd come back for me. He said once he had the land and the house ready, he would come back. That it would take a long time, so I must be patient. He is building a life for us...' She trailed off, the tears falling freely now. 'But no letters . . . for so long. I'm scared something's happened to him. What if he's been hurt or worse? I can't stop thinking about it.'

John sighed, leaning back in his chair, the fire reflecting in his eyes as he rubbed a hand across his face. 'Breda, I know you want to believe he'll come back, and I don't doubt that he meant those words when he said them. But it's been years now. A man can change, especially in a place like the Antipodes.'

Breda shook her head fiercely, clinging to the one thing that had kept her going all this time. 'No, John. He hasn't forgotten me. I know he hasn't. If he's able to, he will come back. He has to. He gave me his word.'

John looked at her with deep concern, his brow furrowing as he leaned closer. 'I just want you to be ready, Breda. For whatever might come. It's been a long time. And . . . life can take unexpected turns.'

'I know that, and I will be strong. I will believe until I hear otherwise.'

'Breda,' he said quietly after a lengthy silence. 'Have you

considered visiting Mrs O'Byrne? She's not well, and I think it might be comforting for both of you.'

Breda's expression tightened at the mention of Mrs. O'Byrne. 'I fear it would only bring more pain.'

'Perhaps, but she's family, and you are connected through Samuel,' John replied, his voice steady but kind. 'I've seen how much you care for her son. It might ease your heart to talk with her and share your worries. You could be a source of strength for each other.'

Breda looked down at her hands, contemplating his words. 'But what if she blames me for his absence? What if she thinks I led him astray?'

'She needs to know that you love him and that you're here for him, even now. Besides, she's hurting too, and sometimes we find healing in unexpected places.' John crouched beside her and rested a gentle hand on hers.

Breda remained silent, torn between her fears and her brother's encouragement. John was a good man, and his advice was usually sound. She knew that it would be the right thing to do, but she didn't want Mrs O'Byrne to write to Samuel or Thomas and tell them of Catherine's existence. She didn't want anyone to know there was a connection to the O'Byrne family.

Finally, she nodded, though doubt still filled her. 'I'll think about it, John. But I can't make any promises.'

John smiled gently. 'That's all I ask. Just know that you're not alone in this. We're family, and we will make a happy and full life for Catherine here, whatever you decide.'

Chapter 33

Kilgarvan Vicarage - Christmas 1850.

Breda's diary.

'As I sit in the garden watching our daughter play, I am filled with conflicting thoughts. She is a bright and spirited little girl, but I often wonder if I am depriving her of something precious. Her grandmother lives only a few miles away, and the thought of Catherine growing up without knowing Samuel or his family weighs heavily on my heart. Am I denying Mrs O'Byrne the joy of a granddaughter when John tells me she is often alone in a house on an estate that has suffered from both the famine and lack of care by Samuel's brother Sean? I wrestle with these feelings daily, and they keep me awake at night.

Receiving a letter from Samuel last month brought me solace. I was overjoyed to receive it and to know that he is well but working far from a port for his letters to travel across the sea to Ireland. It is hard to imagine the distances that he describes.

I will have faith and patience, and I will trust that he will come back when he is able to.'

Breda turned to the back of her diary and took out the letter that had filled her with joy last week. She read it for what must be at least the hundredth time. The morning Patrick delivered the letter to the front door of the vicarage, she ran happily into John's study and waved the paper around.

'Look, John. Look.' Her words tumbled over each other in her excitement. 'Samuel has written me. He is well.'

John's smile warmed her heart. Her brother was so kind to them, and he loved Catherine as though she was his child.

'Does he speak of when he will come for you?'

Breda shook her head. 'No, it will be a long while yet. And I cannot reply as there is still no address. May I read it to you? It makes it seem more real if I read it aloud; it's as though I can hear Samuel speaking.'

August 1850

My dearest Breda,

I am sorry—truly sorry—for the long silence. I hope you can forgive me.

One of the farm workers is going home and has offered to take my letter and post it in Port Melbourne. Poor Harry has been unwell and unable to cope with the unrelenting heat, isolation, and rough living conditions. A close encounter with a snake yesterday was the end for him, and he is travelling back to Port Melbourne as soon as I finish writing this letter. I do hope it reaches you and eases your concern about my lack of correspondence.

I know two years without any word from here must have been very hard for you, and I pray that you have not given up on me. Believe me when I say that not a day goes by when I don't think of you, wondering how you are, and cursing the lack of post out here. Thomas is working with Cousin Richard in the goldfields, and I have been working on remote properties that are comprised of vast tracts of land with huge flocks of sheep and herds of cattle. Australia is a really interesting land, and I am beginning to love it. I am now what is called a "jackaroo"; that is what they call those of us from home who are working on sheep and cattle stations to gain experience so we can eventually become landowners.

We are isolated from civilisation, and my day is made up of work and sleep. There is no mail service this far inland, away from the ports, so it is hard to get news in or out. The lack of communication with family back home has caused many of the younger workers to leave for the "old country". I smiled the first time I heard that phrase, and it is now becoming quite common. There is certainly a difference between the old and the new country. Can you imagine a farm where it takes two days to ride to the boundary fences? That is part of my work. I am alone in the vast spaces, and the stars at night are a wonder to behold. Even though it can be dry and hot, let me tell you what it's like when it rains, Breda. I wish you could see it, and I pray that you will one day. The land, dry and cracked from months of heat, suddenly drinks in the water like it's starved. Everything changes in an instant. The dusty earth becomes soft mud, the rivers swell, and the air is thick with the smell of wet soil and eucalyptus. It reminds me of life itself, how it can be barren one moment and full of promise the next. There's hope in this place, even though it's hard, and I keep that hope alive for us. I will write again and get it to the post when I can.

Yours always, Samuel.

Chapter 34

Maureen's Café - Wednesday, early February.

Róisín and Debra settled into a cool corner of the café, the scent of Maureen's freshly baked bread wafting through the air. It was a rare moment away from the office. Even with Seth away in Canberra, the work had been full on. Róisín had found herself still in the office at seven o'clock last night. The two days with Seth away had flown; she was looking forwards to his return tomorrow afternoon. He'd driven to Broken Hill and caught a flight to Canberra yesterday morning, and today was a day with back-to-back meetings with contacts of the Murray-Darling Basin Authority, the Federal Police, and the Department of Agriculture, Water, and the Environment. For the first time, she'd seen Seth doubt his ability as they'd discussed the strategies he was going to present.

When he'd expressed his worry over one of the strategies in particular, she'd put her pen down and looked at him until he was aware of her attention. He glanced up, and that moment she dreaded arrived—when their eyes locked, sending a rush of attraction spiralling through her. Seth Brodie was a genuinely good man with a kind and considerate nature and far too good-looking for her peace of mind. At least fighting the attraction took her mind off what was happening in Brisbane. Megan had texted to let her know she'd call in her lunchbreak.

'You look like you've got the weight of the world on your shoulders,' Debra said as they waited for Maureen to bring their salad wraps out.

'You've become a good friend already, Deb. You read me well,' Róisín said with a laugh, shaking her head.

'You're very much like Shea, or rather, she's like you, being the oldest. It's not because you're missing the boss, is it?' she teased.

Despite her intention not to react, heat rushed into Róisín's cheeks. 'Not at all. I do miss him because we still have a lot of work to do before we head off next week, but not in any other way.'

Debra didn't let go. 'Pull the other one,' she teased. 'You have to admit he's a looker. And a great guy. And single.'

Róisín grinned at her. 'See, I didn't even know that. For all I knew, Seth Brodie could have been married.'

'And I saw him looking at you the other day when you weren't watching. A dreamy look. And now you know, so . . .'

'So, we'll put our heads down and get back to work.'

'Okay, I'll stop teasing. You and Shea are alike, though. It's a small world, isn't it?' Debra replied with a warm smile. 'I miss my old mates. So many of them have moved away to the cities. It's different out there.'

'Families really do scatter, don't they?' Róisín mused. 'But it's funny how we all seem to come back home eventually.'

'Exactly,' Debra said, her eyes sparkling with shared understanding. 'There's something about roots that pulls you back, no matter how far you go.'

Just as they were deep in conversation, the sound of Róisín's phone ringing interrupted them.

She glanced at her phone and saw Megan's name on the screen. 'I won't be long. I have to take this,' she said to Debra, standing up. 'I'll take it outside.'

Stepping onto the footpath, Róisín found some shade and took a breath of dry, dusty air.

'Hey, Megs, what's happening?' she asked.

'Hi, Ro. Just a quick call to bring you up to speed. The separation order and the AVO were filed last week, and his nibs has obviously gotten them because he called me before.'

'I'm not surprised. That's his way of operating. I assume

you told him you were not at liberty to speak.'

Megan chuckled. 'I hit him with my best legalese. I said that legal ethics prohibited me from discussing anything directly with the opposing party without their own legal representation.'

'And?'

'He said he was his own legal representative because he was the top lawyer in the state. I'm sorry I couldn't help myself. I laughed, and that wound him up even more. He's certainly reactive; he called me a few good names. He's going to be a piece of cake in court. I'll enjoy this one.'

'Be careful. He's got a few judges on his side. How's Linda?'

'Surprisingly good. She likes it out here; she feels safe. She's already enrolled Aurora at the local school and found a small flat underneath a house two streets away from here. She's a goer now that she feels better; she's been for two interviews, and it looks like she's picked up a part-time job in the local supermarket.'

'That's fabulous news. Thanks so much. Now that I know she won't need my apartment, I'm going to put it on the market. I won't be coming back to Brisbane.'

'Don't be hasty, Ro. Don't let this lowlife ruin your career.'

'No, it's all good. I love this new job. It's challenging, and

I love being back out in the west. My city days are over.'

'As long as you're sure. Looks like I've got a long drive to come and visit you.'

'I'd love you to come visit when you can.'

'I will when this case is done and Linda gets what she's entitled to.' Megan hesitated. 'There's just one more thing, Ro.'

'What's that?'

As she listened to Megan's words, a cold wave of shock hit. Somehow, Greg knew. He knew Róisín was behind Linda in seeking her rights, knew where she was, and even knew she was working out in the west.

'How could he possibly know all that?' she asked, struggling to keep her voice steady.

'I don't know,' Megan replied, her tone urgent, 'but the threats, Ro . . . they were nasty. He said you'd be sorry. You should be careful out there. Maybe even consider getting an AVO yourself.'

'I'll be fine out here. He wouldn't come looking for me. And even if he did, what would he gain?'

'Just be careful, okay?'

'I will.'

Róisín walked back into the café thoughtfully, forcing a smile as she approached the table.

'Everything okay,' Debra asked. 'Your face is red.'

'All good. It's hot outside. Just a friend in Brisbane who's going through a tough time.'

Debra nodded, and Róisín focused on her lunch, fighting the fear that Greg would follow through on his threats.

Chapter 35

Maureen's Café - Thursday, early February.

The next day, Seth glanced around Maureen's café, appreciating Róisín's company as they sat with their coffees. It was Debra's flex day, and he and Róisín had come in to grab a quick lunch. As their conversation flowed between work and personal topics, which seemed to be no longer taboo to either of them, she asked how his meetings had gone.

'Well,' Seth said, leaning back slightly. 'The Federal Police were very supportive. They know what's going on here; it's just up to us to get the data onsite so they can come in. They want our schedule sent ahead of time—just in case something goes wrong. They'll have someone on standby.'

Róisín chuckled. 'A bit dramatic, don't you think? We're just checking water use, not busting a drug ring.'

Seth grinned. 'Yeah, I know. But they're being cautious.'

She nodded. 'Well, better safe than sorry, I guess.'

As they continued chatting over lunch, Róisín asked if Seth was familiar with Canberra, curious if he'd enjoyed his time there.

'Yeah, I know it well,' he replied, smiling. 'I went to school there, actually. Made a lot of good friends. It's a bit quiet for some people, but I like that about it.'

Róisín raised an eyebrow. 'Really? You don't miss the bigger cities?'

Seth shrugged. 'I don't mind the pace. It was home, you know? It still feels like it when I go back.' He leaned back and asked, 'What about you? Where did you go to school?'

Róisín smiled slightly. 'Local primary school at Louth first, and then I went to boarding school.'

'Boarding school, huh? How did you like that?'

She paused for a moment, thinking. 'It was alright. Not easy at first. I got used to it, though, and made some good friends. But being away from family wasn't the best. What about you? All local?'

He nodded. 'Yeah, never strayed far until going away to high school, but I guess boarding was . . . different.'

As they shared stories, Seth leaned in. 'What was the best part of boarding school for you?'

Róisín chuckled softly. 'Definitely the friends I made. We

were like a little family. But I missed home a lot, especially at first.'

'Yeah, I can relate to that,' Seth replied. 'It was tough being away, but I liked the independence. I remember the late-night study sessions and the shenanigans in the dorms.'

'Sounds familiar,' she said, grinning. 'We had some wild nights, too. Sneaking snacks after lights out was an art form.'

'Exactly! Those little moments made it all worth it.'

As their conversation continued, Seth noticed a hint of hesitation in Róisín's voice when she spoke about her past. He decided to steer the discussion away from family, preferring not to get into his background. It wasn't something he shared. The army was the closest thing he'd had to family, and look how that had gone pear-shaped.

No, he was a loner these days, and that's the way he'd stay.

'So, did you have a favourite subject at school?' he asked, genuinely curious.

'Definitely history,' she replied, her eyes lighting up. 'Something is fascinating about how the past shapes us. How about you?'

'Maths was my thing,' he said with a smile. 'But I think I enjoyed the company more than any of the subjects.'

Despite their shared experiences, the topic of his family remained unspoken.

They finished their second cup of coffee and headed back to the office.

She smiled as she walked into his office with the schedule printed out. 'I've finalised the route we discussed for the best way to attack the properties—' She laughed. 'I mean, you know, the order in which to visit. And all the accommodation is booked. You will have a bed and not a swag'—she chuckled— 'but I can't vouch for the quality of the beds in a couple of the pubs.'

'Teasing again?' Seth grinned, but as their hands brushed briefly over the table and their eyes met for just a second too long, they both instinctively pulled back. There was that tension again, the unspoken understanding they both seemed hesitant to acknowledge. He felt something stir inside him, a feeling that crept up unexpectedly. But he kept his expression neutral, focusing on the work discussion.

'Not this time,' she said.

Seth pulled out a map, and they reviewed the order of properties they'd visit between Wilcannia and Bourke.

'Okay, so the first stop is a hundred ks north of Wilcannia, then we can head north along the eastern side of the river,' he said, marking down points on the map. We need to work out where we'll get fuel.'

'Yes, the eastern side.' Róisín leaned in, pointing to a

cluster of properties. 'These should be first. I figure we hit them on the way up, and then we can come down the western side of the Darling. It's the most efficient route. If we fill up before we leave, there's *usually* fuel at Tilpa and Louth, but in the worst-case scenario, we should have enough to get to Bourke, where there is a fuel depot.'

Seth nodded, noting the fuel stops. 'Good call. All that's left is for me to make the calls tomorrow to say that we'll be calling in. I hope it won't be difficult for you with those you know through your family.'

'It'll be fine,' Róisín smiled. 'You can collect me on Wednesday, and then on Friday, you can drop me home after we're done.'

'No problem. One car's enough.' Seth gave her a playful look, knowing there was a spark of something more between them, but he kept it light. 'And who knows, I might even get a meal and drink at your place on the way home.'

Chapter 36

Kilgarvan Vicarage - December 1852.

My dearest Samuel,

It has been more than five years since you left for the Antipodes, and though the ache of your absence grows deeper by the day, I write this with love still in my heart. How could I not? Each moment I spend thinking of you keeps my spirit alive despite the hardship here in our country.

Things are still difficult here, as I am sure you can imagine. The famine still tightens its grip on the land, and we've had to make do with so little. We live day by day, and I am overwhelmed each day by the generosity of the parish, who always ensure that we have enough food and peat to keep us fed and warm.

It is so wonderful to have an address to reply to. I will place all of the letters I have written since you left me in one parcel and ask John to take me to Kenmare Post Office as soon as he can.

I pray each day that one day soon, you will find your way back to me.

Yours in hope and love,

Breda

Breda's diary

'Oh, how wonderful to receive a letter from Samuel on the day of Catherine's fifth birthday. It is almost as though God is telling me to keep faith. He told me that he would soon be travelling south to meet up with Thomas and that they would be settling on the long river called the Darling.

John was quite fascinated when I showed him the rough sketch that Samuel enclosed. It gave us both a greater understanding of the vast distances in Australia. Samuel drew a map of Ireland and put it on the map of their new country. He said that Australia is more than one hundred times the size of our country.

For the first time, I felt trepidation at travelling such a long distance to such a country, but the thought of being with Samuel soon overcame my fear. I have replied immediately and at long last, I have an address so that I can send all of the letters I have written to Samuel over the past four years. He said they will be held there for him, and it could be up to a year before he can collect them.'

Breda smiled all the way to Kenmare. She had bundled the letters she had written into a parcel, and John had offered to take her the eight miles into Kenmare so she could send them on her way. She sat with Catherine nestled on her knee, the rhythm of the cart's wheels carrying them away from the vicarage. The road to Kenmare was bumpy and rough, but the landscape was familiar. As they passed the path into the forest where she and Samuel had walked, Breda blinked away tears. The distance between them caused a sharp ache in her chest.

She clutched the parcel, running her fingers over the brown paper and the rough twine, her heart thudding with every turn of the wheel. Samuel would receive it this time.

Finally.

His name, **Samuel O'Byrne, Sydney Post Office**, was written in her careful hand.

The horse's steady pace didn't match her fast-beating heart as doubt churned through her mind.

What if the parcel never reached him?

What if he gave up on her simply because it was lost on its journey to the Antipodes?

Her mind spun with questions she couldn't ask aloud. She

turned her face away from John, not wanting him to see her worry.

Catherine's sweet voice broke into her thoughts, her little hand pointing excitedly toward a flock of sheep grazing lazily on the hillside. 'Look, Mam! Look!'

She smiled down at her daughter, forcing the corners of her mouth to lift. Catherine's eyes were wide with wonder, her innocence shining in the morning light. *Samuel's eyes.* She had her father's eyes.

'Do you think Da will like the parcel?' Catherine's question was a whisper of hope, so accepting of the existence of an absent father it nearly broke Breda's heart.

'Of course, love,' she replied softly, stroking Catherine's soft curls. Samuel would come back.

Would he?

John thought her foolish when she told Catherine that they were posting a letter to her father.

John cleared his throat, breaking the silence between them. 'What did you put in the parcel?'

'The letters I have written in answer to each of his and a shirt I made for him. Something for him to remember us when he wears it.' She paused, her voice quieter. 'I do hope he gets it.'

John was quiet for a moment. She could feel the question hanging in the air, the same one he'd asked so many times before, but it still stung when he finally spoke. 'And what if he doesn't? Breda, it's been—'

'He'll come back.' Her voice was sharper than she intended, but she didn't soften it. 'I have to believe that.'

John sighed, long and low, but said nothing more. She knew he wouldn't press her now, not with Catherine taking in every word. The rest of the ride passed in silence, the cart's wheels kicking up dust on the quiet country roads, leaving Kilgarvan far behind them.

Kenmare came into view slowly, its few buildings clustered together against the sprawling hills. Catherine gasped, her small hands clutching at Breda's shawl as her eyes took in the people, the movement. Farmers were unloading their carts, women gathered at the shop windows, their voices loud and filled with gossip, and children darted across the cobbled streets, their laughter a stark contrast to the quiet of Kilgarvan.

Their village was still recovering. So many had left, and so many more had been lost. Fields that once held families now stood empty, the stone and mud cottages crumbling into the earth. But Kenmare had life; there was a vibrancy Breda could almost feel as they rolled into the village. The sight of it both comforted and unsettled her.

'Look, Mam! Look at all the people!' Catherine's

excitement bubbled over, her feet drumming on the wooden floor of the cart. Breda smiled, pressing a kiss to the top of her daughter's head.

Yes, there were people here. There was life here. But her life, her heart, her thoughts were with Samuel, in that huge faraway place he wrote about, where rivers stretched wider than anything she could imagine, where sheep grazed on vast lands, untouched by these sorrows that gripped their homeland.

John guided the horse to a stop outside a small stone building that served as the post office. She stepped down, her legs trembling slightly, though she would never admit to it. Catherine skipped ahead, her tiny feet light on the ground.

Inside the building, the air smelled of ink and dust. The postmaster barely looked up as Breda handed over the parcel, her fingers reluctant to let it go. 'Australia,' she whispered, and the man nodded, taking it from her without question. And just like that, it was out of her hands. Out of her control.

As they stepped back outside, Catherine tugged at her hand. 'Is Da going to get it now?'

Breda's throat tightened. 'Yes, love. He will. Soon.'

He has to.

John stood beside her, his face unreadable. He said nothing as they walked down the street, but Breda could feel the doubt he held. If he thought she was foolish, so be it. They found a small tearoom near the square, and she welcomed the warmth of the fire that awaited them inside. Catherine climbed onto the bench, her legs too short to touch the floor, and her eyes, wide and curious, darted around the room, watching the people come and go.

'I do hope it gets there.' John's voice held an apology.

'Thank you. As I do, too.' Her brother had been good to them. He loved them, and he only worried because he wanted the best for them.

When Samuel came to get them, it would be very difficult to leave him alone in the vicarage.

Breda sipped her tea slowly, staring into the flickering flames.

Catherine giggled suddenly, watching a child run past the window outside. Breda smiled softly, her heart twisting. It had to be enough, didn't it? To send the parcel, to keep hoping, to keep waiting. It had to be.

When the tea was finished, they climbed back into the cart, Catherine's head resting against Breda's chest as she grew drowsy, her small body relaxing into the warmth of her mother's arms. The ride home was quieter, the shadows growing longer as they made their way back to Kilgarvan.

Breda stared out at the landscape, her mind drifting across

the sea to the distant place where Samuel was.

To the home he had promised her.

Chapter 37

Darling River, New South Wales - July 1, 1854.

My Dearest Breda,

I can hardly contain my joy as I think of you as I write, my heart racing with every word. Receiving your letters has been a balm to my soul, a reminder that despite the vast distance between us, you are still very much a part of my life. Each letter brings your voice back to me, filling the silence of this remote land with your laughter and warmth, and encourages me to work even harder so that the time until I come to Ireland to collect you will come more quickly.

I must confess that when I picked up your letters at the Sydney Post Office, I could not help but shed a tear as I held them in my hands. The words that brought you so vividly into my mind overwhelmed me with emotion. In that bustling place filled with strangers, I felt utterly alone until I read your words, and in that moment, I was transported back to Kilgarvan, right beside you.

Your letters spoke to me of home—the familiar sights and sounds of County Kerry—and I can almost picture you sitting in the woods, the sun casting a warm glow upon your face. I long for the day I can return to hold you close and tell you everything I cannot express in words. You have a way of lighting up even the darkest corners of my heart, and I carry your love with me always.

This land is both a challenge and a blessing. The earth is rich, and we are beginning to see the results of our hard work. I dream of the day when I can welcome you to the home I will build. I can already see you wandering by the river; it is the thought of you that drives me to work harder. You are my strength, Breda, and every letter I read brought me closer to you. Please know that I am doing everything in my power to make this dream a reality. I cannot wait to hold you in my arms again.

I long for the day that you will stand beside me and look out over the river and our home.

Cousin Richard's death was unexpected; it was very generous of him to leave us his land and investments, but life is not the same without him. I did not learn of his passing until after I travelled back to the goldfields to meet up with Thomas and Caitríona. We will be forever grateful as it has meant that we can build up our property so much more quickly.

We were delayed settling here for two years because of the flood of 1852. There was unusually heavy rainfall, which began in late 1851 and continued into the next year. Thomas stayed in the goldfields for another year while I took over Richard's business interests. This prolonged wet weather led to substantial riverine flooding. The Darling River and its tributaries overflowed, affecting many settlements and agricultural areas. Many farms were submerged, leading to substantial losses of crops and livestock. Thomas and I have learned not to build our houses close to the river.

I arrived at our land three months early in 1853 before Thomas and Catriona, and by the time they arrived, I had built a small wattle and daub cottage for them to live in. I camp out on the land as I work and join them occasionally for meals. It will be strange to live within four walls again when I build our home over the river.

The beauty of this place—our land—is hard to convey in words. The Darling River flows gracefully through our land, a lifeline for all that we hope to achieve here. The banks are lush and green, and the air is filled with the sounds of nature waking up around us. It is very different from the softness of home but holds its own wild beauty.

We have settled in well, though the work is hard and the days long. Thomas and Caitríona are happy, and I am grateful for their company. Caitríona has taken to the land beautifully, as I am sure you will. Her laughter echoes through their small hut, reminding me of the joy you always brought into my life. Their three children, James, Maeve, and baby Erin, give us much joy.

With all my love,
Samuel

Chapter 38

Wilcannia - Friday morning.

'Good morning, Mr McGillvray.' Seth held Róisín's gaze across the desk as the call connected, his voice calm and steady. Mr Reg McGillvray of *Dunleavy Station* was the last call to be made. Each of the earlier calls resulted in co-operation, and a firm appointment was made. The only one that they hadn't succeeded with was the one owned by a property run by a company called *Scaramouche*. The property was up near Bourke. The name niggled at Róisín, but she couldn't place it. Seth left a message on voicemail and sent an email to the administration address.

'Who's this?' A gruff voice crackled through the speaker. 'Who are you?'

'My name is Seth Brodie. I'm with the Murray-Darling Authority. We're conducting a survey on water usage down at this end of the Darling River for the next couple of weeks.'

Róisín leaned back in her chair, listening to Seth's smooth, professional tone. It was a voice that could diffuse tension—something she knew would be useful right now. She knew old Reg well.

'I don't need to talk to nobody about my water,' McGillvray barked. 'What business is it of yours?'

Seth glanced at Róisín, raising an eyebrow before answering. 'We're just gathering information to improve the health of the Darling, Mr McGillvray. Everyone's input will benefit all landholders along the river in the long term.'

'How do I know you ain't here to steal my water? Should I be talking to you at all?'

'I can send you my credentials if you'd like—'

'I don't need no photos or fancy degrees!' McGillvray cut him off sharply. 'I don't think I want to talk to you at all.'

Seth opened his mouth to say something, but the line abruptly went dead.

Róisín exhaled slowly, a half-smile tugging at the corner of her mouth. 'That went well,' she said, her tone dry. 'As well as I expected.'

Seth chuckled, a sound that momentarily softened his serious expression. 'I had my suspicions about him. We might need to pay him a visit. I've heard Reg McGillvray can be . . .

difficult.'

'Seemed like a good phone interview example for me,' Róisín teased.

'Did I pass?' Seth grinned. When he smiled, his face transformed, the lines around his hazel eyes crinkling in a way that made him seem younger. With his tanned face and sun-tipped short hair, he would have looked at home on a beach carrying a surfboard. Róisín pushed the tempting image away.

'Don't worry. I've had tougher calls. My first job threw me into the deep end with those,' he said.

'You haven't mentioned that job,' Róisín remarked, curious.

He shrugged. 'Not much to tell. I walked in fresh out of uni, thinking I'd made it big at a prestigious firm. It turned out I was a glorified assistant, fetching coffee and doing data entry for the first two years. Didn't really get into interviewing clients until the last twelve months.'

'AI has probably replaced half of that work now, huh?' Róisín smirked.

Seth nodded. 'Yeah, but there's something AI can't replace—human emotion, the nuances in conversation.'

'Exactly,' Róisín agreed, her eyes brightening. 'It's one thing to analyse data, but picking up on the subtleties . . . that's where we humans come in.'

'Couldn't have said it better myself,' Seth replied. 'Though AI's handy for sifting through all the info we collect. But there's always that human element that can't be ignored.' He chuckled. 'No doubt in the nuances in Mr McGillvray's tone.'

'I'm ready for a coffee,' she said. 'One for you too?'

'Yes, please.'

'A coffee bag do? I'm not going to walk around to the café,' she said with a smile.

'I guess so.'

Seth glanced at his tablet when Róisín carried in two mugs of coffee from the small kitchenette.

'Thank you. So, I think we might just turn up at *Dunleavy.* We tried to speak to him. We'll wing it on Wednesday.'

'Sounds like a plan. I'm excited about the trip.' Róisín shifted in her seat, her gaze distant. 'I've never done the full Darling River Run. After we cover the routes over the next few weeks, I can tick that off my bucket list. Should be interesting.'

'Sounds like a holiday. I guess you're familiar with driving on dirt roads. More than me. Maybe you can drive the work Land Cruiser.'

'I can manage,' Róisín replied, her tone casual, though she glanced away for a moment, lost in thought.

Seth noticed the brief hesitation. 'You are okay with

travelling together?' he asked, lowering his voice.

'Why wouldn't I be?' Róisín gave a light laugh, but her eyes betrayed a flicker of uncertainty.

Seth leaned back, studying her for a moment. He wondered if she was dealing with something else too—something more than the worry of her father's recovery. There was a guardedness about her at times. Maybe it wasn't damage, but poor judgment—he wasn't sure.

Róisín had been staring out the window as though lost in memories, when she finally spoke. 'I loved growing up on the Darling, you know. The highlight of the year was always the races at Louth.'

Seth saw her smile, a nostalgic warmth creeping into her expression. 'Good memories?'

'Yeah,' she murmured. 'Family memories. We'd all get together—Mum, Dad, my sisters. The races were a big deal. It was the one time we'd all go out together. Even when I was away at boarding school, I'd come home for the races.'

'Must've been a change, moving to Brisbane after all that,' Seth said, still sensing there was more beneath the surface.

'It was,' Róisín admitted, her voice softening. 'City life is . . . different. More exciting in some ways—there's always something happening, always someone new to meet. But out here . . .' she hesitated, then sighed. 'Out here, you might go months without seeing anyone but your family. I missed that stillness.'

Seth nodded. 'You prefer it out here, don't you?'

'Yes,' she said simply, but Seth could hear the depth of feeling in that one word.

'What about you?' she ventured. 'You've never mentioned your family. Do you see much of them?' Róisín asked, her curiosity piqued.

Seth paused, glancing down at his coffee. 'No family. It's a bit complicated. I was a foster child, you know? Moved from home to home for most of my childhood.'

Róisín's eyes widened. 'That must have been tough.'

'It was, but I learned to adapt quickly. Made a lot of friends along the way, though.' He shrugged, trying to downplay his situation.

As she stared at him, he decided to be honest. 'Most of the homes I was in were purely for the financial gain of the foster parent. Sure, I had clothes and food, but there wasn't much else. If you ever notice I'm a bit closed off, I'm sorry; I'm not good with that sort of thing.'

'I can't even imagine,' she replied softly. 'Do you ever see any of them now?'

'Not really,' he admitted. 'They were just part of that

chapter in my life.'

'Okay, time to get back to work,' she said, and Seth hoped the suggestion wasn't to spare his feelings from memories that might seem sad to her.

They spent the rest of the morning working on the schedule for the following week. They'd planned two visits a day to various properties along the Darling River. The properties had been chosen carefully, each close to the next, allowing for the rest of the day to be spent travelling to the next property or overnight stop.

Róisín had been impressed with the way Seth had selected the stations where he had decided visits were necessary. When he outlined his reasoning—based on both the reports and the phone interviews he'd conducted—she found herself respecting his methodical approach, even when she teased him about the failed call with Reg McGillvray.

'You should've impressed him,' she said with a smile. 'Out of all of them, Reg McGillvray was the one you should've been able to charm.'

Seth gave a wry smile. 'That was a disaster—McGillvray's like an old bull, stubborn and territorial. I don't think anyone could charm him.'

'I've picked him first, for Wednesday late morning,' Róisín

said, raising an eyebrow.

'I noticed that. Bold move,' Seth said with a grin. 'Maybe I should have done the schedule. You, with your local knowledge, are supposed to make this easier for us.'

'None of it's going to be easy, Seth.'

'He'll be easier in person, I think,' Seth said, his confidence evident.

'Time will tell,' she said.

Seth nodded, looking at the screen. 'Okay, I'll come to pick you up on Wednesday morning. I'm driving up to Bourke on Monday morning and plan to spend a couple of days there, setting up the second office.'

'Already found a space to rent?' Róisín asked.

'Yeah, it's not far from the old post office,' Seth said casually. 'Anyway, after McGillvray, we can drive back south through Tilpa and take the road on the other side of the river to *Twin Trees* in the afternoon. Then up to Bourke for the night after that.'

Róisín glanced at him. 'Okay, sounds the most sensible way.'

Seth noticed her pause but didn't push. He shifted the conversation to more mundane matters, like instant coffee. 'You know, I'll bring my coffee machine,' he said with a grin.

Róisín laughed. 'Good plan. Nothing worse than instant

coffee.'

##

An hour later, Seth stood at Róisín's door. 'It's time you were heading home. You've got a long drive on dirt roads this afternoon. You were supposed to be gone by two, and it's almost half past.'

'Thanks, I lost track of the time,' Róisín replied, gathering her files while he watched. He would miss her company over the weekend. At one point, he almost suggested he could pick her up on Sunday night, and she could come to Bourke with him, but it wasn't necessary that she be there.

Work relationship, he reminded himself, but that thought faded when she turned to him with a contented smile. 'Well, I have everything. I'll hit the road now. Don't work too late, will you?'

'I won't,' he said, forcing a smile. 'You emailed me all those files?'

'I did,' she replied.

She lingered as if hesitant to leave, and he walked over to her desk, where she hovered. 'I'll walk you out.'

When they reached her car, he opened the passenger door for her. 'Thank you,' she said softly, and before he could think twice, he took her hand and leaned over, pressing a gentle kiss to her cheek.

'You take care, Róisín O'Byrne. I'll see you next Wednesday at about ten.'

'At *Ceann Mara*,' she said. 'You can't miss the sign. And remember to take the road from Wilcannia on the east side of the river.' He noticed the blush that stained her cheeks, and then a sweet smile lifted her lips. 'You have a good weekend and watch those kangaroos,' she teased.

'Yes, boss.' Seth waved as she drove out. When he stepped back into the office, the place seemed empty. Before he could think about why, he sat at his desk and checked his email to read the files she'd sent.

Chapter 39

Ceann Mara - early February, Wednesday, 10.30 a.m.

Seth pulled up to Róisín's place and stepped out of his car, a smile spreading across his face when he spotted her walking down the steps towards him. She looked vibrant, her hair catching the sunlight and her eyes sparkling with anticipation.

'You found the place easily?' she called, a hint of laughter in her voice.

'I did,' he replied, trying to keep his tone light despite the fluttering in his stomach.

Róisín led the way down the path, her enthusiasm palpable. 'I want to show you something special before we hit the road,' she said, glancing back at him with a smile that made his heart skip a beat. 'You've missed meeting Cat and Logan—my sister and her partner. They had to go over the river to Logan's place.'

'I'll meet them on Friday afternoon when we check on

Guntana.' He glanced at Róisín, but she looked happy enough with that.

They walked side by side, the grassy path bordered by clusters of native bluebells and river buttercups swaying gently in the breeze. Seth couldn't help but admire the way Róisín moved with confidence, comfortable in her surroundings. 'What's this special place?' he asked, curiosity piquing.

'You'll see.'

As they approached the riverbank, the gentle sound of flowing water filled the air, and Seth inhaled deeply, taking in the fresh scent of the river. Róisín stopped, gesturing to the riverbank ahead. 'This is where my family comes for picnics and celebrations. It's kind of our place.'

Seth looked around. A flat mowed lawn sat in the middle of the tussock grass on either side and a wooden table with two long benches overlooked the river. 'It's beautiful. I can see why you love it here.'

Róisín smiled, her expression softening. 'This river holds a lot of memories for me. Mum brought us here to play when we were little; Dad dug a bit of a dam down there, and we used to spend hours playing in the shallows.'

She pointed to a few rocks jutting out from the bank. 'That's where we used to sit and fish. My father taught me everything I know about fishing right there.'

'What about your family now?' Seth asked, genuinely interested.

'They're all scattered across the state now, but we all try to come home when we can.' She paused, looking out over the water. 'Life gets busy, but this place always grounds me. I forgot how good it was when I was in Brisbane.' She looked off into the distance for a moment, and a fleeting sadness crossed her face.

'I can understand that,' he said, stepping closer to her. 'It's a beautiful place. I could sit there all day.' He gestured to the table. A sense of calm relaxed him as he stood next to Róisín. He was drawn to her, enjoying the shared moment beside the beauty of the river. Gentle waves rippled across the water beneath the breeze, and morning sunlight danced on the water.

After a few moments of companionable silence, Róisín turned to him. 'Thanks for coming out of your way to collect me.'

'No problem,' he replied. 'It saved you extra driving, and you would have had to leave your car somewhere anyway.'

The visits ahead were their purpose, but he could easily have spent the rest of the day beside the river with Róisín.

She must have sensed his reluctance. 'Come on, boss, it's time we head back to *Dunleavy*,' she said, her tone light. 'Did you notice it as you came past?'

'I did,' Seth replied, recalling the ramshackle sign and the dry paddocks dotted with scrawny cattle. 'It's hard to believe it's a thriving station.'

Róisín nodded, her expression thoughtful. 'I'm yet to be convinced it is. We have our work cut out for us, don't we?'

'Definitely,' Seth said, reminded of their goal for the day. 'Let's get started.'

***

As they approached *Dunleavy*, Reg McGillvray's property, a knot tightened in Róisín's stomach at the sight of the poor cattle, their ribs protruding under the harsh sun. 'There's no water in that paddock,' she said, her voice trembling. 'I'm going to report him. He's always been a lazy station owner, and his reputation is terrible across the district.'

The road to the old homestead was winding and rutted; the ground cracked and dry, each bump jostling their thoughts. Near the gate, a thin dog on a chain barked ferociously, but Róisín was undeterred. 'He's got no water either. I'm going to let him off,' she insisted.

Seth hesitated, concern knitting his brow. 'He might bite you.'

'No, he'll know he can get to the river as soon as he's off,' Róisín replied. As she spoke, the dog sat patiently, its barking fading as she unclipped the chain. It took off in the opposite direction, heading toward the river, and she turned to Seth with a small triumphant smile. 'See? I won't say I told you so.'

The gate was triple padlocked, preventing their entry. 'We'll have to walk in,' Seth said, glancing at the overgrown landscape around them.

'Do you need a hand getting over the gate?' Róisín teased, pulling a face, before climbing over.

'I was about to ask you the same thing,' Seth replied, quickly following her.

A couple of old cars and three rusted trucks lay abandoned in the house paddock, surrounded by tall grass that swayed in the gentle breeze. 'Watch out for snakes,' Seth warned, scanning the ground. 'We don't want a snake bite this far from help.'

As they approached a high, rusted gate that led to the house yard, Seth's instincts kicked in, and a shiver ran down his spine when he heard a click.

'Get down!' Róisín yelled, grabbing his arm and pulling him to the ground as a shot whistled past them.

'I told you not to come on my property!' a voice laced with menace called out from the shadows at the western side of the house.

'Don't get up!' Róisín's eyes were wide with fear. The landscape around them felt suddenly hostile, the surrounding paddocks now threatening danger. They had to get out of here; Reg McGillvray was crazy enough to shoot them as they turned their backs.

'We're not going to get in here,' Seth said, frustration creeping into his voice. 'I'll ring him and tell him we're leaving without any trouble.'

'Do you think he's hiding something?' Róisín asked, worry etched on her face. 'I heard he lost the plot a bit after his wife died, and it doesn't look like poverty has treated him well—especially the cattle.'

Seth pulled out his phone, quickly scrolling through his contacts for McGillvray's number. It answered immediately.

'Get off my land!' came McGillvray's voice, followed by another shot that sent a chill down Róisín's spine. She glanced down at their dust-covered clothes, the reality of their situation sinking in. If they got out of there alive, they certainly wouldn't be dressed for a visit to *Twin Trees*, the next station on their list.

'Can we come and see you, please?' Seth asked, his tone reasonable.

'Get off my land!' his voice roared through the phone.

'Okay, we're going. Stop shooting! We'll stand up and

leave peacefully.'

'Give me the phone,' Róisín whispered, urgency lacing her words.

Seth frowned but handed it over. 'Reg, this is Róisín O'Byrne, Tom's daughter. Did you know my dad had a heart attack?'

'What's that got to do with you being on my land?' he shot back.

'We just want to talk to you. We're not here to cause any trouble.'

'How's Tom?' Reg asked after a long silence, his tone slightly less hostile.

'He's okay. He's in hospital in Sydney. Can we talk to you? It's important.'

'Stand up. I won't shoot you. I'll come out and talk to you out here. No one's been in our house since Betty died.'

'Okay, we'll wait here,' Róisín said, handing the phone back to Seth.

'Game to stand up?' Seth asked. 'Looks like local knowledge works.' His voice was laced with wry humour as they stood. They shared a hopeful glance, but were still aware of the danger of their situation. 'Can we trust him?'

'Maybe,' she said.

They waited for ten minutes, but there was no sign of him, but at least no more shots were fired.

'We're not going to get near the river to check his meterage,' Seth said, frustration seeping into his voice. 'I'll ring him and tell him we're leaving without any trouble. This is one for the boys in blue.' Seth called again, but this time, the phone rang out. He shrugged. 'Time to give up, I guess.'

'Hang on.' Róisín put her hand up to shade her eyes. 'Here he comes.'

Róisín's heart ached for Reg McGillvray as he approached them. His gaunt, yellowed face spoke of deeper problems than his land; he looked as though he was in the last stages of some awful disease.

'What do you want?' he barked, his eyes cold, the rifle still clutched in his hands.

Her sympathy dissipated as the harshness of his tone rang through the air.

'We just need to talk to you about your water license,' Seth said, keeping his voice calm.

The gun lowered slightly, and Róisín instinctively squeezed Seth's arm.

'We just wanted to check you were all right. The dog was tied up, and the gate's locked,' she added softly.

'No one comes on my place. It's not open to anyone,' Reg

yelled, his resolve firm.

Seth took a step ahead, ready to reason with him, but Róisín tightened her grip on his wrist, sensing the rising tension in Reg.

'Okay, as long as we know you're okay, we'll go. Can you unlock the gate for us to get out?' she asked, her voice steady despite the uncertainty swirling around them.

'Nope,' he replied flatly. 'You can get out the same bloody way you came in. If my dog doesn't come back, I'll bloody sue you too.'

Róisín's heart sank, but she stared at him until he finally turned away and went back to the house. They climbed the gate and walked back to their vehicle.

Seth shrugged, a wry smile playing on his lips. 'I guess I've got a bit to learn. It's not all cut and dried like data or paperwork, is it? What were we saying about AI the other day? We need the human element? Well, if that's the human element, I think I prefer AI.'

Róisín chuckled. 'Dad told me he might be difficult. Apparently, no one's been in there since Betty died. Like he said.'

'Does he even leave the place?' Seth wondered aloud.

'Apparently, his food is left at the mailbox for him,' Róisín replied, sadness creeping into her voice.

Seth brushed himself off and reached over, gently pulling a blade of dead grass from Róisín's hair. 'Where to next?' he asked.

Twin Trees. The Scaramouche property.

Róisín's eyes widened as it hit her. 'What's wrong?' he asked.

'Nothing,' she shook her head. She was sure that she'd seen files in the office in Brisbane for a company called Scaramouche. She'd seen the logo on Greg's desk one day and had smiled because Bohemian Rhapsody was one of his favourite songs.

'One of yours?' she'd asked idly as she waited for him to put his tie on. They were going down to the bar under the office for Friday night drinks. She'd been surprised when he'd picked it up and shoved it in his drawer, his tie still unknotted.

'No, a client,' he said briefly. Then he turned to her to change the subject. 'Where's the dress I told you to bring to go out tonight?'

'I forgot it,' she said, lightening her tone.

'You look like a bloody secretary,' he said. 'Go home and get it, and I'll meet you down there.'

To her shame, she had. But that was where she'd seen Scaramouche; maybe it was a coincidence. At the time, she'd thought little of it. Now, the connection to Scaramouche was too coincidental to ignore.

Róisín was quiet as they travelled down to Tilpa and then the seventy-five kilometres up the eastern side of the river to *Twin Trees*. They stopped just before the property, and Seth went to the back of the Land Cruiser, where he had packed a thermos of coffee. The camp fridge held milk and some sandwiches, but Róisín waved her hand. 'Just coffee for me, thanks.'

*****

As he poured the brewed coffee he'd made just before he left Wilcannia, Róisín walked across to the riverbank, deep in thought as she watched the water flow past. Seth could tell there was something on her mind.

The banks of the Darling River shimmered with life after the recent rain that had broken the drought, vibrant green grass and wildflowers sprouting in patches along the shore. Towering red river gums loomed above them, their gnarled trunks and sweeping branches providing dappled shade.

However, as Seth gazed along the bank, he spotted dead carp, their lifeless bodies a stark contrast to the otherwise thriving environment. The mingling scents of damp earth and decay lingered in the air, underscoring the fragile balance of this ecosystem.

'Are you upset about Reg McGilvray?' Seth asked, making her jump as he stood behind her. Róisín hadn't heard him approach.

'Yes, a little,' she said. They walked back to the car together, and he noticed she had tipped most of her coffee out. Something was bothering her. Seth held the sandwiches out to her again, but she shook her head. He put them back into the camp fridge.

'No, not hungry. The coffee was lovely, though, thank you.'

'Are you okay? Not car sick or anything?'

That got a slight chuckle out of her. 'Not at all. No, I'm just focusing on what to do about Reg McGillvray's place. We're going to have to get a court order,' she said, pulling a face.

'I know, either that or we get the police to come with us. I'll talk to the Feds and see what they recommend. We'll have to go back out there in the next few days.'

'After we make the second trip down south?'

'I'm not sure. It'll depend on how long the Federal Police take to get back to us.'

Róisín climbed into the passenger seat as Seth closed the back of the Land Cruiser and walked around to climb in.

'Ready for the second visit?'

Her smile was tight. 'Yeah. I hope we don't face any rifles

this time.'

They were surprised when they reached the front gate of *Twin Trees*. It was open, and the entry to the station was unkempt, with no sign of any livestock. They hadn't even passed any goats on their approach.

Róisín stepped out of the car, dust swirling around their boots as they took in the sight in front of them. The property stretched out, barren and silent, far too quiet for a place flagged for booming cattle sales. A dry, cracked landscape greeted them, withered grass clinging to life in patches and not a single beast in sight.

'This can't be right,' Róisín muttered, scanning the horizon, her brow furrowed in confusion. 'Where are all the cattle?'

Seth shook his head, squinting towards the house in the distance. 'We've been hearing about huge sales, but it doesn't add up. This place looks abandoned.'

They walked further down the track, their steps the only sound in the oppressive stillness. The river shimmered faintly in the distance, but the land leading to it was parched and cracked from the recent drought. There were no pumps, irrigation systems, or signs of recent activity—just dry paddocks and an empty house.

Róisín stopped, hands on her hips, turning in a slow circle. 'There's nothing here, Seth. No cattle, no signs of recent movement. How are they claiming such high production out of this?'

Seth stood still, trying to make sense of it all. 'We've got records showing them moving hundreds of head of cattle. Where are they?' He kicked at a dry clump of dirt. 'They couldn't have disappeared overnight.'

They reached the dam, expecting at least a sign of water usage, but found only a dusty, cracked bed. The dam was dry, untouched by the recent rainfall or irrigation.

'This place should be thriving, or at least surviving,' Róisín murmured, her voice trailing off as she shook her head in disbelief. 'There's nothing to suggest water misuse. If anything, they look like they were barely holding on and walked off the place.'

The two of them exchanged a glance, equally perplexed. *Twin Trees* was on their list because it had survived the drought so well—prosperous even—but the reality on the ground told a very different story.

'Something's not right here,' Róisín said quietly. 'I don't know what's going on, but this place is hiding something. It has to be.'

Seth nodded slowly, instincts prickling as he stared out at

the property. 'We need to dig deeper. Get the water authorities and the agriculture department involved. This doesn't add up.'

They walked back toward the car, both unsettled by the stark contrast between what they'd been led to expect and the ghostly, lifeless landscape that lay before them. *Twin Trees* was dry, empty, and silent, but the mystery surrounding it had only begun.

Chapter 40

Darling River Run - early February, Thursday.

As they headed south again after visiting the six properties on their list over the three days, Seth was pleased that Róisín's relaxed manner seemed to have returned. She could still be distant at times, but they had spent the evening in Bourke in deep discussion about what they found at *Twin Trees*. He had called his contact at the Federal Police, who suggested they talk to the local police at Louth and arrange a time for Seth and Róisín to go back to *Dunleavy*, accompanied by local officers.

Seth's reaction to what they found at *Twin Trees* was fast. He fired off a couple of emails to the Department of Agriculture and Primary Industries to double-check that they had the right place. The reply from his contact there was instant, with figures showing the cattle that the property had allegedly sold at sales over the past three years.

'Not right,' Róisín said. 'I think we've definitely got some data here we can use. Why would they say they were selling cattle at sales? The land's been neglected; it hasn't been used in some time.'

'That's where the money laundering comes in,' Seth replied.

'How? I've heard of it but how does it actually work?'

'Okay,' Seth said, leaning back in his chair. 'Fictitious livestock sales. *Scaramouche* buys water licenses ostensibly for agricultural use. These licenses allow them to access and use water from the river, usually tied to land for irrigation. But the thing is, the land they own is fallow—unused, barren. No legitimate farming or livestock activity is actually happening. And no water use.

'Then they pretend to run a cattle operation. They create fake records—water usage, cattle purchases, breeding, sales— all fiction. No cattle ever were bred and raised on that land. It's just a front to launder money. They report high productivity, even though the land is sitting idle. The so-called "income" from those cattle sales is actually money earned from whatever illegal business they're really running.

'Without the review seven years ago, they would have gotten away with it,' Seth continued. 'Resourcing has increased. Thus, our jobs came into existence'—he smiled at her—

'because that review showed that our state's resources were way lower than the other states. Plus, the penalties for non-compliance were often insufficient to deter illegal activities. Sorry, I get carried away sometimes,' he apologised. 'You probably know that already.'

'I'm interested. I haven't had time to read that whole review yet.'

'Plus, proving it is tough when everything's under a company name like this one. They can hide behind shelf companies—pre-registered businesses that sit inactive until they need a front. It makes it harder to trace who's really pulling the strings. You've got to dig through layers of ownership, shell after shell, until you find the real people involved. Even then, the transactions look clean on the surface. It's subtle, but once you spot the inconsistencies, you can start pulling the threads together.'

Róisín shook her head and said nothing. She would do some digging and tell him her suspicions tomorrow.

Seth looked over at her. 'You sure you're okay? You've been awfully quiet since we went to *Dunleavy*.'

She forced a smile. 'I'm fine. But there is something I want to talk to you about when we get back.

This was their last night in Bourke before heading south again. They spent the evening at the desk in Seth's motel room, working through the data and sending it off.

'There's one more place we need to see,' Seth said.

'I know. *Guntana,* Logan's place. I don't have a problem with that.'

'I know you say he's clean, and I trust you, Róisín, but we still have to follow the process.' Seth's tone held a warning, but he knew there wasn't any subterfuge on her part. She trusted her brother-in-law and how he operated.

Maybe he thought her trust was misplaced, though.

'I'd like to interview him. Logan?'

'Yes, Logan Wainwright.'

'Do you think it'll be possible for me to catch up with him tomorrow afternoon when I drop you off?'

Róisín straightened up slowly. 'I've been thinking about that. It's a long way for you to drive from *Guntana* to Wilcannia, and it'll be quite late by the time we get there tomorrow afternoon.' She took a deep breath. 'How about I give Cat a call and we organise to meet up tomorrow night? We can have a barbeque, there are plenty of spare rooms at the homestead, and you can stay there overnight and head out Saturday morning.'

Seth thought about it and nodded. 'That sounds like a plan. We can all be in on the meeting. I'm sure everything is above board. But you realise we have to look into it because of the water usage figures there.'

'I do, but like I said, I've been there. I've seen it. It's not happening. I'll give Cat a call now.' Róisín picked up her phone and dialled Cat's mobile.

'How's it going?' Cat asked. 'Having a good trip?'

'Yes, it's been interesting,' Róisín said slowly.

'That doesn't sound good.'

'It's all good. Have you heard anything from Mum and Dad?'

'Yeah, looks like they're coming home in about ten days.'

'Oh, that's great news!' Róisín smiled at Seth

'Yep, just some physio still to happen for his leg, but they're happy with his heart.'

'We've been out of service for a bit. I'm sure Dad tried to ring me.'

'He knew you were away, so he asked me to pass it on when you got home. He's so excited about these letters, Ro. He's been in a whole stack of databases, and he's put it all together, he thinks. The National Libraries in Australia and Ireland, Ancestry.com, and it looks like we finally found our Samuel. The letters were apparently found in a house in Melbourne owned by a Samuel Burns. The new owners found them in an attic and donated them to the National Library here. Sorry, I'm rabbiting on. Do you have time to listen to me now?'

'Yeah, I've got a minute. I just wanted to ask you

something anyway.'

'It looks like *our* Samuel went by the name Burns. He travelled back to Ireland in 1860, and it appears he brought a wife and a child back on a boat called the *Ariel*.'

'Wow, Dad's made great progress.'

'He's beside himself, we both are,' Cat said. We just have to find where he built his house called *Luachmhaire*.'

'I just hope he doesn't get too excited.' Róisín glanced at Seth, but he was staring at his computer screen.

'So, what did you want to talk to me about?'

'Well, Seth and I are leaving Bourke tomorrow and should get back home around mid-afternoon. I offered for him to stay for dinner and overnight before he heads back to Wilcannia. But only if you're happy to do a barbie down at the camp kitchen and have one of the spare rooms ready.'

'That sounds good.'

'Is Logan handy?' Róisín asked.

'Yeah, do you need to talk to him?'

'Yes, please. Can you put him on for a minute? See you tomorrow. Love you, bye.'

Logan came to the phone, and Róisín pressed the speakerphone button so Seth could hear, too. 'Hi, Ro. What's happening?'

'All good,' Róisín said. 'It's a bit difficult, but no drama. You don't use any water at *Guntana* yet, do you?'

'No, I haven't had a chance to get any of that set up. Too busy with the fences for the goats and working at your dad's. Why? Is there a problem?'

'Well, the records from the property over the last couple of years are a bit haphazard, and Seth and I, as part of the team, need to talk to you about what you know about the licenses and things.'

'Yeah, not a problem at all. I can dig out any paperwork I've got. I had some emails back and forth with your uncle when I bought the place, but I don't think there was any mention of water licenses then.'

'Okay, we'll see you tomorrow afternoon. Nothing to worry about. We're going to have a barbie—Cat's going to do some salads.'

'Okay, see you then. Bye.'

Róisín turned to Seth. 'All good. See? Logan's happy to talk, and Cat's happy to cook a barbecue.'

Relief washed through Seth. The guy had sounded genuine. 'It'll be nice to have some social downtime after we talk to him. It's been a pretty hectic week, what with being shot at, seeing *Twin Trees*, and all the travelling.'

'Yeah, I'm a bit tired,' Róisín said. Seth looked at her

quizzically. She was still more distant than she had been over the first few weeks.

***

As they approached Louth on the eastern side of the Darling River, Róisín frowned. Seth glanced at her.

'What are you thinking about?'

'Well, I'm trying to figure out whether we're better off driving down this road to *Guntana* or if it would be easier to turn across the bridge and go down the western side so we have the car at *Ceann Mara*.'

'You use a punt to get across the river, don't you?'

'Yes, I do, but I was thinking if we want to look at any files, the internet connection at Mum and Dad's is better than at Logan's, and there's a lot more room to work if we want to spread out. It'll be hard to take everything over in the punt. Plus, if I need anything like a change of clothes, I can quickly hop back across. Anyway, you'll probably want to cross in the punt to check the water meters, won't you? We can do that tomorrow morning if that suits you.'

'I'm in your hands.'

'Does that mean you trust me?' Her eyes were steady, even

though the thought of being in his hands sent a pleasurable ripple down her back.

'I do. I'll be honest. I wondered why you were leaving a firm in Brisbane for a totally different area of law, but once you told me about your reasons and after working with you for three weeks, I trust you implicitly.'

More tingles fired her nerve endings, and she smiled as she held his eyes.

'Do you mind if I call you Ro? Róisín can be a bit of a mouthful.'

'People I like are allowed to call me that,' she said, her eyes twinkling as she looked back at him. 'So, yes, you can call me Ro.'

This time, he let the spark of attraction stay. 'How far to Louth?' he asked.

'Not far at all. We might stop at the general store and pick up something for nibbles. Cat will be cooking up a storm now that she knows we're coming. She's got a lot of Mum's cooking talent.'

As they approached Louth, Róisín pointed to the general store at the turnoff to the bridge. 'I haven't caught up with some friends who bought the store since I've been back, so we'll call in and see what they've got.'

'Sounds good to me.'

Not only was Mandy in the store, but Teddy was there as well. Róisín's eyes lit up when she saw him.

'Hey, Teddy! How's it going?'

'Hi! Good to see you!' His gaze flicked to Seth, who had walked in behind her.

'I'm on a work trip, Teddy. We've been up to Bourke and back. This is Seth Brodie, my boss. Seth, this is Teddy Brewster.'

As Seth and Teddy shook hands, Mandy came around from the counter and wrapped her arms around Róisín.

'So good to see you, Ro! You don't look any different.'

'It's been a long time.' Róisín turned around, spreading her arms wide. 'Look at this! What a trendy little shop we've got here—so different from when Mrs Higgins had it.'

'We're pretty proud of it,' Mandy said. 'We get a lot of people coming in from the properties now to buy stuff here instead of getting it flown in. What are you after today, or did you just stop in to say hello?'

'We're stopping at Mum and Dad's on the way home, and Cat's cooking a barbecue, so just some nice nibbles. Maybe dip and bikkies.'

'We can do better than that.' Mandy led Róisín over to the delicatessen section of the general store. Róisín's eyes widened at the array of cold meats, cheese, and olives.

'Wow! You must have a lot of customers if you can keep this much stock!'

'I enjoy doing it. Yes, we had a bit of waste at first, but it's really built up now. We get a lot of tourists. Grey nomies heading to the station stays stop in to pick up nibbles here, and we've got a freezer full of meat. The word has got out on social media. Next purchase is a coffee machine.'

Seth was in conversation with Teddy when Róisín went over to them while Mandy wrapped the order.

'What do you think? Should we get some meat too?' Róisín frowned. She should have asked Cat when she called, but she was too excited about the family research.

Seth shrugged. 'I've got no idea. I haven't been to a family barbeque at a property before.'

'You're in for a treat at *Ceann Mara*,' Teddy said. 'Ro's mum has a reputation for being the best cook in the district.'

'Haven't you heard?' Róisín asked.

'Heard what? Is everything okay?' Teddy asked.

'Actually, I suppose it hasn't spread around the district yet.'

'I've been down at Menindee for a couple of weeks while Mandy's been running the store.'

Mandy put a hand to her mouth. 'I'm so sorry, Teddy! I forgot to tell you—I heard Tom had a heart attack.'

'Oh, shit! That's not good,' Teddy said.

'But all good,' Róisín assured them. 'Apparently, they're coming home from Sydney in the next week or two.'

'That's great news!' After making their purchases, which Seth insisted on paying for, Róisín was aware of Teddy's thoughtful expression as they walked out together. She held the back of the car open for him to put the cold stuff in the camp fridge.

'I guess that's going to start a bit of gossip in the district, isn't it?' Seth said with a grin. 'Your boss is going home to your parents' place.'

'No, it's not going to start gossip. Teddy is a good bloke, but you've got him thinking. Even though there's nothing to think about, is there?' she said, holding his gaze directly.

'Not yet, but I'd like it if there was,' Seth said.

Chapter 41

Darling River, New South Wales - October 4, 1857.

My dearest Breda,

The sun beats down fierce here in the Antipodes, and the land is vast—far beyond what I could ever have imagined. Each day, I rise before dawn to set out on horseback, surveying the land and marking out the boundaries of our future. We've named the property on the western side of the river Ceann Mara, *as a reminder of what we left behind and what we're building anew.*

The work is hard, harder than I thought, but we're making steady progress. Thomas tends the sheep and looks after the store we've built to trade along the Darling River. The river is a lifeline here—goods come and go, and I've already seen the potential in it. The store brings in a fair trade of people travelling in small boats and by cart and horseback on the narrow road. With the store and our dock, we'll build something more for our future. I've been clearing land on the east side of the river these past weeks. It's rough country, but I see its promise. It's there, Breda, that I'll build a house for you —our home when I finally bring you across the sea.

I wish I could tell you it'll be sooner, but it will be at least another two years before I can come for you. The land needs more clearing, and our flock needs building. Please be patient, my love. I beg you to wait for me. I promise, with all my heart, that I will return. Hold on to the thought of what we're building here—our life, our future.

Until we are together again, my love, keep writing to me. Your words are my lifeline, and I cherish them more than I can say. I will travel to Sydney each year, so be patient until I write back to you. Please wait for me.

With all my love,

Samuel

***

Kilgarvan - Christmas Eve, 1858.

Dear Samuel,

I hope this letter finds you well and in good spirits as Christmas approaches. I wanted to wish you a joyful holiday season. I think of you often and hope for your return.

I visited your mother a week before she passed; my heart

aches for you and Thomas and your brother. Sean told me that he had written to you about her passing.

I told your mother that our love would reunite us soon, and she expressed her confidence in you. She told me she had no doubt you would return if you gave your word. It was comforting to hear her speak so assuredly, and it filled me with hope for the future.

Please tell me more about your new home, and how the store is going. I long to hear about your plans for the house you will build across the river.

Take care of yourself, Samuel. You are always in my thoughts.

With love,

Breda

Chapter 42

Kilgarvan Vicarage - November, 1859.

My dearest Samuel,

I was so happy to receive your letter and to hear that you have started building a home for us. Thomas and Caitríona's house sounds wonderful. I cannot imagine living in a building that size after living in the vicarage. The drawing that you included of both Ceann Mara *and* Luachmhaire, *our future home, filled me with happiness, and I must admit that I cried. I read it over and over, holding each word close to my heart. I know you are far away, but hearing about the work you are doing and the land you have cleared for us makes me feel as if I'm right there with you, standing by your side. I close my eyes and imagine I am with you at our home. I promise you, Samuel, I will wait. No matter how long it takes, I'll be here, ready for you to take me with you.*

The description of the paddle steamers planned for the river widened my eyes. Being used to our narrow streams here, I can't imagine such a huge river. Hearing that you are building one, too, made me realise that you have truly become a businessman in your new country.

Knowing that the day you will return to me is drawing closer and that we'll be together again soon fills me with the utmost joy. I hope and pray that you will be happy with me when you arrive here.

I am a very different person from that young girl that you met at her mother's grave all those years ago. Take care, Samuel, and know that no matter the distance, my heart is always with you.

With all my love,
Breda

Breda leaned back and closed her eyes, wondering if she had said too much in the letter. Perhaps she had been wrong not to tell Samuel about Catherine, but it was too late now. Knowing that his arrival could be soon, she realised she had to plan for their departure. A part of her also knew she had to prepare herself for Samuel's reaction when he learned he had a daughter.

She held the letter as she jumped to her feet. It was time to tell her daughter of the exciting journey they would have ahead of them in the coming year—or the journey she hoped they would have. Her embroidery basket fell to the ground as she knocked over the small side table, which in turn knocked the fire tongs, poker, and ash bucket onto the hearth with a loud crash.

John hurried in from his study. 'What was that? Are you hurt, Breda?'

'No, I was careless as I hurried.' Breda's hands shook as she held the letter out. She turned to John, her voice catching in her throat as she tried to steady her emotions.

'Samuel says it will only be another year or so before he's here,' she said. 'He's building a home for us. He included a drawing . . . he's called it *Luachmhaire*. It's everything we've dreamed of.' She wiped away a tear and handed the letter to John. 'I have written him back and told him how much it meant to me.' She began to read aloud from her reply, her voice growing stronger with every word.

'*My dearest Samuel, I was so happy to receive your letter and to hear that you have started building a home for us. Thomas and Caitríona's house sounds wonderful. I cannot imagine living in a building that size after the vicarage. The sketches you included of both* Ceann Mara *and* Luachmhaire *filled me with joy, and I must admit that I cried. I read it over and over, holding each word close to my heart.*'

She paused, looking up at John. 'It's so hard to imagine all of it, isn't it? How he's building this life so far away, and yet he's . . .'

Her voice broke for a moment, but she continued.

'*To know that the day when you shall return to me is drawing closer and that we'll be together again soon fills me with the utmost joy. I just hope and pray that you will be happy with me when you arrive here.*'

'But I am starting to doubt, John.' Breda put down the letter and looked at her brother with a tearful smile. 'What if . . . when he finds out about Catherine—'

John stepped closer, placing a hand on her shoulder. 'Breda, Samuel loves you. He's doing all of this for you. He's building you a life over there. And how could he not love Catherine?'

'But I'm not the same girl, John,' she said softly. 'I'm not the young girl he met at the graveyard. I am a grown woman now, and I am a mother. What if he doesn't want this life when he meets me again?'

'If that is the case, we will still make our own way.'

'What do you mean? We?'

John hesitated, then spoke. 'I've been thinking, Breda . . . if you go, I will probably go with you.'

Breda blinked, startled. 'What? You'd leave Kilgarvan?'

'I have nothing left here,' John said quietly. 'This vicarage is too big and empty for me alone, and I would miss you and Catherine more than anything if you left. Maybe it's time for me to leave, too. They'll need clergy over there, won't they? Perhaps I could help, find a new calling, start afresh . . . just like Samuel.'

Breda's heart ached with both love for her brother and uncertainty for what lay ahead. 'You'd come with us?'

'If you'd have me,' John said with a faint smile. 'We could all be together again, as a family.'

Breda stared at him, his offer sinking in. It was a flicker of hope, a glimpse of a future where she wasn't alone. But Samuel . . . what would happen when he arrived? The bailiffs might still be a danger to him here, and there was Catherine to consider— would Samuel accept their daughter after not being told the truth? The uncertainty gnawed at Breda, but as always, her faith held strong, and she allowed herself to hope.

'Maybe, John. Maybe we will all find a way to a new life.'

Chapter 43

Ceann Mara - Friday.

Seth parked the ute where Róisín directed, just at the front of the house. The wide verandah of Ceann Mara blocked the afternoon sun, casting long shadows across the yard. Logan and Cat emerged from the house, Logan wiping his hands on his jeans, his eyes quickly scanning Seth from head to toe, sizing him up. For a moment, Róisín noticed the tension in Logan's stance, but as he took in Seth's easy smile, his shoulders relaxed.

'Seth, this is Logan,' Róisín introduced them. Logan extended his hand with a nod, no longer guarded. 'And this is my sister Caitríona,' she added, gesturing to the woman beside him. 'Usually known as Cat.'

'Welcome to *Ceann Mara*.' Cat smiled warmly. 'I hope you're ready for some real country hospitality.'

Róisín led Seth inside, showing him the downstairs guest room Cat had prepared.

His eyes widened as they entered the homestead. 'This is incredible. It is actually the original 1800s homestead?'

'Much of it.' Róisín smiled, wishing their mother was here to see his reaction. 'Mum's done a great job to make it look authentic. 'It's simple but comfortable,' she said, opening the door to the guestroom. 'There's your bathroom just through there, and towels are on the bed. Take your time. I'll be upstairs getting changed.'

Seth nodded his thanks with a smile, already peeling off his work jacket. As he headed into the bathroom, Róisín went upstairs. She closed the door behind her, leaning against it for a moment, gathering her thoughts. It felt strange, having Seth here—familiar, yet new. Nice.

As she went to her wardrobe, Cat pushed open the door without knocking, flopping down on the bed with a dreamy sigh. 'So, what's the story with this Seth?' she teased, her eyes gleaming with curiosity. 'Anything there, or just your boss?'

Heat rushed to Róisín's cheeks. 'Nothing yet,' she mumbled, trying to sound casual. 'But maybe …'

Cat laughed, raising an eyebrow. 'I knew it. Well, about time, girl. Much better than your last boss.'

Róisín quickly busied herself with changing, ignoring the teasing grin Cat was giving her. They headed back downstairs, where Seth was already waiting, looking fresh from his shower. The three of them walked up to the camp kitchen, the smell of cooking drifting in the evening air. Logan was already there frying onions before he put the meat on the barbeque. He offered Seth a beer and poured a wine for Cat and Róisín.

Róisín arranged the nibbles from the general store on a platter: cheese, olives, and crackers, listening as Seth and Logan chatted as they stood together at the barbeque. The conversation flowed easily. Logan told Seth about his time as a policeman up in Queensland, handling everything from rowdy pub fights to more serious incidents out in the bush. Seth, in turn, shared a bit about his army days—nothing too detailed, just the camaraderie and discipline, the way it shaped how he approached problems now.

'It's different work out here,' Logan admitted, sipping his beer. 'But after years of chasing after trouble, it's not so bad helping Tom with the goats and keeping this place running.'

'Yeah, it's peaceful,' Seth agreed, glancing out over the property, the rolling hills fading into dusk. 'We'll get to that water stuff tomorrow.'

'No problem,' Logan replied easily. 'Give me your email, and I'll send you everything I've got from Gary. He's the girls' uncle who owned the place before me. They moved away, and I bought the property. Built the house, but since then I've mainly been running a small herd of goats and helping Tom over here.'

Seth nodded. 'Sounds like the ideal setup.'

As the night wore on, the conversation settled into a comfortable rhythm. The firelight flickered softly as they shared more stories, enjoying each other's company. A few times, Róisín noticed Cat's considering look as she watched Seth, and she blushed when her sister gave the thumbs up.

***

The next morning, Róisín left Logan and Seth to pore over the water records for *Guntana.* They inspected the meters together, going through each detail carefully. By mid-morning, Seth was satisfied. He straightened up, dusting off his hands, and smiled as he turned to Róisín when he came back.

'No issues here; everything checks out,' he said as they made their way back to the house.

Logan and Cat came out to see Seth off as he prepared to leave.

'Thanks for everything,' Seth said, shaking Logan's hand. 'I'm sure I'll be seeing you again soon.'

Cat grinned, casting a knowing glance at Róisín. 'I'm sure you will,' she said with a wink.

Logan and Cat headed inside, leaving Seth and Róisín standing together at the car.

'So, you were happy with what Logan showed you?' she asked, trying to stay professional despite the flutter in her chest. Their relationship had changed in the social setting last night.

Seth nodded. 'Yeah, no problem at all. But let's not talk business. I've had a great half-weekend here. I love your parents' place, and I really enjoyed Logan and Cat's company. Hopefully, we can do this again sometime.'

Róisín looked up at him, her heart skipping as he held out his hand. She took it, and as their eyes met, Seth gently pulled her closer. 'I'll see you Tuesday morning when I pick you up.'

'Are you sure you don't want me to meet you at the office?' she asked, a little breathless.

'No, I'll be on my way back from Bourke, so it makes sense to get you,' he said, his voice warm. 'But let's not talk about work, Ro.'

His hand lifted, cupping her cheek. For a moment, everything around them faded. His lips met hers in a soft, lingering kiss. When he pulled away, the look in his eyes said everything words couldn't.

'I'll see you Tuesday,' he said before getting into the car and driving off.

Róisín stood there for a moment, feeling the warmth of his

kiss still on her lips. A smile spread across her face, and she knew—this time, it felt right.

Chapter 44

Ceann Mara - August 1859.

'Samuel, I cannot fathom for the life of me why you have this sudden urge to return home.' Thomas pulled tightly on the wire securing the wooden fence post he was setting at the corner of Samuel's house paddock.

Samuel was more than satisfied with the progress of the work. The building of his home over the river from *Ceann Mara* had begun a few months ago. The foundations were laid, and the timber frame was almost complete. The availability of timber from the river gums on their property hurried the building along; they had learned a lot when they had built the homestead across the river at *Ceann Mara*.

With the help of an upriver settler, Samuel had built a kiln; the natural clay of the Darling River flood plains was extremely suitable for making bricks. Enough had been made, dried in the sun and fired in his kiln. Labour had been hired, and with Thomas' supervision, the interior would be completed when he returned from his journey home.

No, he corrected himself. This was home now and always would be.

'I will return. Just once,' he replied as he reached over and took the load of the wire from Thomas.

'But why, in heaven's name, do you need to go back? It doesn't matter what Sean does there. We've done well here since our Richard's death; God rest his soul. His passing ensured that his property came to us, and we shall never want for anything in this new land. Mother has passed away, and our life is here.'

Samuel grunted as the rope strained and the fence post pulled upright. 'I don't care about Sean. From all accounts, he spends little time in County Kerry anyway.'

'For God's sake, will you tell me why you must leave? It will not be safe. You know they'll always be watching, waiting for our return.'

'It will be well, brother. You need not worry. I am sailing on the *Brucklay Castle* from Port Adelaide to Liverpool, and on the ship's manifest, I appear as Samuel Burns.'

'But you're not going anywhere near County Kerry?'

'I must,' Samuel said quietly.

'You *must*? Why, in God's name, *must* you? You realise that if something happens to you over there, I've no chance of managing the business interests you now hold. I'm a farmer, Samuel. I do not have your business skills, and I know nothing of what businesses you now hold.'

'I will be fine. I shall return.' He sent a sideways glance to his brother. Thomas' face was red and glistened with sweat. 'And I shall not return alone.'

Thomas, startled, looked at him. 'What are you saying? You will not return alone?'

'I'll be bringing a wife.'

Thomas ran one hand over his face. 'Look at me—this worry is giving me a fever. Can't you find a wife here?'

Samuel spluttered with laughter. 'I believe it is the heat of the day making you sweat. If that's all you can say to convince me to stay, you will have no success. To ease your mind, brother, I am returning to County Kerry to fetch my wife, or rather, the woman who will be my wife when we return.'

'Your wife?' Thomas paused, frowning. 'But you'll not go anywhere near *Ceann Mara* and Sean, will you?'

'You're not interested in who she is, then?' Samuel ignored his question.

'Of course I am!' Thomas said. 'Who is she?'

'Her name is Breda. Breda Atkins. Her brother is the vicar at Kilgarvan.'

'The vicar's sister? Where did you meet her?'

Samuel smiled. 'I met her in the graveyard at Kilgarvan a year before we left for Liverpool.'

'And she has agreed to marry you?'

'Yes. I would have brought her with me when we came here, but reason intervened. And I needed to be sure that we could build a successful life before asking her to join me.'

'Are you sure she hasn't married someone else?'

'No,' Samuel said firmly. 'Breda would not marry anyone else. She promised to wait for me. I told her it would be some time, as I wished to establish myself here first. I am ready to collect her, and nothing will persuade me not to.'

##

Liverpool Docks - January 1860.

As the *Brucklay Castle* neared the docks of Liverpool, Samuel O'Byrne stood at the railing, the icy wind cutting across his face. After months at sea, the thought of seeing his Breda again consumed him. She was his sole purpose for returning to County Kerry. He had imagined their reunion more times than he could count, yet alongside his anticipation was the unease and the uncertainty of what lay ahead. He rubbed his cold fingers against her last letter, the letter that had been in his pocket since he had left the Darling River.

Breda had held faith for many long years, and so must he.

Sean had written two years ago to tell Samuel and Thomas of their mother's passing. Samuel had no desire to visit *Ceann Mara* and did not intend to tell his youngest brother of his temporary return; he was well aware of the danger of returning to Ireland. He had worked hard to bury the past, but the memory of that afternoon at Lissyclearig lingered. He didn't know if the law still searched for them, but the possibility of danger was there. Returning to Irish soil could mean risking everything. He would not jeopardise their safety, even thirteen years later.

He had made a promise. He had fought too hard to build a future for Breda, and he wouldn't let fear stop him now.

He and Thomas had created a good life on their land on the Darling River. Their sheep had become very successful. The expansive plains of western New South Wales provided vast tracts of land that were ideal for grazing, and they had expanded quickly. Settlers along the river could readily draw water for their flocks, making sheep farming viable even in areas with little rainfall. Samuel had built a store on the western side of the river to take advantage of the river trade. Their good fortune and the bequest of Richard's land contributed to their successful venture, and they purchased more land each year with their profits. Samuel had commissioned a paddle steamer for his business as he had travelled along the Murray River to Port Adelaide. The steamer would be ready when they returned to Australia, as would their home.

Yet as the ship creaked closer to port, his thoughts turned back to Ireland, the place he had fled and the woman he had left behind.

Breda's letters were filled with love, but he knew her life had not been easy without him. Her brother, the vicar, had provided a home for her, but doubt tugged at him. Would she be willing to leave everything familiar for him? Her brother, her home, all she had known—to follow him to a place as distant and unknown as a sheep station on a remote river? A river that was worlds away from the clear babbling streams of County Kerry.

As the ship docked in Liverpool, Samuel took a deep breath, the salty air filling his lungs. Whatever lay ahead, he would face it. He had survived the challenges of Australia, and now he would confront his past.

A week later, he boarded the steamer in Liverpool, full of excited anticipation. The crossing was short, but each mile churned up memories the closer he got to Ireland. Stepping off in Galway, he kept his head down, blending into the crowds as just another man looking for work. Ireland had changed, but the air still felt thick with loss. The famine had passed, but he saw the empty cottages, broken stone walls, and gaunt faces hardened by hunger.

No one looked twice at a man like him. He made his way east, sometimes walking, sometimes hitching rides in carts, each mile adding to his excitement. The joy of getting closer to Breda with each mile that passed dispelled all his concerns.

By the time he reached Kilgarvan late one afternoon, his pulse was hammering in his throat. It had been almost thirteen years since the spring he had left her here.

The muddy lane to the woods wound before him, familiar and filled with happy memories. But the trees, now bare of leaf in the depth of winter, provided a sombre backdrop, lightened only by the watery sun shining from a cloudless sky. Samuel had imagined this walk a thousand times, but now that he was here, his chest felt tight, his breathing ragged.

And then he saw her.

Kneeling in the garden, just as he had pictured her in his letters. Breda's face, partially turned away, was still achingly familiar. Sitting on a garden seat close to the gate where he stood was another woman. As he moved closer, he could see she was a young girl, about the same age as Thomas and Catriona's son, James.

Samuel's breath hitched, his stomach twisting into a hard

knot as the young girl noticed him and stood. He stopped, staring, frozen by the sight of her. Dark hair, delicate features—a younger version of Breda.

But there was something else too, something of himself, staring back at him even from this distance.

He did not doubt in that instant that he was looking at his daughter, the daughter he had never known existed. A soft groan broke from his lips as a surge of regretful guilt shot through him.

Samuel stood there, his breath coming too fast, too shallow, caught between the urge to leave and the crushing need to face what he had done. He had left Breda behind and she had been with child.

He stood at the gate, breathless, as Breda worked in the garden. She was focused on her work, her hands buried in the soil, separating bulbs for spring. Eventually, she looked up, her brow furrowing in confusion as her eyes scanned the unfamiliar figure before her.

Despite his rough appearance—his beard, worn clothes, and hat pulled low over his face—there was something about him that seemed to resonate with her. And then, in an instant, her expression shifted, recognition sparking in her eyes.

'Samuel?' she whispered, her breath catching in her throat as she pushed herself to her feet. 'Oh, my dear Lord, Samuel!'

Her eyes locked onto his, and it was as if the years melted away. Samuel stood frozen, his heart racing, the world around them fading.

She lifted her hands to her face, uncertainty flickering in her eyes, and without him being aware of moving, they were in each other's arms. The familiar scent of his Breda enveloped him, a mixture of earth and warmth that brought memories he had held for so long. She buried her face in his chest, and tears soaked into his shirt as she pressed against him. It was as if no time had passed since they last held each other.

'Oh, Samuel, I have longed for this moment for so long,' she said, lifting her face to meet his gaze. Her hand reached up to caress his face. 'Look at you. Your skin is so brown, and you have a beard.'

'My love,' he murmured, an overwhelming sense of happiness filling his heart as Breda's familiar giggle erupted.

'And now you have dirt on your cheek,' she said.

Then, from behind them, a soft voice intervened.

'I'm presuming you are my da? The one we have been waiting for? My grandmother said you would come.'

Samuel slowly lifted his head and turned to see a young girl, almost as tall as Breda, watching him with wide, curious eyes.

'Your grandmother?' He frowned.

'Your mother, Samuel. She met Catherine the week before she passed.' Breda took a step away from him. 'Please don't judge me, but yes, this is Catherine, your daughter. I named her for *your* grandmother.'

His daughter. There was no mistaking it. Her eyes, the shape of her face—part of her was Breda, but much of her was unmistakably him. He reached out, his hand shaking slightly as it rested on her shoulder.

'Aye,' Samuel said softly, his voice rough with emotion. 'I'm your Da.'

Catherine tilted her head as if studying him, and then, without hesitation, she stepped closer and wrapped her arms around his waist. Samuel closed his eyes, pulling her into the embrace, feeling her heartbeat against his chest as he reached his other hand to pull Breda close. It was more than he deserved, more than he had ever dared to hope for. He held his daughter and Breda close, the years of separation and doubt melting away in that moment.

For the first time in a long while, Samuel felt whole again.

##

Kilgarvan Vicarage - A month later.

Samuel sat beside John, glancing at Breda, his wife of two weeks, as she packed the last of her mother's china into a box. She handled the fine ceramic with the same care she gave to everything in their lives. Catherine sat reading in the window seat nearby, the evening sun casting long shadows over the garden. Samuel felt a rare sense of peace, knowing his family was with him and always would be, but his mind was already turning to their departure the next day.

'You'll like the Darling,' Samuel said to John, his voice steady. 'It's good land, and the river keeps everything flowing. The Merino sheep—we've got them settled, and their wool's fetching a price in the markets you wouldn't believe. Britain can't get enough of it.'

John nodded, a quiet understanding passing between the two men. 'I know, Samuel.'

'Have you definitely decided yet, John?' Breda looked anxiously at her brother. 'You haven't changed your mind? The bishop didn't dissuade you when you met with him in Kenmare today?'

'Did you not notice, dear sister, that I have packed several boxes in my study?'

Breda chuckled. 'You know I am not allowed to touch anything in there, but yes, I was hoping.'

'I'm coming with you,' John said. 'I advised the bishop

three weeks ago, and when you were all out walking last Sunday, I told the congregation and the churchwarden.'

Samuel smiled at that. It was a relief to know John was committed. 'Good. I thought you might, but I still wasn't sure. We will have no trouble getting you a passage.'

'I will pay my way,' John said firmly.

'If you insist, but please be assured that there will be a home for you at *Luachmhaire* for as long as you wish to stay.'

'I can tend to the settlers' spiritual needs from what you have told me,' John replied. 'And there's work for me there, too. Those settlers—well, they'll need more than land and sheep. They'll need a place to gather, to pray. I could start a church there.'

Samuel's smile widened. 'Aye, that's true. We have also built a small chapel at *Ceann Mara* on the western side of the river. You'd be doing something important, something lasting.' He paused for a moment, his expression turning sombre as he continued, 'It would have been good to have a vicar there for Sinead, Thomas and Caitríona's daughter, who was stillborn and rests in the graveyard. Her absence is felt deeply, and having a proper service would have brought some comfort to us all.'

'I will say a prayer for her.' John turned back to Samuel. 'It's not just about the land, is it? It's about life being created in a new land. A place to raise families and build a church for the community.'

'That's right,' Samuel said. 'The settlers—you will see how they're scattered. The distance will be no hardship for them. A church will give them somewhere to come together.'

John nodded slowly. 'I've been thinking the same. The people need more than just work. They need faith. And I can be there for them.'

'You'll be giving them something they can't do without,' Samuel agreed. 'It's not just about surviving—it's about living, building a future. For all of us.'

He glanced at Catherine, who had wandered over again, her curiosity shining through her bright eyes.

She tugged on his sleeve, and her smooth brow was creased in a frown. 'I'm pleased Uncle John will have a church, but where will I go to school? Is there a village school?' she asked, her voice full of anticipation.

Samuel chuckled. 'I have already made plans for that, Catherine. There will be a governess at *Ceann Mara* who will teach you and your cousins. I have written to your Uncle Thomas and asked him to fill the position.'

Catherine's concern transformed into a smile, and she walked back to the window seat and settled into her book again.

'Won't that be very expensive, Samuel?' Breda asked

quietly.

'We are very comfortable on the land, my love. You will want for nothing. And that is why I have arranged for some weeks in London for you and Catherine to shop while I visit the London Wool Exchange to meet some new buyers.'

Breda came and stood by him as the last rays of sunlight began to fade. 'It sounds as though we're all going to be adjusting to something new.'

Samuel reached out and took her hand, feeling the warmth of her skin against his. 'Something new and wonderful. I cannot wait until you see *Luachmhaire.*'

Chapter 45

Guntana Station - Tuesday morning.

Róisín stood in the kitchen, her anticipation building as she heard the soft rumble of an approaching vehicle as it came in from the road. She'd worked from home yesterday because Seth was picking her up on his way south from a meeting in Bourke, and with their early departure for Wentworth tomorrow, it had made sense for him to stay the night. But the thought of him being here with her made her stomach flutter.

But in a good way.

The kettle started to steam, and she moved absently to prepare two mugs of coffee, hoping Seth would like the pods she found next to Logan and Cat's coffee machine. She focused, trying to shake off the nerves that were making her hands shake.

Despite her vow to keep things with Seth strictly professional after what had happened with Greg, it appeared she had fallen into a vulnerable position again. But this time, she knew she could trust the man who had kissed her when he'd left on Saturday morning.

Seth's gentle kiss had brought a smile to her face all weekend. He'd called her to chat on Saturday night when he reached the motel at Wilcannia, and they'd talked about all sorts of things, avoiding work topics. She knew she had to tell Seth today about the connection with Scaramouche, and she hoped it didn't destroy his trust in her. She still couldn't figure out the connection between her previous place of work and the property on the river. Greg had never had any interest in anything outside city boundaries.

Hearing the vehicle get closer, she put one of the pods in the machine and turned it on, before glancing out of the kitchen window, expecting to see the Water Authority vehicle pull in. Instead, her breath caught in her throat.

A red ute.

Her body went cold as the familiar vehicle rolled to a stop near Logan's shed. It was that guy they'd asked to leave *Ceann Mara* when he was camping illegally. The same man who had been extremely aggressive and refused to go quietly at first. What was he doing here? Looking for a campsite?

As the ute's engine stopped, Logan's dog, Molly erupted into frantic barking. Róisín stood frozen for a moment, fear tightening her chest. The last time she'd seen this man, Logan had been with her. But now she was alone, and his presence felt far more menacing than before.

A woman alone in his sort of company was risky. Logan had said he thought he was an itinerant, hiding out in various camping sites out west. At the time she'd thought "hiding" was a strange choice of word.

She watched, her pulse quickening as he stepped out of the vehicle and reached back into the cabin. Her next indrawn breath turned into a gasp as she saw the rifle he held. His posture was as hostile as she remembered, his bearded face set in a scowl. He stood there for a moment, scanning the paddocks and the house, and then slowly, his gaze moved towards the shed where her car was inside out of his line of sight.

He bypassed the shed and walked to the side fence, where the paddocks to the north stretched out in a patchwork of green and brown, the grass still wet from recent rains, and Logan's goats dotting the landscape. The scene outside was calm, but Róisín's instincts told her that something was wrong. The skin on her arms rose on gooseflesh despite the heat of the afternoon.

What was he doing here? It looked like he was casing the place.

Her hand gripped the edge of the counter as her mind raced. If he didn't see the car in the shed, he wouldn't know she was here.

Molly's barking escalated, snarling at the intruder, but he didn't seem to care. He walked towards the shed, slow and deliberate, as if he had all the time in the world. A surge of panic raced through her. She backed away from the window, her heart hammering in her chest. Should she call Logan? Or Seth, to see how close he was?

She grabbed her phone off the counter, her hands trembling. Whatever this man wanted, it wasn't good. She needed someone here. And fast. She pressed speed dial for Cat, and to her relief, her sister picked up straight away.

'Cat! Is Logan around?' Róisín whispered as she held the phone tightly and went back and stood at the side of the kitchen window, watching him look around. He walked past the shed and didn't open the door, so he still didn't know if anyone was there. He wouldn't be expecting her anyway; he'd seen her over at Mum and Dad's place.

'Yeah, what's up? You sound odd.'

'That guy's here.' She kept her voice low.

'Which guy?'

'The guy in the red ute drove in and he's poking around outside.'

'Where are you?'

'Inside. He hasn't seen me yet.'

'Okay, lock yourself in and stay there. Logan's in the shed. We'll come straight over.'

'Be careful. He's carrying a rifle.'

'Hide inside,' Cat said, her voice full of concern.

As she looked out, he'd disappeared around the side of the house. She stood there for a moment, thinking hard. Both front and back doors were unlocked but closed. If she locked the back door, and he was close, he'd hear the lock snick, and then he'd know someone was inside.

Come on, Seth, please get here.

She looked out the front, and there was no sign of the guy. Maybe he was walking down to the river to look for a campsite. Now she worried about Cat and Logan bumping into him.

Maybe she could get to her car while he was gone and drive out and meet Seth?

Or was she overreacting? But why was he carrying a gun?

Leaving the front door unlocked so she could get out quickly, she crept to the laundry to look out the back and lock the door.

She screamed as the door swung open, and before she could react, strong hands grabbed her shoulders. He spun her around before one hand clamped over her mouth. She tried to scream, but his dirty hand stifled it.

'Shut up.'

Panic surged as she fought against him, but he was stronger, dragging her backwards into the kitchen.

'Missy, we're going on a little trip,' he said, the smell of sweat and dirt overwhelming her.

Róisín's heart raced as she struggled against him, adrenaline coursing through her veins. She opened her mouth, moved her head slightly and bit down on his fingers, the sour taste of his skin making her gag.

'Let me go!' she tried to shout, but her voice was muffled against his hand. She kicked and squirmed, desperate to escape, but he held her firmly, one arm around her and the other over her mouth. She wondered where the rifle was. With that not here, she had a chance to fight.

'Stop moving, or I'll make it worse for you,' he growled. In a fit of fear-fuelled determination, she elbowed him hard in the gut. For a brief moment, his grip lessened, and she thought she might have a chance. But then he retaliated, removing his hand from her mouth and forming a tight fist. She screamed as he drew his fist back, extending his arm.

***

Róisín reached out for her water bottle at the side of the bed, but for some reason, the table was further away than she thought, and she couldn't reach it. She waved her hand around, and her headache got worse. She had been having the most awful dreams, and she was busting to go to the bathroom. She tried to roll over, but for some reason, she couldn't move. She frowned. Her bed wasn't against the wall, but she was wedged against the wall as she became fully conscious. She wasn't in her bed, and the events from some time ago—she didn't know how long she'd been here—came flooding back.

She tried to sit up and gagged as the pain in her head increased. She closed her eyes and focused. She was in the back of the red ute. Light filtered in from a couple of high openings on each wall, and her head rested on some sort of rag that smelled like oil. She lifted a shaking hand to her right temple, and her fingers came away sticky. She had enough awareness to put her hand in front of her nose, and she could smell the metallic odour of blood.

Focus. Focus. Try to remember what happened, she urged herself, fear coursing through her. She pushed herself to remember. She lay there for a moment, her head pounding as the constant hum of wheels surrounded her; the vehicle was on a rough road. Gradually, snippets of the events came back to her. The red ute. He'd been in the yard, around the house, and he had a gun. He'd come through the back door, and he'd lifted his arm.

He must have punched her.

She remembered trying to hide and then, with great relief, recalled talking to Cat on the phone. At least they knew it was the guy in the red ute.

Her heart pounded with a mix of terror and defiance; they must have already travelled away from *Guntana*. She could hear cars driving past constantly; there wasn't that much traffic on the *Guntana* road.

Where was she?

She closed her eyes and drifted off again for a few minutes.

Or more.

Or less.

Her head was spinning, and she wasn't thinking straight.

Blinking rapidly, she looked around the confined space; she was confined in the solid dog cage on the back of the ute. The air was stale—the vents were small—and panic gripped her heart.

'Help! Someone help me!' she screamed, her cries echoing in the confined space.

She clawed at the walls; each movement filled with desperate energy. 'You won't get away with this!' she shouted, hoping someone would hear her.

Where were Cat and Logan, and Seth? She needed to stay calm and find a way out before he drove too far away.

Her mouth dried as the vehicle slowed and the motor stopped. A door slammed, and footsteps crunched on gravel, and the back of the ute creaked open.

The guy stood at the back, a sinister smile playing on his lips. 'I told you, Missy, it's a long trip. Just relax, will you? Stop yelling. No one can hear you.'

She closed her eyes to rest for a moment; her stomach gripped with fear until she drifted into unconsciousness.

When she opened her eyes again, she could hear that the ute was still on a dirt road.

The sound of a bolt sliding roused Róisín the next time, and the back of the ute opened with a clang. Bright light flooded the dark interior, and she put her hand up to her eyes.

'Oh, so we're properly awake this time, are we?' he said, holding a flashlight in her face. 'Nice bump on your head.'

She stared at the man, forcing her fear back. That wouldn't help her; she might be trapped, but she wasn't going anywhere without a fight.

'What did you do to me? What did you give me? Where am I?'

'I didn't give you anything apart from a bit of a clout on the head because you were fighting and biting me like a little bitch.'

'What do you want? Is this payback because we wouldn't let you stay on our property.'

'Is that what you think this is all about? I got off when that bloke of yours told me to.'

'What bloke?'

'The one you were with. He came back to see me a second time, and he made me very, very angry, but I left. It wasn't time to get you then.'

'Get me? How did you know I was across the river? What do you want with me?'

'Got a tracker on your car,' he bragged. 'Apparently, you're in a lot of trouble, sweetheart. I've got to deliver you to a friend of yours.'

She swallowed, the dry metallic taste of blood filling her mouth as fear overwhelmed her. 'I've got no idea what you're talking about. What friend?'

'Your friend in Brisbane.'

'I don't know what you mean.' She couldn't see his face; all she could make out was the shadow of his bulk in the space. 'I need to go to the toilet.'

'I thought you might. If it was up to me, I'd chuck you in the river, but your friend is paying me a nice little bonus if I deliver you intact. Then again, he's pretty pissed off. Maybe you won't see home again.'

Róisín's head spun with his words. 'Honestly, I have no idea what you're talking about or who you're talking about. You've made a big mistake. Can you please just let me go?'

'And miss out on thirty grand? Not a hope in hell, sweetheart.'

She fought back the rising fear again and lifted her chin. It made her head hurt more. 'I said I need to go to the bathroom.'

'There's no bathrooms out here, so don't do anything stupid.' He grabbed her ankle and slid her out the back of the ute. Her legs hung over the side, and she gripped the edges, trying to sit up, but her head was spinning.

'You're going to have to help me out. My head is giddy.'

'Jesus Christ,' he muttered. Rough hands grabbed her wrist and jerked her up. Excruciating pain shot down the back of her head and into her neck.

She whimpered, putting her hands up to her eyes as the flashlight seared her vision before he flicked it over to the dark. They were parked in a paddock near a river, but it wasn't the Darling River. 'Where are we? I'm not home.'

'You've been out of it for ages. I checked on you a couple of times. Made sure you were still alive. You worried me there for a while. I thought you'd carked it.'

'Please let me go to the toilet,' she whimpered.

'I'll give you a bit of privacy. There are two trees over there.'

Róisín managed to keep standing when he let go of her. She took a deep breath and turned. She could see the trees in the distance. Her vision was hazy, but she put that down to the bright light more than the injury to the back of her head. She didn't think she had a concussion—maybe she did. The headache was bad enough. Her thoughts cleared as she took deep breaths and walked toward the trees. At one stage, she stopped and turned around; her stomach clenched in fear as she saw him standing there, rifle pointed at her.

'No funny business!' he yelled.

She stepped behind the trees and squatted down. The relief of an empty bladder reinvigorated her. She waited there a little longer, looking at the river. It was a wide river, and she could see something strange ahead, like a weir. It definitely wasn't anywhere she'd been before.

She grabbed the bark of the tree as she stood, rearranged her clothing, and stepped out. Shakily, she made her way back to the ute.

'Where are we?' she asked.

'Well, you've got no phone, and you can't tell anyone

where you are, so it won't hurt, I suppose. That's the Balonne River. We've just crossed the border, and we're near St. George.'

'I've never been here before,' she said.

'Doesn't matter to me either way. We're not staying here.'

'Where are you taking me?'

'I told you. I'm taking you to Brisbane.'

'Has this got anything to do with Greg?'

'Loverboy Greg Henderson? You're not as dumb as I thought you were.'

'You mean Greg got you to do this? To take me to him? Why couldn't he have just rung me? I would've gone to see him if it was this desperate.'

'Yeah, but then you would be the boss of yourself and could've left when you wanted. I don't know that you'll be leaving to come home again. He's not a happy camper.'

He pushed her over to the back of the ute. 'Can I please ride up front with you?'

His laugh was loud and nasty. 'What, and give you the opportunity to wave for help and climb out when I stop for fuel? Get a life, sweetheart. Get in the back.'

'I can't climb up there.' She regretted saying that immediately as his beefy hands grabbed her rear and hoisted her up onto the tray. Her elbow hit the back, and she felt a trickle of blood as a sharp piece of metal sliced it open.

'If you want me to get to Greg in one piece,' she snarled, 'I need water, and I need something to eat.'

'What a princess,' he muttered.

The back door slammed up, and he pulled down the overhanging hatch. 'I'll get you something. Just wait there.'

Only seconds later, the top opened again, and a cold bottle of water and a muesli bar were thrown at her. She went to say thank you but thought, no, I'm not giving him the courtesy of a response. If she could get water and food into her, and get rid of this blasted headache, she was going to find a way to get away from him—whatever it took.

Chapter 46

Guntana Station - Tuesday morning.

Seth whistled as he drove toward *Guntana* to collect Róisín for their second road trip. He left Wilcannia before dawn, the thrill of anticipation surging through him. Thoughts of her danced in his mind—her laughter, her quick wit, the way her eyes sparkled when she spoke about her work. The feel of her soft lips beneath his.

But then, out of the morning mist, a kangaroo bounded into the road. He slammed on the brakes, heart pounding.

'Focus on the road,' he muttered to himself, remembering Róisín's warning not to leave too early and to watch out for kangaroos. He was keen to get there and pick her up.

'Remember, Seth,' he reminded himself. This is work, not a holiday.'

When he'd first arrived in Wilcannia, the quiet hadn't bothered him. But when Róisín arrived, filling the office with her smiling face, intelligence, and quick wit, the days had become full. The weekend alone in Wilcannia seemed to take days to pass, and he ploughed through a lot of work to fill in the time.

Just because he found her attractive and fun to be with didn't mean he could put the investigation at the bottom of his list.

Debra was fun to work with, too, but strangely, he didn't miss her on the weekends like he missed Róisín. He had to take a moment to think about where his thoughts were heading. He'd learned the hard way in Canberra, but he knew Róisín was a totally different person from Sharon.

His eyes had soon opened to the fact that Sharon wasn't just after a relationship; she was using him and his position to get a promotion in the squadron. It hurt for a long time because he had cared for her, and the thought of being used hit him hard.

At first, he had wondered about Róisín and her motives for being there, but he was totally convinced now that he could trust her. She contributed to the investigation, and when planning their routes for visiting the properties, her knowledge of some of the landowners had been invaluable.

On this second trip, they were planning to travel as far south as Wentworth. Even though she wasn't as familiar with that section of the Darling River, her research and phone calls had made the organisation easy for him.

As he neared the sign on the eastern side of the river, six kilometres from town, he took a deep breath, refocusing his mind on the task ahead. This trip was important, and he couldn't afford any distractions. But that little voice in his head was relentless, reminding him that it was hard to resist daydreaming about Róisín when he was so attracted to her.

Seth's excitement ramped up as he approached *Guntana*. He could picture her welcoming smile, the way her eyes would hold his. But the drive demanded his attention; he forced himself to focus. The investigation was important, and he couldn't let his feelings cloud his judgment. As he drove down to the small timber house she'd described, nervous energy coursed through him.

Seth ran lightly up the three steps and rang the bell hanging at the side of the door, expecting Róisín to be waiting. When there was no answer, he frowned, assuming she might be in the bathroom. He glanced at his watch; she knew he'd be arriving about now.

He wandered around the outside of the house, noticing the track she'd mentioned leading toward the punt. They hadn't needed to come over to the house on Friday night when he'd been at *Ceann Mara*. It seemed peaceful out there, but unease soon settled in. After a few minutes of waiting, he rang the bell again, this time for a bit longer, and a bit harder.

'Róisín, I'm here.'

Then he noticed the door was slightly ajar. Pushing it open gently, he called out her name again. The silence that followed sent a chill down his spine.

Seth stepped further inside, his eyes landing on the coffee machine and two cups on the counter. A rush of concern flooded through him as he called her name again, louder this time: 'Róisín!'

Silence answered, amplifying his concern.

He moved towards the back door and noticed it was wide open, the gentle breeze ruffling the curtains over a stainless-steel laundry tub. A prickling sensation crept up his spine. The peacefulness of the surroundings felt deceptive now, and his instincts screamed that something was very wrong.

He walked up the steps leading to a bedroom and bathroom, peering into both. The doors were open, revealing an unsettling emptiness. His gaze fell on her half-packed suitcase and handbag sitting on the bed. He went to call out for her again, but a quiet dread gripped him, urging him to move faster, to find her.

As Seth stepped outside through the back door and headed around the shadowed side of the house, a commanding voice echoed through the air. 'Stop right there!'

He recognised Logan's voice and went to turn around.

'Put your hands up. Where's Róisín?'

Seth complied, raising his hands, the panic rising in his throat. 'Logan, it's me, Seth. I'm looking for her,' he said quickly.

His heart racing, he turned slowly to Logan, who was levelling a rifle in his direction.

'I haven't seen her. I came to pick her up. She's not here. I was just going to walk down to the river to see if she was there.'

His eyes caught a glimmer in the dirt—her phone. Fear washed over him as he realised the implications.

'Jesus, Seth, I didn't know it was you from the back.' Logan put the gun by his side and ran over as Seth bent to pick up the phone. 'She rang us. There was trouble.' He hurried around the front, looking around. 'Shit, he's gone, and I bet he's taken her.'

'Who?' Seth demanded. 'What are you talking about?'

'A guy who caused us some trouble a couple of weeks back.' As he spoke, Cat appeared at the side of the house, panting.

'Is she here?' Her voice was shrill.

'No.'

'What sort of trouble?' Seth asked. 'Why didn't Róisín

mention it?'

'He's an ex-crim who was hanging around *Ceann Mara*.'

'How did you know he's an ex-crim?' Cat put her hands to her mouth. 'What didn't you tell us, Logan?'

'I think we underestimated him.' Logan put the gun down and put his arms around Cat. 'Stay calm. I'll tell you more later. Right now, we have to find Róisín.' He turned to Seth. 'You didn't happen to see a red ute on your trip up, did you?'

Seth nodded. 'I did. He tore past me, heading this way about fifty ks back when I stopped for a break.'

'You didn't see it again as you came from the south?'

'No.'

'Well, he's obviously headed north.'

'I'll go after him.'

'No, he's too dangerous,' Logan said. 'I'll call the police. We've got his number plate.'

Cat put her hands over her face. 'Why. What's happening?'

All Seth could think of was the warning he'd given her the first day in the office. 'Cutting off their cash flow could make them dangerous. You'll be in the crosshairs like the rest of us.'

Chapter 47

Lockyer Valley - late Tuesday night.

It was pitch dark hours later when he pulled into a service station on the highway. Róisín could see the lights of the bowsers and the service centre with the café when he got out of the car. She heard the bowser start up, and when he was done, he got back in the car and moved it, obviously going to pay and maybe grab something to eat. As she thought about that, her stomach gurgled.

He parked the car in a dark area at the back of the garage, where only one faint light shone. When she heard him get out, she tapped on the back window. He came around.

'Don't you dare yell out,' he said. 'There'll be trouble.'

'I need to take something for my headache,' she said. 'And I need to go to the toilet. I mean, I really need to go.'

He stood there quietly for a minute, then walked to the front of the ute. He came back and handed her a bottle of water and a rag.

'Wash your face, clean your hands, and sort your clothes out a bit. I'll take you inside, but if you so much as speak to anyone or indicate in any way there's a problem, I've got a gun in my pocket, and I'll shoot the first person I see in that service centre. Is that clear?'

She nodded. 'Yes. I just need to go to the toilet, get something to eat, and I need some Panadol.'

'I'll take you to the toilet, and I'll wait outside the door.'

Róisín lowered her head as he linked his arm through hers, walking her around the side of the garage. He took her other hand and placed it over his pocket. 'Feel that? That's a gun. I wasn't bullshitting. Any trouble, someone dies.'

'Okay, I believe you.'

They didn't attract any curious looks when they walked into the garage. She could see the sign for the toilets in the back left-hand corner, opposite the food section filled with tables and chairs. A couple of truckies sat there eating meals, and in the other corner was an older couple—likely from the caravan she noticed when they walked around the side.

'One step out of line, that old lady gets it. Got me?'

'Yes. I just need to go to the toilet. Can you get me some Panadol and a sandwich?'

'No way, love. I'll be waiting outside the corridor while

you do whatever you gotta do.'

As they walked through the café, Róisín noticed a curious look from the older lady sitting with the grey-haired gentleman. The woman leaned over and spoke to her partner as they passed, but Róisín couldn't hear what was said. He pushed her down the corridor until they reached the door of the ladies.

'I'll wait out here. Don't be long.'

Her hands shook uncontrollably as she entered the restroom. There were three cubicles and one basin. She looked around—nothing she could use, nowhere to go. In the corner of the last cubicle was a bucket, a mop, and some cleaning materials. She quickly grabbed the bottle of spray. Could she spray his eyes? Too risky—would he pull the gun and shoot loudly, endangering lives?

As she stood, frozen with indecision, the door opened. She jumped and hurried into a cubicle, but it wasn't him. It was the older woman from the café.

The woman went to speak, but Róisín shook her head wildly and pressed her fingers to her lips.

No, no, don't speak. The woman nodded and mouthed to her: *Do you need help?* Róisín nodded. The woman disappeared into the cubicle.

After a couple of minutes, the older woman flushed the toilet, washed her hands, and, as she walked out, pointed Róisín toward the cubicle door.

'Get in there,' she whispered close to her ear.

Róisín heard the woman speak to him outside. 'Not a good look standing outside the ladies' loo, mate.'

This was no frail old woman—she had backbone.

Róisín's eyes widened as she spotted the broken window above the cistern in the cubicle the woman had sent her into. If she stood on the toilet, she could climb up and push herself out. Ignoring the jagged edges of glass, she flushed the toilet, making a noise as if she were vomiting.

'Hurry up.' He pounded on the door and then stopped, obviously realising he was drawing attention to them.

'I need to vomit again,' she called out, climbing onto the cistern and pushing herself through the narrow opening. She balanced on the frame, the glass cutting her hands. Thank God for all those gym classes, she thought, and swung down, letting go just centimetres above the ground.

Without looking back, she took off. The service centre was isolated in the middle of the highway and only dimly lit at the back. Heart pounding, Róisín scrambled behind the garage and spotted the older couple walking towards their car.

'Please help me, help me!' she whispered urgently, grabbing the woman's hand.

'Quick!' the woman said, leading her behind the caravan so they wouldn't be seen. 'We were going to call the police. I knew there was something wrong.'

The man pulled out a set of keys, unlocked the caravan door, and said, 'In, quickly!'

Róisín darted inside. The door slammed shut, and she heard the lock click. Minutes later, the van was on the highway. Tears of relief streamed down her face.

What happens now? she wondered. She wasn't ready for the police, not yet. She had something to do first.

***

Alan—she knew them now as Alan and Marilyn—had driven for about an hour until Alan pulled over and said he was absolutely sure the brute wasn't following the caravan. He said that when he pulled out of the service centre, there was no sign of the big man in the café either, and he assumed he was still waiting for her in the corridor.

Róisín was so relieved to have escaped that she could barely speak when they unlocked the van's door.

Marilyn switched on the light near the step, her eyes widening as she looked at Róisín. 'Oh my God, sweetheart, you're covered in blood.'

'I'm so sorry for the mess I made in your caravan.' Róisín's hands and arms were lacerated from climbing out the window, and she had a big cut on the side of her hip that wouldn't stop bleeding.

'That's not a worry at all. It'll clean up. We just need to get you patched up and get you to a police station.'

She shook her head. 'No, please don't do that. If you do, it's going to mean . . . I need to get to my friend's house. It's a safe house. She's a lawyer and works with women in trouble.'

She wanted them to think it was a domestic violence situation. They wouldn't know she had been in the back of that ute for who knew how many kilometres. She noticed the road sign outside the caravan and realised they were only about forty or fifty kilometres from Ipswich, where Megan lived. She was so lucky they hadn't gone any further because she was sure Greg was waiting for her. Apparently, he'd paid his thug thirty thousand to bring her home.

For the life of her, she couldn't understand why. Was it to do with Linda's situation and Megan representing her? Was it Greg's pride being hurt over her leaving him? Or was it something to do with their sniffing around Scaramouche, which she was really starting to wonder if Greg was involved in?

Two hours later, Alan and Marilyn said goodbye as Megan

met them at the end of a quiet street in Gatton.

Róisín's fingers and arms were covered in Band-Aids, and she had a plaster on her hip. Marilyn had wanted to give her clean clothes, but Róisín hugged her. 'It's fine. Thank you for helping me. I don't know how to thank you for what you've done.'

'I think we might've saved you from a nasty situation by the look of that guy you were with. Next time, Rose . . .' Marilyn paused. Róisín still hadn't given them her real name at this point. 'You choose more wisely, okay?'

She nodded but made sure to get their name, address, and phone number before they left. One day, she would go see them and tell them everything. She was certain they had saved her life.

Megan's face was set as they drove from Gatton to Ipswich, Róisín beside her, shivering from the aftermath of fear. When Megan noticed the lump on the side of her forehead, she insisted on taking her to see her friend, who was a doctor, to be checked for concussion.

'Don't worry, it's all confidential. If we need to go to emergency, we'll deal with that as it comes.' But after the doctor examined her, she was cleared.

'Just keep an eye on her when she's asleep,' the woman said to Megan. 'Make sure she doesn't sleep too deeply. Keep waking her up. And tomorrow, it wouldn't hurt to go to the hospital and get checked out properly.'

When they got back to Megan's house, she sat Róisín down and gave her a strong, hot coffee. 'That'll help keep you awake anyway. What do you want to do now?'

'I need to make a phone call, then I need to have a shower, and after that, I need to go into the city.'

'The city? What the hell for? You're not driving in this state.'

'I need to get into the city,' Róisín repeated. 'As soon as I can.'

'Okay, make your phone call. You haven't got your phone, obviously.'

'No.'

'Use mine. I'll give you some privacy.'

Chapter 48

Megan's house, Ipswich – Tuesday, midnight.

Róisín sat on the edge of Megan's couch, her heart racing as she dialled Seth's number. The ringing felt like an eternity, each tone echoing her anxiety. When he finally answered, relief flooded though her and tears filled her eyes.

'Thank God, Ro! What happened? Where are you?' Seth's voice held alarm.

'That's not important right now. I just wanted you to know I'm safe,' she replied, trying to keep her tone steady. 'Tell Cat and Logan.'

'They're with me. I'll put you on speakerphone.'

Róisín could hear the shuffle of movement, then Cat's voice broke through. She was crying.

'Oh, Ro! Are you alright?'

'I am,' Ro reassured her, though her limbs felt like lead, and her head was throbbing.

Logan's voice came next, sharp and probing. 'What happened?'

'I got away from him. I'm at Megan's now.'

Seth's voice was urgent. 'We've got his number plate, Ro.'

Her stomach twisted. 'He changed it. He did that before we reached the highway. The new one is a Victorian plate, IPV 323.'

Logan repeated the number, his tone steady. 'We're on it. Well done, love.'

'Give me the address you're at. I'll leave now,' Seth insisted.

'Megan's house is in Ipswich,' Ro said, hoping that Seth's care was personal and not professional. After the events of the day, her emotions were jangling.

'We'll come too,' Cat chimed in. 'I want to make sure you're okay.'

'I'm okay, Cat. Really, I am,' Ro assured her, but her hands were shaking so much she could barely hold the phone. 'Seth, I need to tell you something in case something else happens. Scaramouche is a company belonging to Greg Henderson, my old boss.'

Róisín's heart dropped. She heard Seth's sharp intake of breath and she hurried to explain. 'And before you think I knew, I didn't. Now I know why he's been after me. Not just because of Linda.'

'I don't know anything about this, Ro. What are you talking about? Who's Linda? And of course, I know you're not involved,' Seth said, his voice firm but concerned.

'Cat knows about Linda. Ask her,' Ro replied, her voice dulling as a wave of fatigue washed over her. Her head ached, and she wanted nothing more than to close her eyes. 'I have to do something tonight, but I'll be back at Megan's by the time you get here.'

Megan stepped into the room, determination in her eyes. 'I'm going to drive you to the city.'

'No—' Ro started, but Logan interrupted, his voice rising. 'Ro, don't you go doing anything stupid!'

'I need to know,' she said simply, her resolve hardening. 'I'll see you tomorrow at Megan's.'

She disconnected before they could ask her what she was doing.

Chapter 49

Brisbane city - Wednesday, 1.30 a.m.

As Megan drove into the city, Róisín remained silent, her mind racing with the possible consequences of her decision. The glow of the expressway lights flickered above them, casting fleeting shadows in the car. Each flash was disorienting, increasing her unease.

She pressed her hand to her mouth instinctively as nausea threatened to rise. Megan glanced over, concern on her face. 'Are you okay?'

'I'm fine,' Róisín lied, her voice barely above a whisper.

'You know this is a foolish plan, Ro,' Megan said, her tone gentle yet firm.

Róisín turned to look out the window, the blurred city lights reflecting her turmoil. She had to know. She had to confront whatever awaited her, no matter the risk. Deep down, she understood the danger, but the urgency of the situation eclipsed her fears. As they continued down the highway, an unsettling mix of resolve and dread settled in her chest.

'I know,' Róisín replied, her voice trembling slightly. 'But I have to know. For me. For Linda.' Her words hung in the air, her determination evident.

Megan nodded, her expression turning serious. 'I understand. Just be bloody careful.'

Róisín appreciated Megan's concern, but the urgency of her intended actions overshadowed her fears. She needed answers, and she was willing to face whatever dangers lay ahead to uncover the truth.

'If the building code has changed, I won't be able to get in, and I'll come home with you,' Róisín said, her voice tinged with anxiety as they approached their destination.

Soon, they turned onto Coronation Drive. The city lights flickered around them, and the parking lot was nearly empty since it was well past midnight.

'Can I come in with you?' Megan asked, glancing at Róisín with concern.

'No, you wait here. If I'm not out in an hour, call the police again.'

'Oh, Ro, do you have to?' Megan's voice wavered. 'Can't you wait for them to get here before you go in?'

Róisín's resolve hardened; no matter how ill she felt, she would do this.

'I do. I need to make amends for my poor judgment. I need proof. Once Greg finds out I got away, he'll be in here destroying any evidence. I just hope he doesn't know already. We've wasted time. I should have come straight here. I'm hoping that fat bastard who took me is too much of a coward to tell him I escaped.'

Megan's silence spoke volumes as Róisín steeled herself for what lay ahead.

Megan had lent her a pair of black jeans and a black T-shirt. Pulling a baseball cap over her head, Róisín tucked her hair under it.

'Take care, Ro. I'll keep an eye out,' Megan said, her concern evident.

As Róisín approached the familiar office building, a surge of adrenaline mixed with fear filled her with energy. Putting the code into the office pad felt strange, but she focused on the task at hand. A grim smile crossed her face when the door clicked open, and she stepped into the dark foyer. She avoided the lift; it would be a dead giveaway. Dead, she thought, the word echoing ominously in her mind.

She made her way up the fire stairs, her ears attuned for

any sound. The tension kept her taut, easing the headache from the painkillers she'd been popping like lollies for the past three hours. When she reached the third floor, she pressed her ear against the door. All was quiet.

Cautiously, she opened it. To her satisfaction, the office was shrouded in darkness. She knew exactly where to go; Greg had a small filing cabinet in his ensuite. She had seen it once when she used the bathroom there, and she was determined to uncover whatever evidence she could find.

As much as Greg thought he was an ace businessman, he had little knowledge of technology and depended on others for that. Róisín was certain the files she was looking for would be printed documents stored in that filing cabinet. She quietly opened the top drawer of his desk and pulled out the keys she knew were in there.

Slipping into the bathroom and turning the dim recessed light above the vanity on, her heart raced as she tried key after key, frustration mounting until the last key clicked and unlocked the cabinet. Opening the drawer, she was pleased to see each file clearly marked. Of course, it wasn't labelled 'Scaramouche,' but the folder marked **QUEEN** in uppercase was a dead giveaway.

She pulled it out and glanced at the contents in the dim light. As soon as she saw the code for the water licenses, she knew she was on the right track. A grim satisfaction filled her as she closed the filing cabinet, locked it again and turned the light off. But she froze when she heard the door to Greg's office open, and voices drifted into the small bathroom.

Her heart pounded as she slipped the keys into her pocket, looking around wildly. The shower? No, the screen was glass. Within seconds, she'd quietly opened the toilet door and slipped inside. Thank God she'd locked the drawer; she'd left no trace of anyone having been in the office—unless they went looking for the keys. But she knew that Greg had a set of keys to the cabinet on his car keys.

Róisín held her breath, listening intently and fighting back nausea.

Please don't open the desk drawer. The voices outside grew louder, and she could hear Greg's unmistakable tone mingled with an unfamiliar voice. She pressed her back against the cool tiles, willing her racing heart to settle. Time felt suspended as she waited for the voices to fade, praying that she wouldn't be discovered.

The other man's voice was louder as they opened the door to the ensuite. 'I told you she was trouble as soon as she got that job in the west. I still think they planted her here, and you bloody lived with the bitch.'

'I told you, she knows nothing, John,' Greg replied, his

voice whiny.

'If that's the case, we're alright. If not, this will all go to shit, and we'll end up in jail. You've been a total fool keeping paper files, and this is a fucking stupid place to keep them. In the bloody bathroom.'

'I'm the only one who uses this bathroom.'

'I don't care if the King of England uses it; it was bloody stupid. Now, get them all out. I'm taking them with me.'

'For fuck's sake, John. I told you why. I don't trust computers.'

'These are going in the shredder tonight.'

'And what about the files on your computer?'

'Don't worry about them. The only issue now is washing the cash from the load coming in from Colombia tomorrow. And finding that bitch.'

Róisín stifled a gasp and squeezed her eyes shut. She leaned on the wall, only a flimsy door between her and death. If only she'd thought to flick the lock, but there was no way to fix that now. She would have to wait here as quiet as a mouse and risk it.

She heard the filing cabinet open, followed by Greg's sharp breath. 'What's wrong?' the other guy asked.

'Nothing,' Greg said.

'Are they all there?'

She heard the hesitation in Greg's voice, and she knew he'd noticed the file was missing. 'Yes, I think so.'

'Are they all there?'

He didn't answer this time.

'Show me the Scaramouche file.'

'I mustn't have printed that one out,' Greg said.

Róisín could see the light from the bathroom shining under the toilet door. She held her breath until she thought she was going to burst, and then the drawer closed. The bathroom door shut, and the light went out. She sat there, still holding her breath, until she absolutely had to inhale.

Thank God. They were leaving. She drew in a long, slow, silent breath.

A moment later, three shots rang out, and she forced herself to stay there as fear flooded through her. She heard a thud. 'Stupid bastard,' the other guy said.

Róisín's heart raced. What had just happened? She needed to stay hidden, but the instinct to flee surged through her. Every second felt like an eternity as she tried to steady her breathing, focusing on the dark, cramped space around her. The situation was spiralling out of control, and she knew she had to act quickly.

The door closed, and then all was quiet. Róisín held her

breath, straining to hear any movement beyond the door. The silence felt oppressive, each second stretching out as she lowered herself onto the closed toilet lid. She couldn't shake the feeling that she was still in danger, and her mind raced with thoughts of what could happen.

What if they were still in the building, searching for her? She had to think and plan her next move carefully. As she waited, she considered her options: stay hidden and wait for an opportunity to escape, or risk it and try to slip out now while the coast seemed clear. The tension in her body was palpable, the lack of sound from the adjacent room feeding her anxiety.

Finally, after what felt like an eternity, she carefully eased the bathroom door open a crack to see if he had actually left or if it was a trap. Silence surrounded her, dense and suffocating. Each breath tightened her chest more, and nausea churned in her stomach. Scared out of her wits from the shots she'd heard ring out, she dreaded opening the door and going back into the office—she knew what was waiting for her there, but she didn't know who it was.

Chapter 50

Megan's house, Ipswich - Wednesday morning.

The seemingly endless journey crawled as they drove towards Brisbane. It seemed like days had passed instead of hours. They were in Cat's parents' Land Cruiser, which was spacious and comfortable. It was ideal for the long distance, with its extended fuel tanks allowing for fewer stops. Cat was curled up in the backseat, asleep, when Logan took over the driving from Seth.

Seth stared at Google Maps on his phone, counting off each kilometre as they drove. The glow from the screen illuminated his worried expression.

'Hang in there, mate. She'll be fine. We would have heard otherwise if not,' Logan said, trying to reassure him.

Seth shook his head, the anxiety churning in his stomach. 'I feel responsible.'

'It's not your doing; it's the criminals involved,' Logan replied. He had been listening intently as Seth outlined the situation to him after Cat had fallen asleep. Ro had confided in Cat about Linda, and Greg's actions, which made Seth's blood boil.

'I'm going to go looking for this bloke after I make sure Róisín is alright,' Seth said, determination creeping into his voice.

Logan shook his head, his expression serious. 'I know how you feel, but leave it in the hands of the police. I've made a few calls. They'll be looking for him now.'

As the landscape blurred past the windows, Seth hoped and prayed that Róisín hadn't gone looking for that lowlife.

At twelve minutes past ten, they arrived at Megan's house. Logan was behind the wheel, and Seth was out of the Land Cruiser the moment they pulled up. He moved through the gate and reached the front door in seconds, his heart racing with concern. The door swung open, revealing a dark-haired woman.

'You must be Megan,' Seth said, his voice tight with concern. 'Where is she? Is she safe?'

Megan gave him a reassuring nod, placing a hand gently on his arm. 'She's here, safe, and asleep in my spare room.'

'Is she okay?' Seth asked, his voice softening with worry.

Megan paused for a moment, her eyes searching his. 'Yes,

but she's pretty traumatised.'

By this time, Logan and Cat had caught up and stood just behind Seth at the front door. Megan invited them all in and led them to the living room.

'Come in here and sit down,' she said as they followed her, 'I'll tell you what happened.'

Megan recounted the events of the night before, her voice steady but tinged with tension. 'I waited in the car around the corner, but I was about to go in search of her; she'd given me the building code. Two guys went in, and only one came out. I called the police again when I saw the two guys go in. I was just getting out of the car when four police cars came screaming to a stop, officers rushing from their cars. She'd called them from the office. Two guys went in, only one came out.' Megan said, her voice steady but filled with tension.

Seth's stomach tightened as he listened, relief and fear swirling inside him. Megan's calm delivery helped steady him, but knowing what Róisín had been through filled him with a fierce need to make sure she never had to endure such danger again.

Seth felt a rush of anxiety tightening his chest. 'One, what happened? Did Ro have to talk to Greg?'

'No.'

'What about the police? Did they speak to her?'

Megan nodded. 'Yes, I was surprised they let her come home with me last night. She has to go into Roma Street this morning to speak to the detectives.'

'Why?' Seth frowned, his concern deepening. 'What happened?'

Megan's voice shook slightly as she continued. 'Because they'd already arrested the other guy. He shot Greg.'

'Shot Greg?' Seth's heart sank. 'What happened?' His mind raced with possibilities, but he stayed silent, listening, his jaw clenched.

'Is Róisín hurt? Is she okay?' Cat's voice was filled with panic.

'Yes,' Megan quickly reassured her. 'She's fine . . . physically. But she witnessed a murder. Greg's murder. She called the police as we were driving in, and then she called them from the office. By the time I called them, they were on their way. They were there when his accomplice came out of the building. He was still carrying the gun. When she came out. . . her hands were covered in blood. She tried to save him.'

The room fell silent, Megan's words settling heavily on them. Seth stared at her, disbelief and anger warring within him. His mind scrambled to process it, but all he could think about was Róisín—what she'd been through.

##

Seth sat silently; his heart heavy as he watched Róisín sleep. The peaceful rise and fall of her chest made the chaos of the night before seem unreal. Her dark blonde hair fanned across the pillow, the bruise on her forehead stark against her pale skin. His stomach clenched as his eyes drifted to the lacerations on her hands and arms, and the fury inside him surged again. He knew he could have killed Greg Henderson with his bare hands for this—and that terrified him.

Seth closed his eyes, taking slow breaths to push the dark thoughts away. Róisín didn't need his anger, his vengeance. What she needed was comfort, safety, and someone to be there for her. And he'd be there, no matter what. His hand instinctively reached out to smooth her hair, careful to avoid the tender spots. She stirred, murmuring softly.

Her eyes fluttered open, and her hand reached out weakly, touching his wrist. 'You came,' she whispered, her voice raspy.

'Of course, I came,' Seth replied, his voice thick. He moved closer, pressing a soft kiss to her cheek. 'I'm not leaving you alone again. Not ever.'

Róisín's lips quirked into a faint, exhausted smile. 'Not ever is a long time . . . maybe not until you get sick of me.'

'I won't do that,' Seth whispered back, his heart aching. 'Ever.' He stroked her hair gently, watching as her eyes began to close again.

'Cat and Logan are here,' he said softly. 'Do you want to see them?'

'In a while,' she murmured. 'Just . . . hold my hand while I doze. You make me feel safe.'

'You are safe, my love,' Seth promised, his voice barely a whisper. 'And I'll make sure you stay that way.'

He wasn't sure if she heard him as she drifted back to sleep. But as he sat there, holding her hand, Seth knew one thing for certain—in the short time he had known Róisín O'Byrne, he had fallen in love with her.

Chapter 51

Ceann Mara - March.

For the first time since Christmas, all five sisters were home together again. Tom and Laura were flying home from Sydney that afternoon, and Róisín had volunteered to fly the Cessna to Broken Hill to collect them at the airport.

'Well, I'm off, you lot. Everything set for the welcome?' Róisín said.

'Almost!' Bridget replied, smiling back as Shea gave a quick thumbs up.

Shea and Bridget were up on two stepladders, hanging a huge 'Welcome Home' sign across the entrance to the camp kitchen. Bridget was cranky, weighed down by exams for a scholarship she was desperate to get. Her constant mantra of, 'I'm not staying in school' filled the air, followed by her sisters' laughter.

'Give it a break, Bridge,' Shea said. 'You've got less than a year to go.'

Shea was still working in Broken Hill and could only spare the weekend to come home and see Dad. She'd started studying for her vet nurse qualifications, and she planned to work towards studying veterinary science.

The door in the small building adjacent to the camp kitchen between the laundry and amenities block opened. Cat emerged, chatting with Erin.

'The display's been updated in the history room for the campers,' she called out.

'Priorities? History? We're supposed to be getting ready for a welcome barbeque here.' Róisín shook her head but smiled. 'And what campers? It's the off-season.'

'When they get here in autumn,' Cat retorted with a cheeky smile.

'She's as bad as Dad with the family history,' Erin chimed in.

As well as the history of the station in the camping area, an expanded version of their recent research had been printed and laid out for Dad on his huge desk in the study. Cat and Róisín had made a bet with Seth and Logan that he'd be in there before the barbeque. 'You don't know our father.'

'All updated, and we even found some pictures of the

Brucklay Castle and *Ariel* online,' Erin said as she held the ladder for Shea.

'Still no images of Samuel's paddle steamer, though,' Cat added with a sigh. 'But I'll be getting Dad onto that. We need to find out where they built the house, what happened to it, and why he ended up in St Kilda. And if there were more children.' Her sisters exchanged laughing glances. 'We've got some big Samuel Burns mysteries to solve.'

'Let him have a break first!' Logan said, catching Cat on her way past and dropping a kiss on her cheek. 'My little family history addict. It's a wonder a man gets fed.'

'You know how to cook,' she said, kissing him back.

Róisín noticed the wistful look on Erin's face as she watched Cat and Logan.

Erin had come home alone, which had surprised them. When they pressed her about Jack's absence, they were stunned to learn that her husband was in Africa.

'Africa?' Cat exclaimed, wide-eyed. 'What's he doing there?'

'He's working on a contract with a magazine,' Erin explained. 'His wildlife photography got spotted online, and he's been picking up a lot of commissions.'

'Why didn't you go too?' Róisín asked gently, surprised

that Erin hadn't told the family he was working overseas.

'We can't afford it,' Erin replied with a tired smile. 'My job at IGA in Wagga goes towards our savings.'

Róisín watched her closely. Erin's smile didn't reach her eyes, and her responses seemed forced, just like when they'd met up last month. There was a restlessness to her, and though she tried to hide it, her unhappiness was clear. Róisín made a mental note to find time for a proper talk with her sister.

Erin had always been the quiet one. She'd surprised the family when she met Jack at a music festival in Broken Hill and got engaged within weeks. Mum often bemoaned the fact that Jack had taken Erin away from the O'Byrne family rather than becoming part of it, though he was always pleasant on the rare occasions they visited.

'As long as she's happy,' Róisín thought to herself, but her concern lingered.

'Okay, I'll call when we're about to take off from Broken Hill!' she said as she headed towards the shed.

'Look after Dad,' Cat called.

The reports on Tom's recovery had been excellent, and he didn't have to go back to the specialist for a month. Róisín had sat down with Seth, Cat, and Logan, and they had decided to keep the events of the last month between them for a while. She didn't want to upset Dad and slow his recovery, and she knew that Mum would worry. Her focus needed to be on Dad once they were home. There would be no mention of the dangers of Róisín's new job, but the incidents in Brisbane had reinforced for Seth and Róisín that they must be careful.

Seth had stayed with Róisín when the police interviewed her in Brisbane. Greg Henderson's colleague, John Harris, had been charged with Greg's murder as well as organising the murder of Col Wilson, the thug who had kidnapped Róisín. Megan was immersed in sorting out the legal tangle with Linda's entitlements from Greg's estate but was confident that Linda would receive everything she was entitled to.

'I'll walk over to the shed with you, Ro,' Seth said. He was helping Logan set up the camp kitchen for the afternoon's barbecue. They'd planned for a mid-afternoon meal since Dad would likely be tired from the trip home.

Since Róisín's kidnapping last month, Seth had barely let her out of his sight. Their office had moved to Bourke, and now they were renting a small house together on acreage just outside town, overlooking the Barwon River.

With a final wave, they headed to Dad's shed, her sisters' banter echoing behind them. As Róisín stood by the Cessna, the morning sun reflected off the small waves on the river.

Seth wrapped his arms around her, pulling her close. 'You

take care,' he said softly, his voice almost lost in the gentle breeze.

'I always do,' she whispered, her breath catching as his fingers brushed a stray lock of hair from her face.

For a moment, neither of them spoke; the only sound was the gentle rustle of leaves in the breeze. Seth's hand lingered at the small of her back as he leaned down, his lips finding hers in a tender kiss with a warmth that deepened as he pulled her closer.

Róisín pressed into him, the newly-familiar feel of Seth's embrace still sending pleasant shivers down her spine. She could feel his love in the gentle strength in his arms.

When they finally parted, his forehead rested against hers, his voice low and serious. 'Stay safe, Ro. Promise me.'

'I will,' she replied softly, her fingers tracing the edge of his jaw. 'I'll be back before you know it.'

With a final squeeze of her hand, he stepped back, his eyes following her as she climbed into the Cessna. She smiled at him through the open window before driving away, feeling the warmth of his kiss lingering on her lips as she set off to collect her parents.

As the Cessna began to move out of the shed, she spotted Cat running over, waving her arms.

'What's wrong?' Róisín called.

'Don't tell Dad what we've done in the history room. I

want it to be a surprise.'

Róisín grinned and nodded. She was still smiling as she flew over the stretch of river that had belonged to the O'Byrne family for almost two hundred years.

Chapter 52

Darling River - 1861.

Caitríona O'Byrne sat on the timber bench that Thomas had built on the riverbank, a half-written letter in her lap and a pen poised in her hand. Her gaze drifted towards her children playing at the bottom of the gentle slope. James, Maeve, and Erin were happily splashing in the muddy shallows of the swimming hole Thomas had dug for the children to paddle in. Little Aisling grizzled beside her, wanting to go down and join her siblings, but she was likely to crawl into the strong running current of the river. The children's laughter rang out like music against the tranquil backdrop of *Ceann Mara*. She smiled, keeping one eye on their play as she tried to focus on her letter to her mother.

Thomas waved to Caitríona as he made his way downriver. 'I won't be long!' he called over his shoulder, disappearing into the dense foliage along the bank. Caitríona nodded absently, continuing to write, but her concentration broke when she heard a distant sound—a low, powerful horn blaring from the river.

She jumped up, her heart racing as the sound echoed across the water. The familiar rumble of the paddle steamer stirred a mix of excitement and curiosity within her. She quickly scanned the horizon, then turned and hurried down the steps to call for Thomas.

'Thomas!' she shouted, her voice laced with urgency. 'Come quick. A steamer is coming!'

A moment later, Thomas reappeared, sprinting back towards her. He glanced at the river, his expression shifting from curiosity to joy. 'Let's gather the children!' he said, his eyes bright with enthusiasm.

Caitríona lifted Aisling and rounded up the children, who were still giggling and digging in the swimming hole, their limbs and clothes smeared with red mud. 'Come on, darlings! The steamer's arriving!' she called. The three quickly scrambled up the bank, excitement sparking in their eyes as they had learned that the steamer meant new things.

They all hurried along the bank towards the dock near Samuel's store, their feet lifting dust with Thomas and Caitríona behind them.

'Will there be new marbles, Pa?' James called back.

'And a new doll for me?' Maeve added.

The steamer loomed larger as they drew closer, its engine chugging rhythmically, the smell of wood smoke filling the air. The children shouted a welcome as they recognised the captain in the wheelhouse, their voices rising above the churning sound of the paddle wheels.

As they reached the dock, Caitríona looked up and spotted Samuel standing at the front of the steamer, flanked by a woman and a young child. 'It's Uncle Samuel returned safely!' she called to the children.

Thomas nodded toward Samuel, a wide grin spreading across his face.

'Looks like we've got company!' he said, and Caitríona couldn't help but smile as they waved at the approaching vessel.

'Who is with him?' Caitríona asked, confusion threading her voice.

Thomas, his eyes narrowing as he followed her gaze, frowned slightly. 'You will see.'

Caitríona looked at him curiously. 'Do you know who they are? Did Samuel write to you?'

Her husband shook his head. 'He told me of his hopes before he left, the reason for his journey, but I held no hope. Thirteen years is a long time.'

As the steamer docked, Samuel stepped off first, his familiar figure quickly followed by the others. The children were already running towards him as Caitríona hurried behind Thomas to the wharf, her curiosity mounting. As soon as Samuel spotted them, his face broke into a wide grin, and when they reached him, he embraced Thomas in a firm hug, the brothers laughing in delight.

Caitríona stood back, puzzled, until Samuel turned toward her, his arm around the unfamiliar woman's shoulders. 'Caitríona,' he began, his voice filled with an emotion she couldn't quite place, 'I'd like you to meet my wife, Breda.' He gestured toward the young girl clinging to Breda's hand. 'And this is our daughter, Catherine.'

Caitríona's hand flew to her mouth, her eyes widening in surprise. 'Oh, Samuel . . .' Her voice trailed off as her gaze shifted to the man beside them. 'And who is this?'

Samuel smiled, nodding toward the tall, serious-looking man. 'This is Reverend John Atkins, Breda's brother. He's decided to join us out here and to minister to the settlers.'

For a moment, there was silence. Then Thomas, ever practical, clapped Samuel on the back, his grin broad. 'Well, it's about time, brother. You've brought them all home!'

Soon, they were all talking at once—Catherine shyly smiling at her cousins while Caitríona, still blinking in amazement, warmly welcomed them all. 'Come,' she said, gathering herself as she beckoned them back toward *Ceann Mara*. 'We'll have afternoon tea, and you can rest after we hear all of your news.'

As they made their way to the homestead, Samuel walked beside his brother as they spoke about the journey. 'After we have tea, I'll take them over to *Luachmhaire*.'

Thomas nodded. 'It's ready, Samuel,' he said with quiet satisfaction. 'And it is beautiful. I hope you will be pleased with the workmanship.'

Before Samuel could respond, Caitríona interrupted with a smile, 'And the gardens are established, too. You'll have roses and fresh vegetables in no time.'

They all reached the homestead, and when Caitríona invited Breda into the kitchen to prepare the refreshments, the brothers sat with John on the verandah while the children took Catherine over to the house paddock to meet their horses.

Samuel grinned at Thomas as the gentle evening breeze drifted in. 'It's taken many years, Thomas, but we are all finally home.'

Epilogue

Ceann Mara - June.

On a warm June afternoon, the day before Cat and Logan's wedding, Róisín and three of her four sisters sat in a circle on the lush green grass by the billabong, their backs to the soft breeze. A flock of corellas called from the trees, and up in the thermals, a pair of wedgetail eagles soared high above. Swans glided by in pairs, the ripples from their path breaking up the mirrored surface of the billabong.

Cat leaned back on her hands, closing her eyes as the breeze swept through her auburn curls. 'Feels like the old days, doesn't it?' she murmured.

Bridget, tracing patterns in the grass with a twig, nodded but kept her focus on the water.

'It's almost too peaceful,' Shea said, glancing up as a flock of birds passed overhead, their wings beating rhythmically.

Róisín smiled, though her mind wandered to the river and the ongoing investigations that had been filling her days. She let it go, inhaling deeply, savouring the calm. It was time to focus on tomorrow, the day the second of the O'Byrne sisters was going to be married. Róisín had been so happy when Logan asked Seth to be best man, and as the first bridesmaid, he would be her partner at the wedding.

Cat must have read her mind. 'Make sure you catch my bouquet tomorrow, Ro.'

'Too soon for that, Cat!'

'Never too soon,' her sister retorted.

'Hi, you lot. Hoped you saved me some bubbles.' Erin, the last of the O'Byrne sisters to arrive, walked toward them, her steps light.

'Erin!' Bridget jumped up, rushing to greet her. Shea followed, and the two youngest sisters embraced her in a flurry of hugs and laughter. Róisín and Cat held back a moment, looking at each other.

'Good to see you, Erin,' Róisín said warmly, though she couldn't stop looking at how thin Erin was. Her skin was sallow, and she looked tired.

Erin grinned, though it didn't reach her eyes the way it used to. 'Good to see you all too. It's been far too long.' She hugged Cat and Róisín in turn as Shea filled a glass for her.

'Dad looks great,' she said, 'and Mum's got food all over the kitchen benches and in both fridges. I thought you were getting caterers in.'

'We are,' Cat said. 'But Mum's worried there won't be enough food.'

Erin nodded. 'She said she'd come out here in a while.'

They settled back down, pulling Erin into their circle. Bridget and Shea fell into easy chatter, catching Erin up on their latest news as Bridget boasted about her scholarship, and Shea told her about her new job at a different vet practice in Broken Hill, but Róisín leaned in toward Cat, her voice low.

'Do you think Erin's lost weight?' Róisín asked, her brow furrowed in concern.

Cat's eyes flicked towards Erin before quickly turning back to Róisín. 'I noticed it too.'

'Too much,' Róisín whispered, unsettled. 'Something's not right.'

Cat nodded, her face clouding. 'We'll have to find a quiet moment to talk to her.'

They shared a brief, worried glance before turning back to the others. The warm breeze rustled the leaves behind them, echoing their unease.

This afternoon, they would simply appreciate being

together, ready for Cat and Logan's special day tomorrow.

Book 3

Daughters of The Darling

Erin O'Byrne returns to *Ceann Mara*, her family's remote property on the Darling River, seeking peace after a painful marital breakup. Camping by the tranquil billabong, she hopes the solitude of the Australian bush will help her heal. While exploring the land, Erin discovers a long-forgotten memorial to a World War I soldier. Her sister, Cat, and father, Tom, who have been researching the family's history, are thrilled by the find and eager to uncover its secrets. But Erin's journey takes an unexpected turn when reclusive Miles McKenzie sets up camp beside her. Though initially guarded, she and Miles gradually develop a friendship that sparks a powerful attraction. Her family, however, worries that she's moving too fast after her breakup, questioning whether she can truly trust Miles. As Erin struggles with her growing feelings and her family's concerns, she must decide whether to follow her heart—or listen to the doubts that surround her.

Erin's story, the next book in the series, *By the Billabong*, will be published in April 2025.
It is available in print for pre-order at Annie's store.
https://annieseatonstore.ecwid.com/
eBook pre-order:
http://books2read.com/u/b6BEvE

Acknowledgements

The Darling River is one of the most beautiful areas in outback New South Wales. In the spring of 2023, Ian and I travelled the Darling River Run from Brewarrina to Menindee in our caravan, exploring this beautiful landscape.

We stayed at *Trilby Station,* where the inspiration for this story was born. *Ceann Mara* is based on this contemporary station.

Thank you to station owners Liz and Gary Murray for allowing me to use information from the historical museum at the campground on *Trilby Station*. We stopped at various sites from Brewarrina to Menindee on the Darling River Run and discovered the beauty of the river. We sat by the water at sunrise and sunset and absorbed the aromas, the beauty of the trees, and the sound of the birds. It is truly a magical place, and if you get the opportunity to travel out there, make sure to do so. There are many beautiful landscapes in Australia, and the Darling River Run is right up there with them.

Over the River is the second book in the *Daughters of the Darling* series, and I'm looking forward to researching more of the series when we travel out to the Darling River Run again next spring.

Many people supported me in writing this book, and I would like to acknowledge them here.

To the many friends I have made in the writing world over

the past fourteen years who constantly support me on my journey, I often say I have found my "tribe," and I value the daily contact with like-minded people all over the world. Again, a special mention and thank you goes to my dear friend, critique partner, and editor, author Susanne Bellamy, and to my wonderful proofreaders, Kristen Woolgar and authors Roby Aiken and Rhonda Forrest.

A huge thank you to my reader and online friend, Dr Christopher Johnson whose input was invaluable when checking my medical information when Tom had his accident.

To my loyal readers, who look forward to the release of the next book, come to my library talks and contact me by mail and social media to tell me they enjoy my stories. Without readers, there would be no need for stories!

It would be impossible to write without support in your personal life:

To Ian, the love of my life and my partner in research as we travel this magnificent country seeking stories each winter. I could not do this without you. My driver, my chef, my bringer of wine, my fisherman, and my husband of almost fifty years.

To our children and their partners and our grandchildren: thank you for your love and support.

Again, my love and appreciation go to my wonderful aunt, Maureen Smith, who not only supports me but supports so many Australian writers by reading, loving and sharing their stories. Aunty Maureen can no longer read due to failing eyesight, but she always tells me how proud my parents would be.

And to you, the reader: thank you for choosing this book. I hope that you enjoy it and talk about it; word of mouth is the best thing for an author.

Maybe you will want to visit this wonderful part of

Australia. I hope you enjoyed Róisín's and Breda's stories. Erin's story will be released in April 2025.

Please sign up for my fortnightly newsletter to hear about my research and my new books. You can find it here: **http://www.annieseaton.net**

I would love to hear from you.

Drop me a line at **annie@annieseation.net**

Reviews on Goodreads are always welcome and much

appreciated!

eBook links:

https://www.annieseaton.net/books.html

Print Store:

All books are available in print at Annie's store and on

Amazon in paperback.

https://annieseatonstore.ecwid.com/

Awards

2023: Winner - Long contemporary novel category, RUBY award for *Larapinta.*

2023*:* Finalist - Australian Romance Readers Awards for *Kakadu Dawn,* the sixth and final book in the Porter Sisters series.

2018 and 2020: Finalist - for the NZ KORU Award.

2017: Winner - Best Established Author of the Year 2017 AUSROM

2017: Winner - Author of the Year 2014 AUSROM Best Established Author, Ausrom Readers' Choice.

2016, 2017, 2018, 2019: Longlisted - Sisters in Crime Davitt Awards

2016: Finalist - Book of the Year, Long Romance, RWA Ruby Awards for *Kakadu Sunset*

2015: Winner - Best Established Author of the Year AUSROM